# CONNEMARA GIRL

## THE GALWAY MURDERS BOOK 1

### DEREK FEE

*For Aine, Bobbie, Sean and Jack*

## CHAPTER ONE

Mweenish Island, Connemara, Galway

THE YOUNG MAN stood on the edge of the pier and threw up into the sea. He wiped his mouth with a paper handkerchief and threw it away before climbing back into the passenger seat of the car. The driver looked at him with disgust.

At close to five o'clock in the morning, it was unlikely that they were being observed. The small island's pier was invisible to most of the scattered inhabitants. The tide had been coming in since they had arrived, and they watched the three boats tied at the pier rise with it. It was almost time. Neither had spoken for over an hour. Each was lost in his own thoughts. There was a hint of light in the east. Dawn couldn't be far away and it was important that they get on with their task.

The driver looked across at the young man in the passenger seat. 'For fuck's sake will you stop fidgeting. You're getting on my nerves.'

'What if somebody sees us?'

'It's pitch black and there isn't a soul for miles around. Relax, the tide is almost in.'

'Just because we can't see anyone doesn't mean that there isn't some fecker out there with binoculars glued to his eyes. You know the way people are around here. Maybe we should be digging a hole.'

The driver opened the car door and exited. The air was fresh and tinged with the smell of ozone. He walked to the edge of the pier. The small fishing boat was clear in the half-light and its gunwale had reached the level of the pier. He turned and signalled to the young man who exited from the car. The two men made their way to the rear of the Land Rover and opened the rear door. They stood in silence for a moment before the driver began to pull at a large plastic fish box containing a mass tied up in two black bin bags. The young man hesitated before leaning into the rear and pulling at the opposite end. They hauled out the box and held it between them, then walked crablike towards the boat until it was directly beneath them. Without speaking they lowered the box to the ground and the driver clambered on board. As soon as he was balanced, he held out his arms. The young man lifted the package and let it slide into the waiting arms, then he returned to the car, removed two large stones and a coil of rope, and tossed them onto the rear of the boat. Before jumping on board, he released the mooring ropes from the bow and stern. He sat at the stern and looked directly into the box which had been stowed at his feet. Looking up, he saw his companion was already in the wheelhouse. The engine gave a couple of turns and coughed before catching, sending a plume of black smoke shooting across the calm waters of the tiny harbour. The boat moved away from the pier and headed out into the silent darkness of the Atlantic Ocean. They cleared Golem Head and made in the direction of the Aran Islands. The early morning mist enveloped them as they crested the waves. The only sound was the rhythmical putt-putting of the engine as they travelled for six nautical miles before the driver cut the engine and exited the wheelhouse. 'Here.'

The young man stood and waited for the driver to join him at the rear. They each took a coil of rope, circled it around the mass in the bin bags, and tied it securely. They looped their coil around one of the stones, hoisted the bin bag and its contents onto the gunwale and waited for a moment before jettisoning the package into the ocean.

'I need my breakfast,' the driver said, heading back to the wheelhouse.

The young man didn't reply but stood watching the package on its way to the bottom of the ocean.

## CHAPTER TWO

Detective Sergeant Fiona Madden sat at a table outside the Quays Bar in Shop Street in the centre of Galway. The weather wasn't perfect for sitting outside and only two of the pavement tables were occupied. It was early May and the 'season' wasn't yet in full swing. Galway in summer was a scene of madness and mayhem as thousands of visitors thronged the narrow streets and alleyways buying their Aran sweaters and searching for that perfect pint of Guinness that they'd heard about. But that was a month or so away though there was still a decent enough crowd of tourists and students to keep the bars and restaurants working at full pace. There was a constant flow of people past the pub, but it was thin enough to pick out individuals. Fiona was dressed in jeans with a biker-chick leather jacket over a black tee shirt and leather boots.

'Hi.'

A young man had slipped into the seat facing her.

She stared at him. 'Piss off.'

'What?'

'You heard.' She flashed her warrant card and the man rose and disappeared in the direction of the River Corrib, hopefully to throw himself in. Every girl in Galway cursed Ed Sheeran for putting a target on their backs.

She looked up the street and saw her new partner, Detective Garda Sean Tracy, lounging against a wall. He had been watching the pickup scene and was smiling. Sean was a good-looking boy when he was suited and booted but today, he was dressed in indigent chic and looked the part. She removed a small photograph from her pocket. The face of the woman in the photo was misshapen and bloodied. The reconstructive surgery was going to be a bitch. It was nearing midday and showtime was close. She slowed her breathing. Tracy was in her peripheral vision, but she saw the nod. The man they were after was walking in her direction. She finished her orange juice and moved to a position where she blocked the entrance to the bar.

'Excuse me,' the man said.

'Patrick Molloy,' Fiona said. 'Garda Síochána.' She looked into his eyes. He was weighing up the odds. Fight or fly. Then his eyes crinkled around the edges and she knew he had decided. He opted for fight. It was a no-brainer. She was a five-foot six skinny bitch who weighed a hundred and forty pounds and he was six foot two and weighed two hundred and thirty pounds. It was the mismatch of the century. She anticipated the punch well before he threw it. She had already gone through the moves in her head. She slid deftly to her left and grabbed his fist as it missed her head. She pulled him off balanced and at the same time kicked him in the right kneecap. He buckled a look of total surprise on his face. As his head came down, she punched him with her left fist on the right temple. The fight was over and he hit the cobblestones like a sack of potatoes. The action had taken less than twenty seconds. Tracy arrived and cuffed his hands behind his back.

'Holy cow!' a man sitting two tables away said.

Fiona noted that he was filming her with his mobile phone.

She took out her mobile to call the cavalry. 'We've got him. Send a wagon.'

A crowd had gathered, and Fiona could see that the mobiles were already out. She held her warrant card aloft. 'It's all over. Please keep moving. This is a police matter.'

'What's the problem.' The bar manager exited the pub.

'Your dishwasher is wanted for attempting to murder his wife.'

'Cool,' the manager said. 'I better put a new help-wanted sign in the window.'

'And be careful who you hire in future.'

'When you clear up the mess, there's a pint and a sandwich for you and your partner inside.'

'We'll take you up on that.' She walked to where Tracy was pulling Molloy to his feet 'Patrick Molloy, I am arresting you for the attempted murder of Róisín Molloy, you do not have to say anything when questioned but anything you do say will be taken down and may be used in evidence. Do you understand?'

Molloy had come to. 'You fucking bitch, you broke my fucking kneecap.'

'Unfortunately not,' Fiona said. 'I really wanted to but that might have invalidated the arrest though if you'd like to continue our bout, I'd be glad to accommodate you. And I promise to break a few of your bones next time.'

Three uniforms had arrived and they took a hobbling Molloy away to where two police cars were parked at the end of Shop Street.

'Fucker,' Fiona said as they led him away.

'Next time give me a chance to get in on the action,' Tracy said. 'What kind of moves were those?'

'Aikido.'

'Of which you're a black belt?'

'I really wanted to hurt that bastard. I had to hold myself back.'

Fiona finished her call and put her mobile on the table. They were seated in the rear of the pub having accepted the manager's offer of a drink and a sandwich. 'He's in a cell in Salthill being examined by a doctor. Two detectives are on the way from Dublin to collect him. Good riddance to bad rubbish.' She sipped her orange juice.

'That was impressive out there,' Tracy said. 'How long have you been doing martial arts?'

'Eighteen years, I started when I was sixteen.'

Tracy stared at her. 'You don't look thirty-four.'

'Spare the compliments. You don't compliment Madden. Or hadn't you heard?'

Even in the half-light of the pub, she saw him redden. He'd been given the tour of the station on arrival. There's your desk, the male toilet is around the corner and the cafeteria is on the first floor. That's Madden. Don't try it on with her; she's a dyke bitch.

'I thought you were going to be duffed,' Tracy said.

'That's also what he thought.'

'They were some sweet moves.' He bit into his ham and cheese sandwich.

'I teach classes in a dojo in town. You're welcome to join. How are you settling in?' Tracy had recently transferred from Cork.

'As well as can be expected. I've been here for two weeks and nobody has nicknamed me *Dick* yet.'

'Give them time. Have you already checked all the stalls in the male toilet?'

'Why?'

'The first guy to give you a nickname will probably be the shithouse poet.'

'There's a shithouse poet?'

She laughed. 'There's a shithouse poet in every police station in the country. You should see the female toilets. You live in town?'

'Yeah, for the moment, I might move west later. The city is compact but it contains everything. Where were you before Galway.'

Fiona finished her sandwich and pushed her plate away. 'Dublin.' There was a look of envy on Tracy's face. *Poor sod. Wait until he ran into the arseholes that inhabited the capital. Half the complement of her base at Store Street station were suffering from either PTSD or depression.* 'Finish up, that's enough bonding for now and we need to get back to the station.'

# CHAPTER THREE

The building housing Mill Street Garda Station started life as the main building of the Galway Foundry Company. Up to the late 1980 there were still two or three Georgian houses on the site. The original building was only recently renovated and turned into a modern three-story stone-faced office building. The Criminal Investigation Division occupied a suite of rooms on the third floor.

Fiona was writing her report on the Molloy arrest when she felt a presence behind her. She turned slowly and stared into the face of her boss, Detective Inspector George Horgan, who was doing his best to look displeased. She smiled.

'You are some piece of work, Madden,' Horgan said. 'I've just had my arse scalded by the superintendent about your little escapade in Shop Street. That arsehole Molloy is screaming police brutality and there's plenty of evidence on social media to back up his claim.'

Fiona opened the file on the attack on Róisín Molloy. She had replaced the photo of the victim's face and it was appended to the first page.

'I read it,' Horgan said. 'But you're a police officer, not an avenging angel.'

She closed the file and opened another. 'Did you have time to read Molloy's file?'

Horgan sighed.

'Two years ago, he beat her shitless and ran. They found him working in a restaurant in Wexford and sent four guards to arrest him. He put two in hospital. At trial, his barrister said that the guards hadn't announced themselves and Molloy felt under attack by a group of men and responded. He pled guilty to aggravated assault against his wife and received a custodial sentence of one year. He was out after nine months. A few months later, she was in ICU and he was on the run. I'm not a seer but I bet this time the DPP will probably charge him with GBH instead of attempted murder and he'll be on the streets in no time. Róisín Molloy will take years to recover. That is if she ever recovers.'

'You're beginning to sound like a warrior in the gender war.'

'You don't think that there's a male conspiracy against women out there? Husbands are responsible for killing fifty-eight per cent of all murdered women. Abused women carry on being abused for years. You know why? Because they don't trust the legal system to protect them.'

'You've heard the expression crime and punishment...' Horgan paused for effect. 'Well we're the crime part of that phrase. The punishment part is reserved for the courts. We don't hand out the punishment on the streets of Galway.'

She looked over at Tracy who was feigning disinterest in her exchange with Horgan but was, what her mother called, earwigging. 'I wasn't punishing him; I was subduing him. Unlike our colleagues in Wexford, I wasn't going to give him the chance to put either me or young Tracy there in hospital. If I had been punishing him, I would have made sure that he would never again be capable of hurting a woman.'

Horgan shook his head. 'Some day, Madden, some day.' He was holding a file and he handed it to her. 'It's a missing person case, a young girl of sixteen. You won't like it because there's little possibility that you'll get to beat the shit out of someone.'

She took the file from him. 'I love you too, boss.'

Horgan shook his head. 'I have a mountain of administrative work to do. I hate it, but it beats trying to talk sense to you. It's likely that the Ombudsman's Office might want to talk to you.' He went back to his office.

Fiona opened the file. It contained two pages. The first was a missing persons declaration form and the second was a picture of a teenage girl. She closed the file and set it aside. The girl had been missing for three days, which wasn't all that long. As a child, she had run away after an altercation with her mother. Driven by hunger, she'd returned hours later to find that no one had noticed that she was missing. It was her last attempt at running away. She hated missing persons and she particularly hated missing teenagers. All those raging hormones took up too much police time. They spend the night with the boyfriend and the parents go apoplectic. They party on for the weekend. Or they simply go to the shops and don't come home for a couple of days. In the meantime, the worried parents launch a missing persons investigation and never bother to inform the police when the miscreant returns home. She tossed the file to Tracy. 'Check out social media. If she's a normal teenager she'll be on every platform. That should keep you busy for the rest of the afternoon.' She went back to writing her report on the events at the Quays Bar.

'Are you in trouble?'

'No more than usual. It depends on who reviews the arrest and the doctor's report on Molloy.'

'Maybe we could have taken him without the aikido moves.'

'What do you weigh?' She sized him up. 'Seventy-five kilos?'

'Seventy-three.'

'Read Molloy's file. He'd have had you for breakfast.'

Tracy picked up the file and started to read.

An hour later, Tracy dropped an A4 sheet on her desk. It showed a scantily-clad young woman in a provocative pose. The photo emphasised the breasts and the bottom.

'What's that got to do with anything?' Fiona said.

'That's our missing person.'

Fiona picked up the photo. 'You're kidding me. Give me the file.'

The photo appended to the file was a typical school photo and it didn't look anything like the photo Tracy had given her. 'This girl has got to be twenty years old.'

'That's Sarah Joyce as presented on her Facebook profile. There are dozens of photos online showing her attributes to best advantage. She's also on Twitter and Instagram. Same kind of material.'

'They grow up fast these days. Any indication of why she flew the coop?'

'Nothing that I can see. I bet most of the juicy stuff is on her mobile phone.'

'She doesn't look fifteen going on sixteen in those photos.'

'What do we do next?'

'Check the hospitals. Call the parents and see if she's turned up in the meantime. Looking like that, she could be working as a waitress in a hotel in the Outer Hebrides and our chances of finding her would be nil. We'll give it a perfunctory investigation and then file it. Most of the runaways end up going home. A couple of weeks on the streets gives them a better appreciation of home comforts. Those that don't return generally have a good reason for staying away. Call the parents and if she's still missing, we'll arrange a visit for tomorrow morning.'

'Okay, boss.'

'Okay, Sarge.'

'Got it.'

# CHAPTER FOUR

Fiona left the dojo at six thirty. The hour teaching aikido had left her feeling fresh physically and mentally. Molloy and Sarah Joyce were banished from her mind and she was anxious to get back to her small cottage and what she often called her real life. She put on her helmet and sat astride a classic Vincent Black Shadow. Her maternal grandfather had bequeathed his two most precious possessions, his home and his motorcycle, to her. He didn't explain why he had singled her out in his will and the inheritance proved to be a bone of contention between her and the rest of her family. The Irish were funny that way. She supposed it had something to do with the paucity of personal effects to be divided between so many. Those thoughts were certainly not on her mind as she rode along the coast road from Galway towards her small cottage in the village of Barna. The day was fine, the traffic was light, and she completed the journey in fifteen minutes. Just beyond Barna she turned left and descended a short incline. The wide expanse of Galway Bay was directly before her and the evening light danced on the blue of the ocean and the grey of the hills of Clare in the distance. She was a hundred yards from her home when she noticed a young man sitting on the dry-stone wall that surrounded her property. She cut back on the throttle. She'd put more than a few villains away and revenge attacks on police officers were a regular occurrence. As she eased the bike, she saw that the man was no more than a young boy.

'Hi.' Fiona stopped in front of her gate and continued to sit astride her bike. 'Can I help you?'

'Sure. I'm looking for Fiona Madden.'

She stared at the young man and found that her heart had begun to beat faster. She controlled her breathing to regain control. A thought had jumped into her mind and she hoped to God that she was wrong. The man-boy in front of her was the right age. She guessed that he was seventeen or eighteen. The accent was pure American. He was already over six foot and there might have been a few inches of growth still in him. He was a good-looking kid with an untidy mop of fair hair. She had spent years learning to control her emotions but she couldn't stop a tear from exiting the corner of her left eye. 'I'm Fiona Madden and what business might you have with me?'

The young man looked at the ground. 'My name is Tim Daly and I think I you might be my mother.'

The word *mother* hit her like a sledgehammer. She had once been a mother but it had been a fleeting state. Could it be that it was a state that was going to revisit her? She stared at the young man. Did he resemble her? She tried to see herself in his face. Maybe the eyes, or the chin, she wasn't sure. She fought to remain calm. 'Is that so?' She climbed off the bike and opened the wooden gate to the short driveway. 'And what makes you think that?'

'I've always known that I was adopted and two years ago I started researching to find the names of my biological parents.' He fiddled with a backpack that stood at his feet and pulled out a file. 'I got lots of paper to show the trail back to you.'

Fiona's heart had gone into overdrive and she had given up all attempts to control it. It was a scene she had visualised a thousand times but nothing came close to the reality. There were a plethora of physical and mental responses. She could rush towards him and enfold him in her arms. That was the classic scene from the movies. She could simply hug him and call him her darlin' child. Instead she opted for the least emotional. 'Come inside and bring your file.' She pushed her bike down the driveway and parked it close to the front door of the cottage. Tim lifted his pack and followed behind her.

As they stood at the door, Fiona felt his closeness. The key to the cottage felt strange in her hand and she had trouble fitting it in the lock. Eventually, she managed and pushed the door open, indicating that he should enter.

'Why don't I put on some tea?' Fiona said. Tea was the Irish solution to every problem. At least that was what her mother had taught her. The day she had announced that she was pregnant, tea was the first item on her mother's agenda. Fiona's world was falling apart. Tea wasn't part of the solution.

'Have you got any coffee?' Tim asked.

'Sure.' She led the way to the rear of the cottage where the kitchen was located.

Tim looked around the interior of the cottage. 'This place is cool.' He dumped his backpack in the corner.

Fiona started filling the kettle noting the shake in her hands. 'The original building is old, maybe a hundred and fifty years old. My grandfather left it to me and I've modernised it a bit.' She looked around the kitchen. 'This extension is the most modern part. Sit at the table. I'll put the kettle on. I think I have some biscuits around somewhere.'

'It's just like the postcards of Ireland my adoptive parents used to receive.'

This is crazy, Fiona was thinking. This young man has just announced himself as my son and we're talking about the condition of my home.

'You live here alone?' Tim asked.

'No, I live with my partner.' She saw that he was watching her.

'Cool.'

'She should be home shortly.'

'Your partner is a woman?' He couldn't hide his surprise. 'You're gay?'

'I am. Are you surprised?'

'Kinda, when did you realise you were gay?'

'When I was about thirteen. I wanted to kiss girls not boys.' She could see that she was punching a hole in his mother Fiona theory.

'Wow, what's your partner's name?'

She smiled at his ability to recover. 'Her name is Ashling.'

'That's a pretty name. So is Fiona by the way. All the girls at college had names like Ava, Mia, and Madison.'

'Ashling in Gaelic means a dream or a vision.' The kettle sounded behind her and she turned. Maybe this was a dream and she would wake up any minute. She spooned instant coffee into two cups and poured hot water. She took milk from the fridge and put the cups and milk on the kitchen table. 'We don't have sugar.'

He pulled a cup towards him. 'I take it black, no sugar.'

Fiona sat. There was an embarrassed silence. She had no doubt that the young man sitting across from her was her son. The problem was that she had no maternal feelings towards him. She now fully understood Jesus' feelings in the Garden of Gethsemane. Why the hell had he bothered to locate her? Couldn't he have left well enough alone? Did she have even one maternal bone in her body? The young man sitting in front of her was a stranger. He appeared to be a nice boy, which was a credit to his adoptive parents and nothing to do with her. She tried to remember how she'd felt immediately after his birth. As far as she could recall, he was whisked away within days of his appearance on the planet and that was supposed to be the end of the matter for all concerned. In the intervening years, she had rarely thought of the baby that her mother gave away. Looking back on herself as a sixteen-year-old schoolgirl ill-prepared for motherhood, she'd thought that giving the baby to people capable of looking after him was the best solution. 'So, how did we get here?'

'I'm a bit embarrassed.' He put his file of papers on the table. 'My adoptive parents were great. They're still are great. I was well taken care of and loved. When I heard stories from my classmates at school who had biological parents that were abusive, I didn't associate with those stories. But one area was off limits and that was any mention of my biological parents. They told me that I was put up for adoption immediately after I was born.' He looked at her. She was impassive. 'Like any teenager, the place I really wanted to go was where my parents told me not to. So, I started researching. And if there's one thing that I'm good at, it's digging into something I'm interested in. My parents were big supporters of this Catholic adoption agency that brought babies from Ireland. I didn't think much about it growing up but I thought it might be a good place to start.' He pulled out some letters clipped together. 'I started writing to them. At first, they tried to flip me off. I hadn't been in an orphanage. The adoption had been done privately. But I kept after them and eventually they verified that I was adopted from Ireland but they wouldn't give me any information about my biological parents. Then my folks found out what I was up to and my mom went apeshit. They were alright about me wanting to find my biological parents but they wanted me to wait until I was older and more mature. But I couldn't stop. I connected with a group here in Ireland that help people like me find their biological parents. The normal reason for the search is to get some medical information. I had my birthdate, which I was told was accurate. Do you know that sixty-eight boys were born in Ireland on my birthday?'

'No, I didn't know that.' She sipped her coffee.

'Yeah, sixty-eight, so the guys here checked up on the others looking at school records and the like. There was only one boy adopted from that group. The birth certificate was for a Sean Madden and you're named as the mother. The father's name wasn't recorded. Did you have a child?'

'Yes.'

'You look young. What age were you when I was born? Sixteen?'

'Yes, where do we go from here?' Fiona realised that she was ceding control to Tim. Having made the trip to Galway, there was no way he was going to be persuaded to leave. 'What happens if you find that you are my son?'

'I haven't thought that far into the future.'

'You're eighteen. I suppose you've just finished college.'

'Yeah, graduated summa cum laude.'

'Congratulations. So, what about university?'

'I've been accepted at Yale. I was thinking about law school later.'

'Sounds like a plan. Why don't you forget this quest of yours? You appear to have a good life. Why not just be happy with that?'

'I need to know. I've got the summer. We could do a DNA test and the result would be in before I need to go back home.'

'We could. Are you prepared for both a positive and a negative result?' She was asking herself the same question. The creaking noise from the living room indicated the front door opening.

'I'm home,' Ashling called from the living room. 'And I'm dying for a drink?'

'We're in here,' Fiona said.

Ashling stopped at the kitchen door. 'Who exactly are we?'

'This young man is Tim Daly. He's come here because he thinks I may be his birth mother.' She turned to Tim. 'This is Ashling, my partner.'

Tim stood and extended his hand. 'Pleased to meet you.'

Ashling shook. 'Now I really do need that drink.'

'Count me in,' Fiona said.

'Perhaps you and I need a quiet word outside,' Ashling said. 'We'll be back in a minute, Tim.'

Fiona stood and followed Ashling out the front door.

'I told you this would happen one day,' Ashling said when they got outside.

'Maybe it's not him.'

'What's he looking for?'

'He wants to check our DNA.'

'He looks like a nice young man.'

'Looks like he's had a good life with loving parents. I wish he'd go back to it.'

'Do you really mean that?'

'Yes. I may be wrong but there will be a lot of unanswered questions if the DNA works out. He might not be happy about that. This could be a serious complication to our lives.'

'Time for that drink.'

They returned to the living room and Ashling made for the kitchen. 'Tim, like to join us for a drink?'

Tim stood. 'I don't drink. But if you have a Coke.'

Fiona was already making two stiff gin and tonics. Ashling found a Coke in the fridge and handed it to Tim. She took a glass from Fiona and raised it in a toast. 'Welcome to Galway, Tim.'

'Yes,' Fiona said. 'Welcome to Galway.'

# CHAPTER FIVE

Fiona woke slowly. There appeared to be a fog in the room and for a moment she wondered whether the cottage was on fire. She felt the bed beside her but there was no sign of Ashling. That was the point when the drumming inside her head rose to a crescendo. Her memories of the previous evening were sketchy. She could vaguely remember arriving back at the cottage and being confronted by a young man claiming to be her son. There was some drinking over dinner and she and Ashling repaired to a local hostelry where Ashling had treated her like one of her clients while she ladled on the drinks. Fiona hoped that none of these memories were correct especially the one about the young man. Then she remembered his name: Tim Daly. She tried to sit up but her head didn't seem to be connected to her body. She needed to get to the bathroom but this was a two-hundred-year-old cottage so there was no en suite and the way to the bathroom led through the living room and the kitchen. She had designed the modernisation herself and it had been established on the premise that there would be a limited number of male visitors. She slung her legs over the edge of the bed, picked up a dressing gown from the floor and put it on. She needed to pee and she needed a cold shower. As soon as she opened the bedroom door, she got the smell of fried bacon and her stomach heaved. She moved quickly through the living room. Ashling was at the cooker and there was no sign of young Tim. For an instant, she thought he had decamped. She knew that she should feel happy but she was sad.

'Good morning,' she said to Ashling's back and was inside the bathroom before her partner could reply.

After the relief of the toilet, she took off her robe and subjected herself to the shower. She stood under the icy stream and allowed the water to exorcise the demons from her head. Fifteen minutes later, she exited the shower feeling at least semi-human. She must have really tied one on because try as she might she could not remember exactly what had happened after they left the hostelry. Hopefully, Ashling hadn't followed her example. In general, her partner exhibited a great deal more sense in the area of alcohol than she did. Thanks be to God she didn't have too much on at work. She wouldn't fancy taking on the likes of Molloy in her current condition. There was a knock on the door.

'Breakfast is on the table,' Ashling called.

Fiona stuck her tongue out at the mirror. She could feel the fur on her tongue but she couldn't see it. Ashling's voice was too damn cheery. At least it meant she was in better condition than Fiona.

'Eggs and bacon?' Ashling said as Fiona exited the bathroom.

Fiona's stomach did a somersault. 'Just tea, I'm going to need a lift into town.' She looked around. 'Is he still here?'

'You mean your son?'

'This is no joke.'

Ashling wasn't smiling. 'I'm aware of that. He's still asleep. Get your clothes on, I have a lecture at ten.'

'And I have to start the hunt for a missing teenager.'

'Good luck with that.'

. . .

'You LOOK like something the cat dragged in,' Tracy said when Fiona arrived in the CID squad room. 'Hard night?'

Fiona put a large takeaway coffee on her desk. 'What I can remember of it.'

'The next time you buy a coffee, it's traditional to get one for your colleague also.'

'Piss off.'

'What were you celebrating?'

She thought about why she had tied one on. Was she celebrating the return of the child she had so easily given away eighteen years previously? Or maybe she was trying to escape from the consequences of Tim Daly showing up. In either case, Tracy didn't need to know. She sipped her coffee. 'No reason, the music was good and things escalated.'

'I thought people your age were supposed to have more sense. I've checked the hospitals and while there are several Joyces there's no Sarah Joyce aged sixteen registered.'

'Joyce is a big name out here.'

'I've arranged for a visit to Mrs Joyce at eleven. She lives in Glenmore. That's sixty miles west.'

'I know where it is.' Fiona took a slug of her coffee. She was beginning to feel more human and she hoped it was showing on her face. 'What about Mr Joyce?'

'There is no Mr Joyce.'

'You didn't ask why?'

'It didn't seem appropriate. I suppose we'd better hit the road.'

'Appropriate, where did you get that from? You'd better forget the three-syllable words. The Garda Síochána is a one-syllable world. You're driving.'

'Of course I'm driving. You think I'd let you behind the wheel of a car in your condition. We can pick up some breath-fresheners on the way. We wouldn't want the citizenry to think that their protectors are on the sauce.'

She thought about throwing the coffee at him but she needed it. 'There you go again with the three-syllable words. Let's go. I think the citizenry knows more about our peccadillos than we care to think.'

'Peccadillos, I thought that was some sort of sexual aid.'

She threw the remnants of her coffee in his direction and managed to miss.

FIONA SAT BACK in the passenger seat and allowed her mind to wander. She'd told Ashling most of her life story when they'd got together. Since they were opposites and Ashling was the steady clever one, she'd been told that someday her son would look for her and that she should be prepared. That was all right in theory. But practice was another matter. She cried for days after the birth. She begged her mother to let her keep the baby but she was told that the child was gone. The adoption was completed and there was nothing that could be done. She'd never forgiven her mother for forcing the decision on her.

Tracy had selected the road through Oughterard. On a fine morning like this one, Fiona would have preferred the road by the coast. That would have taken her past her cottage and she could have popped in to see whether Tim was awake yet. Was this maternal care or did she want to discover that he'd already packed his bags and gone back to where he came from? She knew that the latter wasn't an option. She'd only scratched the surface of Tim Daly but she knew already that he wasn't the type to cut and run.

She was on the clock so her thoughts turned to the possible whereabouts of Sarah Joyce. Finding a missing teenager was the job that was usually given to the new detective on the squad. In other words, it was a ball-ache. It meant dealing with distraught parents who either don't know why the teenager has absconded or are very aware but don't want to say for fear of incriminating themselves. Tracy and she could play around with the case for the next few days. They would interview everyone they could and establish a file and they could then hand it over and put young Sarah onto the national register. There might be an appeal in the *Galway Advertiser* and a two-second slot on TV. But missing teenagers were a dime a dozen. The motion of the car was lulling her to sleep and she closed her eyes.

THE JOYCES LIVED in a small cottage on the outskirts of the village of Glenmore. Villages in this rural part of Connemara tended to consist of a church, a pub, and a shop, or maybe two. Glenmore was a cut above the other villages, containing as it did a pharmacy, a clinic, a second pub, and that rarity: a Garda station. Tracy had been up on his protocol and had informed the officer in charge of their mission to locate Sarah Joyce and the fact that they would be interviewing members of the family. He wasn't surprised when the resident of the station informed him that he had an urgent appointment that coincided with the time of their visit. The rural officers didn't like the detectives wandering around on their patch.

'We're there,' Tracy said as he pulled up just off the road. The car was parked at the end of a bare earth path that led to a house that Fiona recognised as the standard provided by the local authority. Without entering, she knew that the house would consist of a living room, a kitchen, a family bathroom, and three bedrooms. They rapped on the front door and it was opened immediately.

Nora Joyce was probably in her fifties but she looked older. She wore a faded housecoat and although it was approaching eleven o'clock, her curly dark hair with greying temples had not yet been combed.

Fiona smiled and held out her warrant card. 'Detective Sergeant Madden and Detective Garda Tracy.'

Nora Joyce opened the door wide. 'Fiona Maire *beag, tá aithne agam ort, agus tá aitne agam ar do mháthair*. I know you, I knew your mother.'

Fiona saw the light in Joyce's eyes. It wasn't simply recognition. Joyce knew about her. Knew her story. This was the area her mother came from so her shame had probably been the talk of their small nation. Some stains can never be washed away. She looked at Tracy. His face was blank. No matter how good a detective he would become, and he had the potential to be particularly good, he would never catch the signal that passed between the two women. '*Leabharamid as Bearla, níl móran Gaeilge ag mo cara.* We'll speak English because my colleague doesn't speak Gaelge.'

'*Taraigí isteach*, come in.'

Fiona had an idea that she had seen Nora somewhere but she couldn't remember where. No matter, it would come to her. She led the way into the bungalow. There was a corridor leading to the rear but Fiona instinctively turned to the left and found herself in the compact living room. There were a threadbare couch and two well-worn easy chairs facing a TV that sat in the far corner of the room.

'I'll get some tea,' Joyce said and left the two police officers to select their own seats.

Fiona sat on the couch and motioned for Tracy to join her. She looked around the room. There was an array of photos on the wall. The family photo showed four children, two boys and two girls. There was the obligatory framed picture of the Sacred Heart but there was no sign of Mr and Mrs Joyce, no wedding photo, and no family photo including the parents.

Nora returned carrying a tray. Fiona rose and offered to help her but Nora placed the tray on the wooden coffee table and distributed the tea into three cups and added milk and sugar before sitting down.

'We're here about Sarah.' Fiona sipped her tea.

'I know,' Joyce said.

'Still no word from her?'

'Not a peep, she's been missing since these two days and there hasn't been hide nor hair of her since.'

'When did you last see her?'

'The evening before last. She left the house at about half six. I supposed that she was heading for a shift at the pub.'

'What was she wearing?'

'I think it was a white shirt, blue jeans, and a brown pullover. That's what she normally wore.'

'Did she ever say anything about running away?'

'Never a word.'

'Was she a happy teenager?'

'I thought so. She was caught up with her magazines about fashion and make-up. And she was addicted to that bloody mobile phone, first thing in the morning and the last thing at night. The worst bloody invention that ever was.'

'She attends the local secondary school?' Fiona asked.

Nora nodded.

'Any problems there, for example did she complain about bullying?'

'She wasn't the type to be bullied and anyway she had a brother who would have sorted it out. But she probably wouldn't have confided in me if she was being bullied. She was at the age when they start being secretive.'

'So you have absolutely no idea why she might have run away or where she might have gone.'

Tears began to run down Nora Joyce's cheeks. 'I'm worried sick.'

Fiona removed a packet of paper handkerchiefs from her pocket and offered one to Nora. 'How many children do you have?'

'Four including Sarah, Conor is the eldest. He's at college in Sligo. Cloe is thirteen and Gerald is ten.'

'What about Mr Joyce?"

'He left just after Gerry was born. I haven't seen him since. Some of the people in the village have relations in Chicago. They've heard that he's living there with another woman.'

'Would she have confided in Cloe?'

'You're kidding. She hardly gives her the time of day.'

'Do you work?'

'I work behind the till at the local petrol station.'

A light bulb went off in Fiona's head. That was where she'd met Joyce.

'Can we look at her room?'

Joyce wiped away her tears and stood up. 'She doesn't have a room to herself. She shares with her younger sister.' She led them along the corridor and opened a door at the rear. 'The place is in a mess. I clean it nearly every day but they mess it up again.'

There were two single beds pushed against the walls on either side of the room with a gap between them. The only other pieces of furniture were a wardrobe and a small bookcase on the wall. Fiona looked at the books. They were exclusively young adult and romances. There was no sign of a diary. She moved to the wardrobe. There were a few pairs of jeans and two dresses suitable for attending mass in. She looked around for a computer. There wasn't one. 'Are any of her clothes missing?'

Nora had stopped at the entrance to the room. 'She doesn't have much in the way of clothes. I don't think that anything is missing.'

'What about a suitcase or weekend case?'

'We don't have suitcases or weekend cases.'

'Sarah has the bed on the right?'

'Yes.'

Fiona lifted the pillow. Nothing. The mattress was thin and she lifted it with ease. Again nothing. She could see why a young girl living in the wilds of Connemara whose reading was centred on romantic literature might take flight. However, a couple of days in the real world would usually be sufficient to drive her back to her family. But the opposite was sometimes true. There were undesirables trawling the train and bus stations looking for vulnerable young women and men. Fiona turned. 'Let's go back to the living room.'

'Are you aware that your daughter has a Facebook profile?' Tracy asked when they were reinstalled in their seats.

'No,' Nora said. 'She pays for the phone from the tips she earns by doing a bit of waitressing at the local pub.'

Tracy took out his mobile phone and brought up the picture that Sarah Joyce had posted of herself. He handed the phone to Nora. 'Your daughter posted that picture.'

Nora examined the photo. 'That is not my daughter. That's not Sarah. This girl is much older and Sarah would never have a photo sticking out her behind like that.' Her facial expression belied her certainty.

'I'm afraid that's Sarah,' Fiona said. 'Have you any idea where she got the dress and who might have taken the photo.'

Nora shook her head and handed back the phone. She stared at the carpet beneath her feet.

Fiona stood. 'Thanks for your help. And don't worry. Eighty per cent of teenagers that run away return home. It's a rite of passage for a lot of them.'

'What about the other twenty per cent?' Nora asked.

'Most of them have a good reason for not returning. They've suffered abuse. But since your husband hasn't been around for ten years, familial abuse seems unlikely. Do you and Sarah argue often?'

'About as often as most mothers argue with a headstrong daughter.'

'Do these arguments ever become physical?'

Nora stiffened. 'I have never struck my children.'

'Sorry, I had to ask. Do you know her teacher's name?'

'Eileen Canavan, but you probably remember her as Eileen Folan. She married a local man'

After a slight hesitation, Fiona said. 'I remember Eileen from school. We'll have to speak with her.'

Tracy extended his hand. 'Thanks for the tea, Mrs Joyce.' He started to walk down the path to the road.

Fiona stopped at the door. 'We'll probably be back. In the meantime, I'd be grateful if you would make a list of Sarah's friends. '

'Do you think she'll come back?' The tears returned.

'There's a good chance, possibly with her tail between her legs. Try not to worry.'

'Worrying is part of being a mother.'

Fiona nodded and followed Tracy. The final remark had hit home. Had she ever worried about what had happened to her child? Maybe eighteen years ago she had but not much in the interim. The arrival of the young man claiming to be her son was making her sensitive to certain remarks.

'What do you think?' Tracy said, standing by the driver's side of the car.

'I don't know. She's been missing for three days and in the eyes of the law she's still a child. We'll do a full investigation and then pass the result to the Missing Persons Bureau in Phoenix Park.'

'You're assuming she not coming home under her own steam.'

'This isn't my first missing persons case. The statistics say that most missing persons return after forty-eight hours. We're beyond that already. When we get back to the station, I want you to have a look at the sex offender's register. Let's find out if we have someone in the vicinity.'

Tracy was about to move away but stopped. 'Two points: what's with the Fiona Maire *beag* and why the hesitation after you heard the teacher's name?'

'We deal in patronymics out here or in this case

matronymics. The locals rarely use their surnames instead they give their own first name, the first name of their father and the first name of their grandfather. That's usually sufficient to identify them. My mother is known locally as Maire beag or little Maire, which makes me Fiona Maire beag. And Eileen Canavan and I were in school together. Now get in the car and get us back to Galway.'

Tracy glanced back at the Joyce house before opening the car door. 'If I lived there, I think I'd probably run away as soon as I could.'

Fiona opened the passenger side door. 'I was raised in a house like that not far from here and it didn't do me a bit of harm.'

'That's a matter of opinion.' Tracy got into the car.

# CHAPTER SIX

Professor Ashling McGoldrick surveyed the class of students before her. She had just celebrated her tenth year lecturing at the National University of Ireland in Galway. The lecturing had become perfunctory except that each crop of undergraduates threw up different challenges. The current crop was no different. The composition of the class was eighty per cent female. It appeared that psychology was becoming recognised as a caring profession and only those with a high level of empathy need apply. She was into her well-practised wrap-up when she noticed that she had lost some of the class. This was a rare occurrence. Lecturing was a performance, a mini drama that she was completely in control of. Her lectures were meticulously prepared. Her stories resonated with the subject matter and were delivered in a way to inspire her students to look beyond the lecture. That wasn't the case today. Something was off. She was off. Then she realised that she had allowed her mind to wander during the class. Ever since she'd left the cottage that morning, she'd been obsessing on the arrival of Fiona's son and the impact it might have on their established relationship. She had no doubt that the boy would turn out to be Fiona's son. After all, she was the one who had constantly warned Fiona that this day might come and that they should have a contingency plan. But Fiona didn't want to think about the possibility that her life might one day be turned upside down by the child that she had given away. She quickly finished the lecture and asked the students to write an essay on the use of mindfulness in treating clinical depression. That would wake up some of the dozers. She gathered her papers and made her way back to her office. There were several pictures of Fiona and her on her desk. She sat staring at them for several minutes. Her life had changed in so many ways since she and Fiona got together. She knew they made a strange couple. She was the staid intellectual and Fiona was this female action-figure come to life. Most of their friends saw them as a case of opposites attract. When they'd met, she'd been overweight, not obese but Rubenesque. Fiona soon fixed that. There was no sitting in front of the television. Weekends were for hiking whatever the weather. On those long treks, they had opened their hearts to each other. She loved Fiona with all her heart and she was sure that Fiona felt the same about her. She'd been harping on at her for the past year that they should start a family. Fiona was still young enough to bear another child and there were lots of possibilities available from sperm banks. She fancied some Scandinavian sperm. However, Fiona was unreceptive. That was before her son arrived on the scene. They were faced with the prospect of an instant family and she wasn't sure if that would be positive or negative. It was nearing eleven and Tim would be up and about by now. They hadn't had a chance to talk alone since he arrived so she cleared away the papers on her desk and went immediately to the car park. The drive back to the cottage took only fifteen minutes and she had nothing on her agenda until a staff meeting set for three o'clock. She would run the professional rule over young Tim.

·  ·  ·

Ashling entered the cottage. There was no sign of Tim. She was about to call out when she heard a noise coming from her and Fiona's bedroom. She went to the door. Tim was rummaging through the contents of the top drawer of their bureau. 'You're up,' she said

Tim jumped. He returned some photos he was holding to the drawer. 'Yeah, I bet it looked like I'd sleep through the day. Fiona said she had some family photos she wanted to show me but we didn't have time to get to it last night.'

'Jet lag can do that to you. Let's go into the living room and maybe you should ask before you enter our bedroom.'

'Sorry, you're right, I shouldn't have gone in there without permission. You finished work already?'

'No, I lecture at the university. My schedule is loose. I thought I'd drop back and see how you're getting along.'

'You told me last night that you teach psychology. That means you're smart, right.'

'Are you trying to butter me up?'

'No, but I do want to be your friend. I'm not stupid. I know that you guys have been cruising along and suddenly I drop in here like a bombshell. My mom told me that I should write first. But I was afraid that Fiona would be frightened off and refuse to meet me. I read lots of shit on the Internet from adopted kids whose real parents freaked out when they contacted them. We're like the birds that get kicked out of the nest and the parents reject them because they have a different smell on them.'

'Fiona's not like that and neither am I. Although, I have to admit that your sudden arrival caught us off guard.'

'I'm not here to cause a problem.'

'No, you're here to get answers.'

'I was right, you are smart.'

'Maybe I should have pointed out that I'm a clinical psychologist.'

'That means you're listening to me and getting inside my head.'

'No, it means I'm trying to figure out who you are and how we can move ahead in a positive way.' She smiled; who was she kidding? Being a clinical psychologist wasn't something that she could turn off at six o'clock in the evening. Of course she was assessing Tim. She wasn't yet sure whether he represented a threat or an opportunity. She stared at him. He was young, naïve, and vulnerable. He needed someone to protect him from the emotional distress that was waiting around the corner for him. But she wasn't going to be his protector. Fiona was her main concern. Despite her hard exterior, Fiona's demons sometimes raged within her. Did Tim Daly represent an existential threat to her perfect relationship with Fiona? She didn't know, but it was important to answer that question. 'So what happens when you get the answers to your questions?'

'I haven't figured that out yet.'

'What if you don't get the answers you want?'

'I don't know.'

'Coffee?'

'That'd be great.'

She walked to the kitchen, put on the kettle, and deposited a heaped spoon of coffee into each cup. She told herself that she should try to be conversational rather than professional. When the kettle boiled, she filled the cups and returned to the living room.

'Tell me about your adoptive parents.' She handed him a cup.

'My dad is great. He's an engineer and works for a big consulting company in Boston. He's like one of the big guys in the company. But he works too much. I liked it more when I was young and he had more time for the family. He used to be such a big outdoor guy. Almost as soon as I could walk, we went camping every weekend during the summer. Now he works weekends or he's away at conferences or meetings. We have a summer house on the Cape and we go sailing. But he only comes for a couple of weeks.'

'Sounds like you have a great life there.'

'Yeah, you could say that. Dad's an example of the American dream. His parents were poor.'

'What about your mother?'

'Mom is mom, she's the rock of the family. She teaches at the local kindergarten. The kids adore her.'

She sipped her coffee. 'Sounds like you've got the perfect family.'

'I suppose so. There's a lot of love and we've never had money problems.'

Ashling was juxta-positioning Tim's perfect life with the shattered lives of her private clients. A world full of Tims would be a pretty happy place. 'So, why the quest to find your natural parents? Why not go to university, meet a girl, get a job, and live happily ever after?'

'Like we say in the States, I got an itch that I just have to scratch.' He finished his coffee and took his cup into the kitchen.

Ashling wondered whether Tim's description of his life was the ideal that he described. A tap ran in the kitchen. It looked like his departure signified that their session together was terminated. She finished her coffee and waited. The running water ceased and Tim returned but didn't take his seat.

'I've been in all morning,' he said. 'I think I'll take a walk.'

'Alone?'

'I'm sure you have lots of other things to do.'

She stood. 'You're right, I have a full schedule this afternoon.' She didn't like the feeling that she had just been dismissed. She raised her head and looked into his eyes. There was a look there that suggested they weren't the eyes of a naïve young man.

He smiled and his eyes automatically softened. He

reached to take the coffee cup from her hand. 'I'll wash this for you.'

She let him have it. 'You're well trained.' She watched him walk into the kitchen. 'Don't forget to lock up before you leave.'

'Okay, have a nice afternoon.'

Ashling sat in her car for a moment without starting the engine. It all seemed so perfect but a small alarm bell was wringing in her head. Tim Daly had certainly researched Fiona. Perhaps someone should return the compliment.

# CHAPTER SEVEN

'Ah, Madden, glad you could spare the time.' Chief Superintendent Charles Cranitch closed the file he was working on and indicated the chair in front of his desk.

'Sir.' She pulled back the chair and sat. Fiona had been operating on autopilot since early morning but a lunch consisting of a plate of Irish stew and two pints of water had brought her back to the real world. That meant that she had realised that there was a young man in her cottage who claimed to be the son her mother had given away for adoption eighteen years previously. She wished it wasn't so but she had a feeling that when she returned to the cottage that evening Tim Daly would still be there. One thing she was certain of was that there would be no repeat of the previous night's drinking exploits.

Cranitch moved the file aside, settled himself comfortably in his chair and sighed. The chair creaked in protest. He was a corpulent sixty-year-old who was six months away from his pension. 'I've had various bigwigs on the phone this morning concerning your little performance on Shop Street yesterday. The chairman of the Galway European City of Culture was on the line for a good half hour giving me jip because people around the globe could witness a Garda detective beating the shit out of a citizen.' He held up his mobile phone. 'Apparently, you're a YouTube sensation. Or maybe a Facebook sensation, I'm never sure. Anyway, people can see you on their mobile phones beating up a poor unfortunate. Care to look?'

She shook her head. 'I don't do either YouTube or Facebook. I gave up social media when most of the users plumped for a video of a cat playing with a ball of wool rather than real events.'

'I'll give you a piece of advice, Madden. Don't get fucking smart with me. What the hell were you up to?'

'I didn't beat the shit out of Molloy. I simply restrained him.'

'The great and the good of Galway city don't agree with you. And they're the ones that count.'

'Molloy is six two and weighs a hundred plus kilos, I'm five four and weight sixty kilos soaking wet. And he threw the first punch. I checked yesterday afternoon and he was released after triage. No permanent damage, a bruise on his knee, and a bump on his head. His wife is still in hospital and won't be out for six months or until a plastic surgeon fixes the damage to her face.'

'You should have taken a couple of the heavy mob along to assist with the arrest.'

'Our colleagues in Dublin tried that. It didn't turn out so good for them.'

'His lawyer is talking police brutality.'

'Good luck with that. When the jury gets a look at the both of us, that claim is going to be in the toilet.'

Cranitch pushed over a piece of paper. 'Professional Services want to have a word with you. I'd advise you to be a little more contrite that you're being today. They'll be in touch.'

She picked up the paper, folded it, and put it in her pocket without reading.

'Horgan tells me you're on a missing person case. At least that should keep you out of harm's way.'

'Sixteen-year-old from out Glenmore way. We've only spoken to her mother.'

'Build the file and pass it to Phoenix Park.' He reached out and picked up the file he'd been reading. 'And for fuck's sake stay out of trouble.'

Fiona stood. 'Yes, sir.'


'Are you still on the job?' Tracy asked as soon as she was seated at her desk.

'Just about.' She took the letter about the Professional Services interview from her pocket and tossed it to him. 'Have a read of this. If you stick with me, you'll be receiving one of your own sometime soon.'

Tracy opened the letter and read. 'I assume they'll want to speak to me. I saw him throw the first punch.'

'Nice to know that you'll speak up for me.'

'Do you get off on rejecting people? The appropriate response to my comment was "Thanks".'

'I'm not known for making the appropriate response. Any news from our case?'

'Your old schoolfriend Eileen Canavan can spare us a few minutes after class this evening.'

'She's not my friend.'

'She sounds nice on the phone. And she's very worried about Sarah Joyce's disappearance. She also gave me the names of five of Sarah's friends and suggested that we should talk to them.'

'I wasn't planning on a return trip to Connemara.'

'I could always go alone.'

'On second thoughts you could drop me home when we're finished.'

'I noticed you weren't riding that ancient piece of crap when you arrived this morning.'

'My grandfather bought that bike in the 1960s and completely rebuilt it. It's worth a fortune so don't you diss it.'

'I took the liberty of checking the social media of the names the teacher gave me. There's a lot of comment on Sarah's disappearance.'

'Anything useful?'

'I haven't had a chance to look at it in detail. But I'll do it before we talk to them in person.'

'What time is Eileen expecting us?'

Tracy looked at his watch. 'In about an hour.'

# CHAPTER EIGHT

A shling had a busy afternoon but, as with her below-par performance at the lectern, her colleagues were surprised at her lack of engagement at the departmental meeting. She had been playing back her conversation with Tim. Not just the words but the intonation. She thought about his gestures, the way he presented himself. There was a complete picture to analyse. If he had been a client, she would have made a recording of the session that she could review and take notes. Something had been off but she couldn't put her finger on it and the more she tried the more it eluded her.

'What do you think, Ashling?'

She only heard her name at the end of the question from the head of the department. The subject under discussion was a mystery to her. On another day she might try to fudge an answer but she knew that her colleagues had noted her reverie. 'Sorry, Barry, I'm afraid I'm away with the fairies this afternoon.'

'Perhaps we could have a session later,' Barry said.

Ashling tried to hide her embarrassment. 'I'm rather busy but maybe if we can arrange a mutual time.' The levels of stress within the department were high and it was a requirement that each member of the faculty who dealt with outside clients was subject to a monthly session where their own mental health was examined. She had only recently had a session with Barry but she could see that he might want an update given her apparent self-absorption. She pulled her mind back to the departmental meeting and tried to concentrate on the business at hand.

As soon as the meeting terminated, she went to her office and switched on her computer. She had fifteen minutes to kill before a tutorial with some masters students. She opened her browser and typed *Tim Daly* into the subject line and stared at the screen as a page of text loaded. The bottom of the page indicated that there were at least twelve more pages to examine. There was a knock on the door and she looked at her watch. She would have to abandon her search until she had more free time. She shut down her computer and prepared to meet her tutorial students.

# CHAPTER NINE

Coming back to Galway had been a calculated risk, Fiona was thinking as she passed from the suburbs of Galway into Connemara. The people who say that you should never go back might just have got it right. She'd been unhappy in Dublin. The work was varied and interesting but her colleagues made an issue of her sexuality. The press would rabbit on about the new Ireland and the public acceptance of sexual diversity. But tell that to some copper who had been lured down from the mountains of Tipperary with hunks of raw meat. The pressure was such that she had the option of leaving the force or asking for a transfer. She wondered who had the quiet word with Human Resources that sent her back to the only place she didn't want to go. Connemara is a magical place. It's the land of lakes and mountains but it's also the land of ghosts. It's a place where you constantly run into your past. And if that past brings up demons from the depths, then God help you. Fiona shivered. She thought about the young man in her cottage. Was he a part of her past that she'd thought was dead and buried? Her grandfather had claimed that their family was descended from the leaders of a druidic cult and that they had second sight. She'd thought that the old man was a talented storyteller and a bullshitter. Now she wished to God that he'd been telling the truth. She'd looked into Tim's eyes but she hadn't discerned any truth. She'd always feared that her past would catch up with her. Now, it appeared it had. The question was: would it unlock further secrets she'd prefer to keep buried? If she were being honest, she would say that she'd been looking over her shoulder for the past eighteen years. Knowing that the son she'd borne and given away was out there somewhere meant that there was a possibility that he would come knocking on her door. And yesterday that was exactly what had happened. It wasn't really a surprise when something happened that you've been expecting for such a long time. It just wasn't what she had visualised. There was no warm feeling. No desire to throw her arms around him. Her first thought had been, *Oh fuck*. Fiona knew she was by nature a cold person. Experience had taught her to be wary of compliments and instant friendships. She detested the backslappers who were only waiting for their opportunity to replace their open hand with a clenched fist holding a knife. She shouldn't have returned to Galway. There were too many ghosts. Tim Daly would have found her wherever she was. But every time she envisaged the future; she saw a train rushing in her direction. She tried to banish the dark thoughts. On the positive side, in returning to Galway she had met Ashling and they had gotten together in record time. It seemed like it might last although Fiona knew that she was an acquired taste. Maybe Ashling's job gave her the skills to deal with Fiona's moods.

'Penny for them,' Tracy said.

'I'm thinking about the missing teenager,' Fiona lied. 'I wonder what she's running away from.'

'Maybe Eileen Canavan has some inkling.'

'You obviously don't know much about teenage girls. I doubt that her teacher has any idea where Sarah Joyce might be.'

'Have you worked on many missing persons cases?'

'A few.'

'Care to elucidate.'

'Elucidate? What orifice do you pull these words out of? Cops don't use words like elucidate.'

'Okay, care to share your experience on the cases you've worked on.'

'That's more like cop talk. It's like I told her mother. Eighty per cent return home with their tail between their legs. Fifteen per cent don't want to be found and the other five per cent will never be found. You don't want to hear that your child is in the five per cent. Also, most of the missing children are in care. That's what bothers me most about Sarah Joyce. I know the house we were in this morning was no palace but it was clean and Mrs Joyce seemed like a caring parent. That rang an alarm bell.'

'You think Sarah might have been abducted.'

'Abductions are rare and they generally involve younger children and an aggrieved parent. I wouldn't discount it at this point in the investigation but it's unlikely. I have a feeling that this isn't one of those cases where we'll be high fiving and ordering rounds of drinks when we find her.'

'And what's that conclusion based on?'

'Sixteen years of experience as a copper and a lifetime as a pessimist.'

'You're aware that you're supposed to mentor me and part of that is making me enthusiastic about the job.'

'Then God help you. How long have you been in the job?'

'Six years.'

'And you can still speak about enthusiasm. You're a newly minted detective and your family is as proud as punch of you. Up to now you've been pounding the beat or riding around in a car checking whether some motorist's tax and insurance are up to date. That was the clean end of the stick. The day you agreed to be called "detective" you agreed to exchange the clean end of the stick for the shitty end. You're going to see things in the next years that are going to shake your belief in the goodness of human nature. Whatever bit of humanity you're carrying around with you now will be erased. You will see human depravity at its worst. Initially it will disgust you but eventually you'll be able to see depravity as normality.'

'The philosophy of policing according to Detective Sergeant Fiona Madden. Not an uplifting discourse.'

'You should have done something more edifying with that degree of yours.' She smiled. 'You're having a bad effect on me. I just used a three-syllable word.'

In Glenmore, Tracy parked the car across the street from the school. The parking area was already occupied by what looked like waiting parents. They sat and watched as the doors of the school opened and a flood of children aged from fourteen to eighteen emerged into the playground and made their way to either the waiting cars or the school bus parked at the side of the playground. Tracy opened the driver's side door and climbed out on the tarmac. Fiona was rooted to the spot. She stared at the building. Nothing had changed since she had been a student. The last time she had entered that building she was sixteen years old and six months pregnant. She hadn't shown much during her pregnancy but at six months it was noticeable and her days as a schoolgirl were effectively over. For reasons of decorum, she would never return to this school. The disgrace of illegitimate pregnancy wasn't hers alone but also her family's and even her community's. She'd been wondering since why nobody ever bothered to find out what exactly had happened. Rumours abounded but the truth was unpalatable. It was easier to propagate the story that she was a wanton harlot. She wondered what the believers of that untruth would think if they knew her sexual orientation precluded heterosexual wantonness. She'd hated her mother for giving her baby away but in the fullness of time, she'd understood that in rural Ireland it had been a necessity. Her child would have been a bastard with all that the word connoted. She willed her body to move but remained still, staring at the open doors that led into the place where her shame was exposed.

Tracy came around to her side of the car and opened her door. Fiona steeled herself and reluctantly stepped out. She scanned the faces of the parents in the waiting cars. They looked to be her age but she didn't recognise any of them. Tracy was already at the gate of the school and Fiona made her legs work and followed him across the playground and through the entrance. A group of teachers was standing in the vestibule just inside the double doors that constituted the entrance. They looked harried and tired. Eileen Canavan's gaze fell on Fiona and she immediately broke away from the group.

'Fiona.' Canavan held out her arms for a hug.

Fiona allowed herself to be embraced but didn't respond. Canavan had put on weight and her body felt soft and feminine.

Canavan stood back. 'You haven't changed a bit. When did you get back to Galway?'

'A year ago.' Canavan certainly had changed and it wasn't only the addition of tens of kilos in weight. On Fiona's last day in school, Eileen Canavan had been a bright-eyed, blonde-haired attractive young girl. Now her hair was a mousy brown, her face was pale and tired, and she looked ten years older than Fiona knew she was. There were a small diamond engagement ring and a gold band on the fourth finger of her left hand. If Fiona had to guess, she would assume that there were at least four junior mouths to feed in her household. They hadn't been friends at school. Canavan was a swat while Fiona was more interested in sports. But they hadn't been enemies. Their paths had simply deviated.

'Why haven't you been out to see us?'

'I've been busy.' It was time to put an end to the reminiscence. She turned and pulled Tracy into the conversation. 'This is Detective Garda Tracy.'

'Your partner,' Canavan said.

Fiona nodded. 'Is there somewhere we can have a quiet word?'

'Of course.' Canavan led them along a corridor and opened the door to one of the classrooms.

The outside of the building might not have changed since Fiona had attended but the interior certainly had. The room contained chairs and tables that looked new and comfortable. The walls were covered with charts and maps and the blackboard had been replaced by an ultra-modern whiteboard. It looked like an environment where learning might be fun rather than work.

Canavan arranged three chairs around one of the tables and sat facing Fiona. 'It's great to see you again.'

Fiona smiled. Canavan seemed genuinely pleased to see her.

'I don't think I've seen you since your last day at school. I'd heard that you joined the Garda Síochána but nothing since. Where have you been?'

Was it interest or probing? Fiona didn't want to be probed. She'd carried out hundreds of interviews. Keep it short and simple. 'Templemore then Dublin, now I'm in Mill Street.'

'And where are you living?'

'My grandfather left me a cottage outside Barna. I've been fixing it up.'

'Are you married?'

'My girlfriend lectures at the university.' There, let's get that chestnut out of the way as soon as possible.

Canavan's face registered surprise. That piece of news didn't fit with the local profile.

'It's great catching up, Eileen,' Fiona said. 'But I'm the one that's supposed to be asking the questions.'

'Sorry, you know the way it is out here,' Canavan said. 'We're raised asking questions. Can I offer you a cup of tea?'

'No, thanks,' Fiona said. 'My colleague already mentioned that we're looking into the disappearance of Sarah Joyce?'

Canavan nodded.

'She's been missing for the best part of a week. Would you have any idea where she might be?'

'I have her for several classes. I was wondering why she wasn't attending. I thought she might be ill.'

'Apparently not. What kind of girl is she'

'A middling student, popular with the boys and the girls. She appears well-adjusted, for a teenager.'

'Any problems?'

'Nothing I can think of.'

'Have you ever had someone run away before?'

'You think that she's run away?'

'We're keeping an open mind at the moment.' Fiona waited for the answer to her question.

'Not in my time.'

'Does she confide in any of the teachers?'

Canavan laughed. 'Sorry, but that would be unique. You're not up on your teenage culture. Teachers are basic.'

Fiona's brow wrinkled.

'Basic is the up-to-date word for unexciting, not cool,' Canavan said. 'I think cool went out of use a few years ago. They invent new words quicker than we can learn the old ones. Sarah was a precocious young girl until a few months ago. Then she started to develop what I might call a bit of maturity.'

Fiona looked at Tracy. 'Show her the photo.'

Tracy flicked through his mobile and found Sarah's photo from her Facebook page. He handed the phone to Canavan.

'Holy God, that's not Sarah.' She took a pair of glasses from her pocket and looked at the photo again. 'That

Kardashian woman has a lot to answer for. That photo is way too provocative for a girl of fifteen.'

'Her mother claims she doesn't have a dress like that,' Fiona said.

'I should hope not. I have two girls myself and I'd be mortified if either of them had a photo like that taken at fifteen. If you saw the way she dressed at school, you wouldn't say it was the same person.'

'Perhaps she wanted to look more grown up,' Tracy said.

'My partner was turned on by the photo,' Fiona said.

Tracy reddened. He closed the phone.

'Did she have a boyfriend?' Fiona asked.

'Not that I'm aware of.'

'We need a list of her friends.'

Canavan went to the end of the room and returned with a sheet of paper and a pencil. She started writing names. When she was finished, she handed the paper to Tracy. 'Will you be talking to the children?'

'Definitely, and how much depends on the direction of the investigation. There's a good chance that Sarah will arrive home tomorrow a bit mortified by whatever adventure she went on. Then we can all go home and forget that it ever happened.'

Canavan relaxed. 'I suppose that's the usual outcome. Running away is probably a teenage rite of passage. At that age, they're a mass of emotions and raging hormones. I sometimes wish that I'd concentrated on teaching the young ones. There's so much less stress.'

Fiona stood. 'We've taken up enough of your time.' She was about to extend her hand but resisted the urge.

Canavan led them out of the room. 'I always liked you, Fiona. You were a free spirit and I envied you. I'm glad everything worked out for you. Please don't be a stranger. I'd love to have a coffee sometime.'

'Stranger things have happened.' Fiona motioned to Tracy to follow her.

They crossed the road to the car and Tracy stopped. 'Am I missing something here?'

'What do you mean?' Fiona said.

'There was a message passing between you and Eileen Canavan. It was the same with Nora Joyce this morning. Are you going to clue me in?'

'You're dreaming.' She opened the passenger side door. She had neglected to mention when she joined the force that she was a mother and the fewer who had that nugget of information the better.

Tracy sat behind the wheel. 'If it's relevant to the Sarah Joyce case, then maybe I should know.'

'Give up trying so hard to be a detective. Try to see what's there rather than what you think is there. Now let's get back to Galway. By the time we're there, we'll be off the clock. Tomorrow we'll start interviewing Sarah's friends. Horgan will want us to wind up the investigation as quickly as possible so we can pass the file to Dublin.'

'Case closed.' Tracy started the car.

'For us; we'll let the so-called experts at it.' Fiona looked back at the entrance to the school. Canavan was speaking with two of the other teachers. She wondered whether she was the topic of the conversation. She was transported back eighteen years. Although it probably wasn't a fact, she was sure that everyone in her village was talking about her scandal. She'd quit school before anyone could deface her locker with a spray-painted "Skank" or the younger children could titter every time she passed by. After she left school, she'd been sent to live with one of her aunts in Dublin and her baby son was adopted straight from the hospital. She had a vague remembrance of a stern-looking woman getting her to sign some papers. Two days later, she was discharged. As she'd exited, she'd seen babies being cuddled by their parents and she had been so overcome by sadness that she spent the next two weeks in bed crying. There was no way that she was going back to school or Connemara so she started working in a bar in the village of Blackrock just outside Dublin. The pay was crap but the tips were good. She moved out of her aunt's house and into a flat with two other girls. They kicked her out when she owned up to being a lesbian during a drunken evening. Life could have spiralled downwards except that one of her clients at the bar ran a dojo and forced her to go along for a free session. Accepting that invitation saved her life. She spent every free hour taking classes and studied aikido, tae kwon do, ju-jitsu, and judo and obtained a black belt in each. She started taking night classes and obtained the Leaving Certificate that she'd been on her way to at school. It was a long trip from the village school to the woman who applied for the Garda exam at twenty-one. She looked over her shoulder and saw that Canavan was staring at the departing police car.

## CHAPTER TEN

Ashling generally enjoyed her tutorial with her graduate students but this afternoon the hands of the wall clock seemed to crawl. She tried to focus on the discussion but found her mind wandering to her lunchtime conversation with Tim. There was something there but she couldn't quite put her finger on it. Maybe it was the fact that she had never met someone with the perfect life. She believed implicitly in the saying that into every life a little rain must fall. The fact that there didn't appear to be any rain in Tim Daly's life contradicted that view. She needed to get back on the computer and she needed to intercept Fiona on her way home. The first step in discerning the motivation of any client was to obtain the maximum amount of information about the client and their lives. She had played back her conversation with Tim and realised that he had given her little or no information about himself. The discussion was winding down and the little hand was on five and the big hand was about to hit twelve. Ashling thanked the students for their participation and set their reading for the next tutorial. She sighed with relief when the last student left the room.

'Where are you?' Ashling asked.

'We're almost back at Mill Street.' Fiona had been surprised to receive the phone call. Since Tracy was proving himself to be a better detective than she'd envisaged, she pressed the phone close to her ear.

'We need to talk.'

'I don't like the sound of that.'

'I passed by the cottage at lunchtime. Tim was there.'

'So?' On the trip back from Connemara, Fiona had been concentrating on what might have become of Sarah Joyce. Tim Daly occasionally crossed her mind but only in the context of wishing that he would disappear as quickly as he had appeared.

Ashling filled her in on her conversation with Tim. 'I've been asking myself all afternoon why a young man with the perfect life would have bothered to make such an effort to locate his birth parents. I got the impression that he wouldn't be content in just finding you but he needs some closure in finding his father. Is there something you'd like to tell me about Tim's father?'

Fiona looked across at Tracy. He didn't appear to be listening but appearances can be deceptive. 'No, let's talk later.'

'I'm through here but I want to spend a little time on the computer.'

'And I need a lift home.'

'Let's meet in Taaffes Bar at five thirty.'

'I'll be there.'

Ashling fired up her computer. Everybody on the planet, even the inhabitants of a village in Africa, leaves a trace. In the developed world, that trace is somewhere on the web. She took up her search where she'd left off.

## CHAPTER ELEVEN

Tracy pulled into a parking space outside the station. 'Maybe we should have left this one to the local coppers.' He turned off the car.

'You think?'

'We're going to be yo-yoing between Galway and Connemara. Tomorrow we'll interview the kids so we're back out west again.'

'You'd prefer to be back in uniform? This is part of the job. You're a detective now. It's what most of the ambitious coppers aspire to and you've made it. You'll learn to enjoy it. We'll wrap up the Sarah Joyce case and you can get on to more exciting shit like finding out who's mugging old ladies in Shop Street.'

'I didn't hear that someone was mugging old ladies.'

'Summer's coming and that means so are the muggers.' Fiona opened the door and climbed out of the car. The day shift was pouring out of the station. Most of them were heading off home to their families or maybe stopping at a local pub for a pint on the way home. The government clampdown on drink driving meant that the pint would have to be the only one. There was no point in going to the squad room. 'Why don't you write up the interview with Canavan.'

'Is that an order, Sarge?'

Fiona smiled but the smile disappeared when she saw Horgan exit the station and head in their direction.

'DS Madden and Detective Garda Tracy, nice to see you,' Horgan said.

'We're working the Joyce missing person case,' Fiona said. 'We've spoken to her mother and her teacher.' She looked at Tracy. 'The report will be on your desk tomorrow morning.'

'There's been a bit of fallout from the Molloy arrest. Apparently, they have the Internet in Dublin because our colleagues in Phoenix Park have viewed the footage of the arrest. The commissioner is in the loop and he's sending one of his minions down the day after tomorrow to get your side of the story.' He looked her up and down. 'Block out the morning and dress in something appropriate. We don't want him to think that you're a member of a motorcycle gang in your spare time.'

'I'll do my best, sir. I'll check if my little black cocktail dress has come back from the cleaners.'

'Someday you'll get too fucking smart with me and I'll have the immense pleasure of taking the sergeant's stripes away from you.'

'Sorry, sir, I was trying to make the point that my wardrobe is not that extensive.'

'Point taken. Just don't fuck up, Madden. How much longer will you be on the Joyce case?'

'We'll interview some of her school mates tomorrow and transfer what we have to Phoenix Park.' Fiona looked at her watch. 'I have an appointment, sir. Do you mind if I head off.'

'The day after tomorrow,' Horgan said. 'Dressed appropriately wherever you find the clothes.'

Fiona nodded at Tracy. 'As we discussed.'

Tracy nodded.

Horgan and Tracy watched as she joined the crowd leaving the station grounds.

'She's a royal pain in the arse,' Horgan said. 'But a damn fine detective. You know she got the highest score ever in the sergeant's exam.'

'You've heard that story about the guy in the States who aced the police exam. They didn't accept him because they thought he was too clever to become a cop.'

'You're another one of those clever buggers, Tracy. I prefer the old-time coppers myself. The university degrees can be an impediment sometimes.'

'You mean the old-timers that handed out justice with a truncheon.'

'The streets were safer then. I must follow the party line with Madden but I wish she'd have given Molloy a good kicking. After what he did to his wife, the bastard deserved all he got. I'm going to make sure that Madden isn't going to be punished for doing the right thing. How are you two getting along?'

'Fine.'

'I hate that fucking word. It means nothing. I'll ask you again, how are you two getting along?'

'She's a good mentor. I feel I'm learning a lot from her.'

'That's more like it. You know the story on her preferences?'

Tracy reddened. 'It was part of my introduction to the station. This is your desk and the toilet is in the corridor and Madden is a lesbian.'

'I don't agree with that kind of remark. A person's religious persuasion and sexual orientation is their business as long as it doesn't break the law.' He slapped Tracy on the shoulder. 'You take care of her and make sure she doesn't get into trouble. Have a nice evening.'

'Thank you, sir. The report on the interviews will be on your desk in the morning.'

Take care of Madden, Tracy thought as he made his way to the squad room. That'll be the day.

# CHAPTER TWELVE

For the past one hundred and fifty years, Taaffes Pub has been a Galway institution among the locals. It started life when Galway was only a village and remained intact as the village became a town and then a city. It's the place where the locals go to meet friends, have a drink, or listen to some of the best Irish music played by some of the best musicians in the country. Ashling was already ensconced in the small snug to the right of the entrance.

'What's up?' Fiona plonked herself down beside her partner.

'I don't know.'

'That's a good start.' Fiona looked at the untouched glass of orange juice in front of Ashling before motioning to the barman for a pint of Guinness. 'I'm supposed to be the one who's all over the place and you're supposed to be the rational one. I wouldn't like it if we had to reverse roles.' She stood up, took her drink from the bar, and drank a quarter. 'It's been a tough day. So you went to the cottage at midday and you spoke to Tim.'

'Yes.' Ashling sipped her orange juice.

'So what's the problem?'

'We talked and you know the way things are for me. I'm never really off the clock. When I ask questions, I'm analysing the answers before I ask the next question.'

'I noticed.'

'He mentioned that he felt that he was being analysed. Which means for me that he was giving me answers that he wanted me to hear. I was trying to be as subtle as I could. It was like a fencing match where every time I thrust, he parried.'

'I was never big into fencing. Get to the point.'

'I asked him about his adoptive parents. They were a little too perfect. The family was a loving one. His father was his pal, his mother was an angel in the house. There were no money or relationship problems. School was fantastic. He excelled at sports and his studies. He's set to enter a top college. The future is rosy.'

'I envy him.'

'Then what the hell is he doing looking up the woman who gave him up? And why the references to finding his father.'

Fiona finished her pint and called for another.

Ashling sighed. 'I thought we agreed that last night was an aberration.'

'Maybe you agreed. Every time Tim's name gets mentioned I feel the irresistible impulse to get sloshed.'

'Maybe that's because you're feeling guilty about him.'

'I should feel guilty that he was raised in a loving family. That he attended a school where he was educated and that his life is so perfect.'

'It's obvious that you do. What happened today?'

'I went back west twice today. That means I passed my parents' house twice and I didn't stop to see how my mother was.'

'You really have to do something about the amount of guilt you carry around with you.'

The second pint of Guinness arrived on the bar and Fiona retrieved it. 'Do you want another orange juice?'

Ashling shook her head.

'You're putting me on the couch again.' Fiona sipped her Guinness.

'I'm trying to help you. Someone should have done it years ago.'

'I'm not just your partner and your lover. I'm a project. You found me broken and you're going to fix me. What happens when I get fixed? Will you move on to the next project?'

'I love you and you're not a project. If I had a broken leg, you'd give me a shoulder to lean on. You are so much better than the version of you that you project. You're not the hard bitch you want people to see you as.'

'No, I'm the hard bitch that ignores the fact that she still has a mother. Let's take the spotlight off me. Like I said, it's been a tough day. I had to go back to places I would have preferred to avoid. But at least I decided that I must face the Tim issue straight on. When we go home this evening I want to go through the documents. If I'm his mother, I want to know what he wants from the relationship. If he needs someplace to holiday in Ireland, he can stay with me.'

'What if he wants you to be a mother?'

'Isn't it a little late for that?'

'Maybe not in his mind.'

'Let's cross that bridge when we come to it.'

'What about his father? From what he said, I think finding his father was as important as finding his mother.'

'I told you before. The sex wasn't consensual. I was already aware of my sexuality and therefore I was raped.'

'Okay, his father was a rapist but where is he now?'

'He's dead.'

'You're sure.'

Fiona hesitated. 'Other than having examined his dead body, yes.'

'So you knew his name?'

'Yes.'

'Do you have a photograph of him?'

'Sure, it's on the wall in my mother's cottage between the picture of the Sacred Heart and the faded photo of JFK. Of course, I don't have a photo of the bastard. I want to scrub him from my mind not carry something around to remind me of him.' Fiona walked to the bar and paid for her drinks. When she returned, she remained standing. 'Time to face the music.'

## CHAPTER THIRTEEN

Fiona's nose reacted to the smell of cooking as soon as they entered the cottage. She looked at Ashling who nodded. They walked through the living room to the kitchen annex at the rear. The table was set for three and there was an open bottle of red wine standing in the centre. Tim was bent over at the oven examining something that exuded the heavenly smell that pervaded the entire cottage.

'Good evening,' Fiona said. 'What's all this?'

Tim closed the oven door and stood up. 'Hi, guys, I thought that since I'm being put up for free maybe I should cook you guys dinner.'

'It smells terrific,' Ashling said. 'What is it?'

'Lamb hocks done Italian style with lots of celery, onions, garlic and tomatoes. I normally make it with pasta but since I'm in Ireland, we're having boiled potatoes.'

'Where did you get all this stuff?' Fiona asked.

'I walked to the local shop. They've got a fairly good selection.'

Ashling looked at the table. 'This is a real treat. We usually have something microwaved on our knees in front of the television.'

'You can pour yourselves a glass of wine,' Tim said. 'The food will be on the table in ten minutes.'

'Where did you learn to cook like that?' Fiona asked.

'Mom is a wonderful cook. I think maybe she took a lot of cooking classes when she was young.'

Fiona poured two glasses of wine. 'You're going to make some woman a wonderful husband.' She passed a glass to Ashling.

Ashling swirled the wine in the glass and smelled the bouquet. 'It smells wonderful. Aren't you joining us?'

'No thanks, I'm having water. I don't touch alcohol.'

Ashling sipped her wine. 'Smart boy.' She picked up the bottle from the table. 'This is Barolo. How much did this cost?'

Tim went to the sink and poured himself a glass of water. 'Ten euro, I think.'

Ashling's eyebrows rose. 'It should be a lot more than that.'

'I guess the store owner might have made a mistake with the price.'

'I'm surprised the store owner had a bottle of Barolo on the premises.'

Fiona put her glass on the table. 'If we've got ten minutes, I'll grab a shower.'

Ashling left her glass beside Fiona's. 'That's such a good idea, I'm going to do the same. Sorry, Tim, we'll be back soon.'

TIM WAS as good as his word and the food was on the table when they returned to the kitchen. All three dived in and filled their plates. The conversation centred on the upcoming US elections and Ashling was careful not to get into clinical psychologist mode. By the end of the meal, she was more doubtful of the instant conclusions she'd drawn following her lunchtime conversation with Tim. Over dinner, he'd shown himself to be both intelligent and articulate. There was a touch of narcissism in him but what eighteen-year-old doesn't think that he's the centre of the world. She castigated herself for what she considered an act of hubris. It was common for people in her profession to think themselves better at reading others than the ordinary Joe Soap. It wasn't always the case and she could point to many occasions when she had called it wrong. Thankfully, the fallout from those rare occasions wasn't disastrous. After dinner, Ashling collected the empty plates and shooed Fiona and Tim out of the kitchen.

Fiona sat down on the couch. They could forget about music having the charm to soothe the savage breast. As far as she was concerned a well-cooked dinner and a half bottle of Italian wine would do the job anytime. The food, the wine, and the light conversation were enough to banish the anxiety her trip to Connemara had created. She felt calm so it was as good a time as any to get to the bottom of Tim's quest. 'Let's see those documents of yours.'

'You're sure you want to do this?'

'I'm sorry I reacted the way I did yesterday. It was a hell of a day.'

'I know. I saw the video on YouTube. It's gone viral. You're famous.'

'For fifteen seconds, I hope. The man we arrested had almost beaten his wife to death and then ran. It wasn't his first rodeo, as you Americans say, he'd already done a stretch inside for grievous bodily assault on the cops who went to arrest him; he put two of them in hospital. I wasn't about to let him do the same to my partner and me. How did you come across the YouTube video?'

'I have you on Google Search. Every time you appear on social media, I get a message from Google with a link.'

'How long have you been following me?'

'About six months.'

'Interesting.' Fiona tried to hide the creepy feeling that had suddenly gripped her. She didn't like the idea that this total stranger had been prying into her life for such a long time without her having any clue it was happening. Now she knew how someone who is being stalked feels and it wasn't a positive feeling.

Tim dipped into his kitbag and brought out his folder. 'This is all my search material.' He handed her the folder. 'I've laid it out in chronological order. There's my correspondence with the society that arranged the adoption, then there's my communications with the group here in Ireland that helps people like me to obtain the local documentation, and finally, there's the research I did on the birth records that led me to you.'

Fiona held the folder in her hands but was staring directly at Tim. Yesterday, she had been unsure of his claim. The first thing that had struck her was that there wasn't any Madden in him. Her family was famous for having the same features. She didn't know what it was. Maybe it was the way he chewed the corner of his mouth when he spoke. Or perhaps it was the dark blue colour of his eyes or the shape of his nose. The more she looked at him the more he bore a resemblance to Michael Fathy, the man who had raped her. She was stunned for a moment. Why hadn't she looked for the resemblance earlier? Perhaps she had banished Fathy's features from her mind. She knew that wasn't the case. Fathy was the ghost that populated her dreams. She knew he wasn't coming back in the flesh but that didn't mean his spirit didn't still threaten her. She shook her head to clear it. She needed to dispel the creepy feeling at being stalked allied to her memory of being raped by Fathy. But she was now convinced that the young man sitting beside her bore a strong resemblance to the man who had violated her.

'What's up?'

'Sorry, I was away with the fairies for a couple of minutes there.'

'I know it's a lot to take in. It must be unexpected to find a total stranger outside your cottage who claims to be your long-lost son. I can tell you that it feels pretty weird for me as well.'

She patted him on the shoulder. The fact that he might be her son was probably in the documents but it wasn't in her heart. Perhaps she was transferring the misdeeds of the father to the son. That would be unfair. The son might be totally different from the father. 'I know. Ashling tells me constantly that it's not always about me and this is a case in point. We're going to work this thing out and however it turns out you'll always be welcome here.'

'I'll leave you alone to go through this stuff. The air here is so fresh I think I'll take a walk down to the ocean.' He stood up, smiled at her, and went to the front door.

The smile should have softened Fiona's heart but it didn't.

FIONA WAS HALFWAY through the first batch of communications when Ashling joined her on the couch.

'How's it going?'

'He is very persistent, almost obsessive.'

'It's part of the pathology. A lot of adopted children get on with life and have no desire to find their biological parents. They've grown up in secure, loving homes and slough off the fact that their adoptive parents are not their "real" parents. Sometimes these secure individuals are obliged to search for their biological parents because of the need for a medical history. Then there are cases like Tim's where the search becomes all-encompassing. That brings up the question of motivation. Our conversation in Taaffes segued away from what I really wanted to tell you. I started a computer search on Tim this afternoon. There are thirty-five pages of Tim Dalys on Google so I've only just begun. I've refined the search a bit but so far, I don't find any trace of our Tim Daly. It's early days.'

'He just told me that he's been following me on social

media for months. He's had a Google alert every time my
name gets mentioned. He'd already viewed the video of me
arresting Molloy in Shop Street. When he told me about it, I
got this creepy feeling.'

'You think he's your son, don't you.'

'I think that there's a good chance that he is who he says
he is.'

'But you don't want him to be.'

'It's a past that I've tried to run away from but I never actually managed. You were right when you told me that yesterday
was a day I should have been prepared for. Let's go through
the rest of these documents together.'


An hour later they had finished reading the exchanges of
letters and emails and the basic research that Tim had done on
the birth records.

'It's compelling,' Ashling said.

'But not conclusive,' Fiona said. Who was she kidding?
She hadn't given Ashling the nugget that might have sealed the
deal. Tim was the image of his rapist father. If there was a way
out of this morass, Fiona wanted to find it but she knew she
wasn't being fair to Tim. At the end of the day, she might have
to put up her hand and admit that Tim was her son. But what
then? She had missed changing the nappies, teaching him how
to walk, read him his books, pick him up at crèche. The million
and one events that helped to form the bond between parent
and child.

'What are you going to do?' Ashling asked.

'Go to the limit. I want to check our DNA.'

'Do you really want to go there?'

'I think I have to. There was a chief super in Store Street
who was a bit of a ladies' man. Before he got married, he had a
brief dalliance with a woman who subsequently got pregnant.
She claimed the resultant boy was his and being a good citizen

he accepted her assertion. He was involved in the boy's life for the next thirty years. He was there at every event, communion, confirmation, school plays the whole gamut. Then it comes time to make his will and he wants to include the boy. But his solicitor points out that for the taxman the boy is in the third category because there's no proof that the chief super is the father. They do the DNA and lo and behold sonny is not the chief super's. I think we need to go the distance.'

'It's your decision.'

'First off, I'm going to check with the adoption agency.' She held up the file with the documents. 'I need to get all these documents verified.'

'You're really scared that he might be your son. Most women would be thrilled if the child they gave up at birth turned up eighteen years later and wanted to get to know his mother.'

'I'm obviously not most women.'

'But I can see that you're scared. What are you afraid of?'

'Who says that I'm afraid? You do. Take off your clinical psychologist hat.'

The front door of the cottage opened and Tim entered the living room. Fiona and Ashling were standing facing each other. 'Sorry, am I interrupting something?'

'No.' Ashling answered first and gave Tim a smile. 'I want to watch the international film on RTE2 this evening while Fiona wants to have an early night.'

'If Ashling wants to watch it,' Fiona said. 'it's probably something very deep and Japanese.'

Ashling laughed. 'Actually, it's something Polish and very deep.'

'Did you get a chance to look through the documents?' Tim asked.

'I did,' Fiona said. 'You're a good researcher.'

'Is that all? Was that your only conclusion?'

'I need to talk to some of the people you communicated

with. On the face of it, you make a good case but this is some-thing we need to be sure of. Maybe we'll have to go for DNA.'

'I already did. I put it on an ancestry website and it came back that I'm ninety-five per cent Irish. It also connected me with some people who share my DNA but none of them are close. If there had been someone showing a close connection, I would have gone down that road.'

Fiona could feel the now-familiar shiver. 'I'll have a swab taken as soon as I have time. I'm working a case at the moment but I should be free in a couple of days.' She knew in her gut that Tim was her son. She also knew that the DNA would prove it. The sensible action would be not to waste time. She could simply throw her arms around him and whisper the word "son" in his ear as he kissed her. But she couldn't bring herself to do it, and she didn't know why. Something told her to play the delay card. The DNA would give her three weeks to become accustomed to the idea but in the end, the inevitability of Tim being her son would have to be faced. 'I'm bushed. I drank too much last night and it's been a tough day. Tomorrow promises to be as bad. So if you don't mind, I'm going to bed.'

Ashling kissed her. 'Goodnight, sweetheart. Sleep well.' She picked up the remote and turned the television on.

'Guess I'll give the film ten minutes,' Tim said. 'Good-night, Fiona.'

'Goodnight, Tim.' Fiona entered the bedroom. Before she'd met Ashling, she was often lonely. Her response was to head for the local dojo and practice katas. These days she and Ashling even meditated together. She bent and removed a wooden box from underneath the bed. She located the loose stone in the wall behind their bed and fished the key from behind it. She hesitated before inserting the key and opening the box. She lifted the lid and looked at the contents. This was her "secrets box". It contained those things that only she could see and it had been a long time since she had viewed the contents. She pushed the trinkets aside with her index finger. The signet ring she had bought for her grandfather and that he had left to her was there. She looked at the black and white wedding photo of her parents. Beside it was the photo of her father holding her as a baby. Underneath was a photo with her on the knee of her grandfather. She never understood why but there had been a special bond between them. He told her once that she was more precious to him than his own children. She kissed the photo before replacing it. At the bottom of the box was a series of papers. She lifted the topmost. It was the first love letter she had written. The girl it was addressed to was a classmate and was probably totally ignorant of the torch that Fiona held for her. She replaced the letter and caught what she had been seeking with the edge of her nail. The paper she removed was brown with age and the folds were cracked and frail. She laid it on the bed and unfolded it carefully. When she had finished, she looked at the front page of the *Galway Advertiser* from August 10, 2002. The headline read *GALWAYMAN'S DISAPPEARANCE BAFFLES GARDA SIOCHANA*. Beneath was a photo of Michael Fathy. It was faded with age but still clear. And it was the living image of Tim Daly.

# CHAPTER FOURTEEN

A room had been organised for them in the school to interview Sarah Joyce's friends. There was an empty desk with two chairs on each side. Although Fiona was sure that the police had never interviewed Eileen Canavan in a station, the layout was a good approximation of the interview rooms in Mill Street. The parents of the children had been advised that their children were to be interviewed by two detectives from Galway and that they could assist as adult advisers. All three female parents had accepted the offer. The children and their parents had to wait outside while Fiona's old friend plied them with tea and a cake, she claimed to have baked. Fiona had given the kids the once-over as she passed them. She'd expected sheepish and secretive. After all these children weren't sophisticated city dwellers. They were children from small villages in the west of Ireland. In her day they would certainly have averted their eyes and wanted to hide under the chairs. But these kids were from different stock, they stared back at the two detectives without a hint of fear. Television and the Internet had a lot to answer for.

Canavan held out a photo. 'This is Sarah's class photo taken six months ago.'

Tracy took it from her and showed it to Fiona. 'From the girl in the photo to the picture online, that's quite a transformation,' he said.

'They grow up fast between fifteen and sixteen,' Canavan said. 'Especially the girls. I was gobsmacked by the photo you showed me yesterday. It was way too advanced for a girl like Sarah.'

'Can I take the photo,' Fiona said. 'We'll make a copy and return the original.'

Canavan handed over the photo. 'You can keep it. We got dozens of copies from the photographer. You know, up until yesterday I wasn't too worried by Sarah's disappearance. But I've changed my mind. What happens next?'

Fiona took the photo and handed it to Tracy. 'We'll interview the classmates and pass the file to a specialised unit at HQ in Phoenix Park.'

'Sounds like passing the buck,' Canavan said.

'She could be anywhere. Eight out of ten are back home in a couple of weeks. Our colleagues at HQ are specialised at putting the word out for the other two that don't return.'

'I've been talking to the other teachers,' Canavan said, 'and we're thinking about putting posters up.'

'We can't stop you but that might freak out Mrs Joyce.'

'I'll come back when you've finished with the children.' Canavan left the room.

When they were alone, Tracy asked, 'How do we do this?'

'What do you mean?'

'You know, do we play good-cop, bad-cop?'

'You watch too much television. Chances are that if Sarah was planning a flit, she wouldn't have confided in anyone for fear of them blabbing to their parents. If she did drop a hint, it would have been simply that – a hint, and it was most likely lost in the babble that passes for teenage conversation these days. So, we ask questions as gently as we can and we listen intently to the answers.'

'Will I show the first one in?'

'That would be nice.'

Tracy went outside and returned with a fifteen-year-old and a woman in her sixties. Fiona looked at the name on the list – Alicia Egan. She indicated the chairs in front of the table and waited until Tracy had taken his place. Alicia was a good-looking young lady with curly dark hair and a thin pale face. She was dressed in the school uniform of light blue shirt, dark blue sweater, and grey skirt. There hadn't been a school uniform when Fiona had attended. She recognised the older lady as Alicia's grandmother. She sat stiffly on the chair with a substantial leather bag held on her knees.

'I'm a Gaelic speaker like you,' Fiona began. 'But my colleague doesn't have facility in the language.'

The older woman said. 'I thought it was obligatory for a Guard to speak the language.'

Strike one for you, Fiona thought. 'It is but not at the level we have. I'm Detective Sergeant Fiona Madden and my colleague is Detective Garda Sean Tracy. Don't worry, Alicia, we just want to ask you a few questions about Sarah Joyce.' Alicia had a disinterested look on her face and didn't look in the least worried.

Alicia's grandmother stared at Fiona. 'I know you.'

'And I know you, Mrs Egan. But we're not here to discuss the past. You're here in case being questioned by the Garda Síochána is a difficult experience for your granddaughter. We're busy, so I'd appreciate it if you'd only comment when necessary.' She turned to Alicia. 'You know that Sarah has been missing for the best part of a week?'

Alicia nodded.

'Have you any idea where she might have gone?'

Alicia shook her head.

Fiona didn't particularly like interviewing children. They tended to fall into two categories: the precocious and overly talkative or the shy and retiring who couldn't utter a word. Alicia obviously fell into the latter group.

'You and Sarah talk a lot about what's happening in your life?'

'I suppose. Except not much happens around here.'

'Do you talk about boys?'

Alicia looked at her grandmother.

'It's only natural,' Fiona said. 'All girls do.' She hadn't.

'Sometimes. We follow the local football team and we look out for the fit ones.'

'Does Sarah have an interest in any of the boys?'

Alicia shrugged. 'I suppose so. I think she might have been going out with someone.'

'Do you have a name?'

'She didn't say.'

Tracy made a note.

'Any idea where they might have met?'

'Maybe one of the local dances or it could have been in the pub.'

'So, it might be an older boy?'

'I didn't think of that. She had a bit of a crush on Mikey Canavan. All the girls did. But he's away at the tech in Sligo.'

'Did Sarah ever talk about leaving Glenmore?'

'Most of the kids talk about nothing else. We're waiting until we finish school and then most of us are either going to college or we'll be looking for a job in Galway or maybe Dublin.'

'But did she ever talk about quitting school early and leaving?'

Alicia looked out of the single window in the room.

Fiona recognised the look. 'You want to tell us something, Alicia?'

Alicia turned slowly. 'I don't know but Sarah was funny the last few months. After school, we used to text all the time. Rubbish stuff about music, films, and programmes on TV. The texts got less about three months ago and stopped about two weeks ago.'

'Do you know why?'

'I thought she was ditching me as her best friend but she didn't seem to be more friendly with any of the other girls.'

'What was her mood like?'

'She wasn't as much craic.'

'Can I see your mobile phone?' Fiona asked.

'Is that necessary?' Mrs Egan interjected.

'We want to find young Sarah and return her to her mother.'

'Huh! Her mother is no example for a young girl.'

Fiona ignored the comment, leaned forward, and held her hand out. 'Alicia, may I have your phone?'

Alicia produced a cheap mobile phone from her skirt, turned it on, and handed it over.

Fiona passed it to Tracy who noted the absence of texts. 'There are no texts.'

Alicia smiled. 'Texts are basic we all use Instagram. When the chats are over, we delete them.'

Fiona looked at Tracy. 'Can we retrieve them?'

He shook his head and handed the phone back to Alicia. 'We may need to have another look later.'

Fiona took a business card from her jacket and passed it across the table to Alicia. 'If you remember anything that you think might help us find Sarah, call me. The world is a dangerous place for a young girl on her own. You and Sarah might think you're ready for the world but you're not. We need to get her back to her mother where she belongs.'

Alicia took the card and it and the mobile phone disappeared together.

Tracy led them out. 'Will I bring the next one in?'

'Let's give it five minutes.'

'What do you think?'

'I don't think we're going to find Sarah on our patch. Of

course, I could be wrong. She might be waitressing in Galway or she might have followed Canavan to Sligo. Or we could be looking for a needle in a haystack. We'll do our job and let our friends in Dublin do theirs.'

'What about this Canavan guy? You seem to know everyone around here or at least they all seem to know you.'

'Since he was probably running around here in a pamper when I left here, I have no idea who he is. There was a Canavan attending the school when I was there but he'd be about thirty.'

'The younger Canavan is a lead.'

'For Dublin. Bring in the next candidate.'

## CHAPTER FIFTEEN

F iona watched the departing back of the third interviewee as she left the room. She sighed and made herself a promise that if she ever had the chance to shaft Horgan, she would take it without question. She was having a brain freeze on the Sarah Joyce disappearance. Yes, they'd noticed that Sarah was missing. No, they had no idea where she might be. If anyone would know, it would be Alicia Egan. The two of them were as thick as thieves. They hadn't noticed a change in her mood. For the male interviewee, she had been hot while for the female she was a stuck-up bitch. No, neither of them was her best friend. The male would like to be and so probably would the female if she was being honest. Fiona concluded that Sarah was a popular girl who was a grade up on the maturity scale. It was almost lunchtime so the options were to return to Galway or chance lunch in a local pub. Fiona decided that they would lunch at Tigh Jimmy and have a chat with the publican about his missing part-time waitress.

Fiona was unfreezing her brain and Tracy was finishing up his notes when Canavan entered the room. 'How did it go?' she asked.

'Pretty much as expected,' Fiona said. 'Nobody knows

anything. If Sarah planned on leaving, she didn't take anyone into her confidence.'

'They all plan on leaving,' Canavan said. 'It's just a matter of when. It's a question of economics. There are few enough jobs in the area so the young people head for the bright lights and the chance of a job. And few of them ever return.'

'At least you hung on.'

'Yes, I did, didn't I? I was the dull swot in the class, the one who always wanted to be a teacher and spend my life out here. There are a lot of people who would think that I'm mad but it's a great place to live and bring up a family. But the young people now don't have the patience. By the time they cop on that there's more to life than pubs, concerts, and nightclubs, they're stuck. They come back here every summer just like the tourists and they cry into their beer about the fact that they can't live here permanently. And then they head back to Dublin or London or wherever they live and work. Meanwhile, the population of young people decreases. Schools are closing for lack of pupils. What I suppose I'm saying is that I understand the Sarah Joyces of this world who vote with their feet.'

Fiona felt her passion. She'd been one of those who had voted with her feet but for quite different reasons. 'We're finished here. I don't suppose we'll be back.'

'What about Sarah?'

'After today, Sarah will be the problem of the missing persons unit at HQ. If she's gainfully employed, she'll need a Personal Public Service Number. They'll find her through Social Welfare or Revenue. That's if she's still in Ireland.' She turned to Tracy. 'We're out of here.'

'It's just as well you're finished,' Canavan said. 'I just heard there's a red weather warning for the Atlantic coast. Tomorrow we're going to be blown off our feet while the skies are opening on us. God is having no pity.'

Fiona stopped in front of her former classmate. 'Thanks, you've been very good to us.'

'Drop in next time you pass through.'

They shook hands. Fiona didn't bother to mention that the last time she'd passed through was eighteen years ago.

'Where to?' Tracy said.

'There's a pub a mile down the road. Sarah did some waitressing there. I thought we'd have a spot of lunch.'

'You're inviting?'

'Dream on.'


TIGH JIMMY, which meant Jimmy's house, was established in the oldest and most important edifice in the village which probably indicated the importance the impecunious Irish gave to having a sturdy communal meeting place where alcohol was served. Although it had been through many renovations, the proprietors had been careful to maintain the original walls and despite the increases in insurance the thatched roof had survived into the present.

'*Dia dhaoibh* (God be with you),' Fiona said when they entered.

The four men drinking at the bar returned her salutation while a man and woman seated at a table just inside the door ignored her.

Jimmy, the eponymous owner, stood behind the bar. He was short and rotund and had a face that hadn't aged since Fiona had last laid eyes on him. He nodded at Fiona as she steered Tracy towards a table at the rear of the room.

'Good God,' Tracy said when they were seated. 'This place looks like a saloon from one of those spaghetti westerns. I half expect Clint Eastwood to walk into the room at any minute. The light is so dim I can hardly see my hand in front of me.'

'Would you shut up. If Jimmy hears you, he'll most likely toss us out.'

Jimmy detached himself from the bar and waddled in their direction.

He stood next to Fiona. 'You're a Madden alright. I heard you'd been in the parish. You're the image of your mother. Long time no see.'

'You haven't changed so much yourself.'

'Forget the *ramaish*. I'll be lucky to see out the year. What can I do for you?'

'We'd like a spot of lunch,' Tracy said.

'Who's your man?' Jimmy asked.

'Newly minted Detective Garda Sean Tracy.'

'Where are you from, Sean?'

'Limerick.'

'We have ham and cheese sandwiches as our special today. In fact, we only have ham and cheese sandwiches today. I suppose you'll be having that. And since Miss Madden is a returned local that will be on the house.'

Fiona smiled. 'Thank you, Jimmy, gracious as ever. We'd like to have a private word with you later.'

'On police business?'

Fiona nodded.

'After you've eaten.' Jimmy went back behind the bar.

'I don't get this place,' Tracy said. 'It seems that there are messages passing between you and a lot of the locals.'

'I am a local.'

'You're not going to fill me in?'

'No, maybe when we know each other better.'

'Horgan told me that your last partner joined the priest-hood. I suppose that was a joke.'

'Not exactly, now Sam McAlister is probably the oldest novice in Ireland. Given the situation with vocations, I think he may be the only priest in training in the country. I suspect

I'll be receiving an invitation to his ordination sometime in the future.'

'Are you telling me that you're responsible for some poor bastard giving up the police to become a parish priest.'

She laughed. 'I can take credit for a lot of things but I'm not responsible for Sam's calling. He was what you might call a reluctant policeman. He had an aged mother that he was taking care of. The day she died he handed in his papers and a week later he entered Clonliffe College.'

'That's a relief.'

'Were you afraid that I might have the same effect on you?'

'Not really, but it's a relief all the same. Did you ever consider the possibility that Sarah was groomed by a gang like those guys in Bradford?'

'You mean the gang of Muslim men?'

'Yeah.'

'Have you noticed any Muslims in the area?'

'No, but there might be a group in Galway.'

'I'll keep your theory in mind.'

Jimmy arrived carrying two plates and deposited them in front of the officers. The sandwiches were several inches thick and consisted of two generous hand-cut slices of white bread filled with a large chunk of cheddar cheese and a thick slice of ham.

'That's what I call a sandwich,' Tracy said.

Jimmy smiled and looked at Fiona. 'I had a feeling your friend would be impressed. The tea is on the way.' He went back to the bar.

Tracy picked up his sandwich and took a bite. 'Fucking brilliant,' he said when the mouthful had disappeared.

'Jimmy is a local character. He's trying to show you we're not yokels back here.'

'I'm sorry the Sarah Joyce case is over.'

'It's not over yet. We still must talk to Jimmy. This is where Sarah used to work.'

Fifteen minutes later, they had finished their sandwiches and tea and Jimmy joined them at their table. 'I know what you've been up to: Sarah Joyce's disappearance. There's no other subject of conversation in the village. What do you want from me?'

Fiona looked around the pub. 'You're the proprietor of the local gossip centre. And you're nobody's fool. We're about to pass the disappearance over to Dublin and I'd like to be thorough. That means I'd like to know what you think.'

'I remember you as a nice quiet wee girl but my contacts tell me that you've changed.'

'Life changes us, Jimmy. Nobody is who they were twenty years ago.'

'Your mother is proud of you. When you made sergeant, she was going around telling everybody in the parish.'

'That's good to know.'

'You should go visit her. She's getting on.'

'When I've got the time, I'll drop by here and have a proper chinwag. Right now, Detective Garda Tracy and I are here on police business.'

Jimmy sighed. 'My contacts were right. You've changed. Let's get to it.'

'Sarah used to work here. Did you have any inkling that she would leave without saying a word to her mother.'

'She's been doing the weekends here since Easter. I thought her mother could do with the extra few bob. She was learning the bar and serving drinks and cleaning up. Besides what I was paying her, she was picking up tips.'

'You've a heart of gold, Jimmy,' Fiona said.

He laughed. 'Don't tell anyone. I didn't talk to her much but I didn't think she was the type to walk out on her mother. As you can imagine, we've had every rumour from running off with an Italian count to an alien abduction. I reckon all of them are rubbish.'

There was silence around the table as the two police officers stared at Jimmy.

'Don't keep us in suspense,' Fiona said.

'I have a bad feeling about this one. She was getting a bit flighty with the customers. Acting older than she was. It's always been my opinion that children should grow up slowly.'

Fiona turned to Tracy. 'Show him the photo on Facebook.'

Tracy brought up the photo and handed his phone to the older man.

'Did she ever turn up for work looking like this?'

Jimmy examined the photo. 'If she had, I would have sent her home with a flea in her ear.' He handed the phone back.

'But you're not surprised?'

He shook his head. 'No, and that's the reason I'm worried.'

'Is there anyone we should talk to?'

Jimmy looked back at the bar. 'If I see customers leering at the staff, I show them the door. You know me and you know my reputation. If someone was up to no good with her, it didn't happen here.'

'But it's something that might have happened?'

'Yes, but don't quote me on that.' He stood up. 'I need to get back to the bar. If I were you, I'd drop the harsh act. It doesn't suit you. You'd best get back to Galway. There's a storm on the way and Met Eireann has put out a red warning.'

'Those sandwiches were great,' Tracy said. 'I'll come out here with some mates during the summer.'

'You'll be welcome as long as you bring your money with you.'

They stood beside the car. There was a freshness in the air and towards the west out over the Atlantic they could see the black storm clouds forming.

'I don't remember the storms when I was a child,' Fiona said.

'Global warming, we're fucking up the environment.'

'Let's get back to Galway and write the report for Dublin.'

# CHAPTER SIXTEEN

A shling's morning was so packed that she hadn't had time to think about Tim. She'd been the keynote speaker at a women's conference in the early morning, followed by a lecture and then a lunch with a literary agent from Dublin about a book that a publishing company wanted her to write about avoiding childhood traumas.

She had almost forgotten that she had her monthly meeting with the head of the department. Professor Doherty had a room in one of the older buildings on the university. The National University of Ireland at Galway was relatively new having been founded in the mid nineteenth century. Ashling's room was in an ultra-modern building which had been constructed twenty years previously. She knocked on Doherty's door and entered.

Doherty glanced at his watch when she entered. 'I thought that you might have forgotten about our meeting.' It was obligatory for the senior psychologists to have a session with the dean every month. It was something akin to confession in the Catholic Church.

'Sorry, Dean, I've had a rather busy schedule today.' She sat facing Doherty.

'I hope we're not over-working you.'

'Not at all.'

'I noticed that you've been distracted lately. It's not like you. Anything I should know about.'

'Well actually there is something.' Doherty was aware of Ashling's sexual orientation and her domestic arrangements. She proceeded to tell him about Tim Daly's arrival.

'That must be traumatic for your partner and to a lesser extent for you.'

'I've spoken to Tim and I'm afraid that my psychology training has led me to believe that he may not be what he says he is. I decided to investigate him by looking him up on the Internet but I have to admit that I'm changing my mind.' She told him about the meal Tim prepared.

'You're doubting your first instincts?'

'Yes, he's turned out to be a polite and helpful young man. There were not many eighteen-year-old who would have traipsed to the shops to buy the necessities and then cook a complicated dinner. My psychologist hat was still in place during the dinner but I didn't get the same impression as in our earlier meeting. He was proving himself to be thoughtful and caring. Of course, it could be that my earlier questioning of his motives had alerted him.'

'Interesting, and how do you intend to proceed?'

'The disquiet I felt after my initial conversation with Tim is still there but the urgency, I felt at the time has dissipated. I haven't ditched the feeling that there was something at odds between the life Tim had described and his motive for searching out his biological parents.'

'Was it the dinner alone that dissipated your disquiet?'

'I may have been influenced by the dinner and Tim behaviour. Or maybe I'm daunted by the research it might require prying into another person's life without having them on a couch in the same room. We know that there's a huge difference between reading about someone on a page and delving into the mind through astute questioning. I know how easy it is to cover one's tracks on the Internet. The inability to accept exactly what was put in front of one is the principal drawback of our profession.'

'Your partner is a police officer, what does she think?'

'I think that she's traumatised. I tried to prepare her for this eventuality but I appear to have failed.'

'Does she know that you're investigating the young man?'

'Yes.'

'Are you sure of your own motives?'

She hesitated. 'I can't deny that Tim's arrival is a disruption and, in my experience, the main problem when an equilibrium is disturbed is how far the pendulum swings on the other side. Maybe I should ignore my feelings and butt out. After all it is Fiona's and Tim's business. Having reviewed the documents that Tim produced, I'm convinced that in her heart of hearts my partner is certain he's her son. She's resisting admitting it.'

'I get the impression that your main worry is that the young man's arrival will impact on your relationship with your partner. You still haven't answered my question, what do you intend to do?'

'I can't shake my doubts about him so I suppose I'm going to keep looking into his background. He may be my partner's son and yes I'm worried about the effect on our relationship but I feel it's the right decision.' She looked at Doherty who sat quietly observing her. It was his way of indicating that the session was over and he'd pushed the issue as much as he intended. He had led her to the decision that she knew she had to take. Tim Daly was a closed book that she intended to open.

# CHAPTER SEVENTEEN

Fiona finished up the report and signed the last page. The investigation was as complete as she could make it. Missing persons cases rarely had a swift conclusion. There were cases that were still open after thirty years. She preferred investigations where there was an element of closure. Her last case in Dublin had involved a murdered husband. The victim had been stabbed thirty-eight times and had his head bashed in by a hammer. The wife was traumatised but indicated that it was a home invasion that had gone wrong. An examination of the crime scene didn't corroborate her story and when the tox report showed that the husband had been drugged, the wife's story collapsed and she confessed. The case was solved in double quick time and it was drinks all round for the CID team. In order to complete the file, she needed to append the two photos of Sarah Joyce to the front page. The school photo was of a young naïve teenage girl. But the photo from her Facebook page was of a young woman aware of her sexuality. There was a tale associated with the change that had taken place in Sarah Joyce but it would be someone else's job to discover that story. She felt a tinge of sadness. Jimmy had made her feel that Sarah was at risk and it was her job to do something about it. She wished that life was that simple. While she was detailed to walk the streets of Dublin, she had encountered the prostitutes and the rough sleepers. They all had a story of how they had ended up where they were. Chief among the reasons were drug addiction and mental illness. But behind these there was abuse, physical or mental. Maybe she'd missed something.

'Are you done with the Joyce girl?'

Fiona turned and saw that Horgan was directly behind her. 'You have an unsettling way of creeping up on people.' It was particularly unsettling because Fiona's martial arts training had made her sensitive to movements in her vicinity. 'Are you sure there isn't some American Indian in your family?'

'Maybe I was an Apache in a previous life,' Horgan said. 'I think it more likely that you were so deep in thought that you didn't notice my approach.'

Fiona knew that it was dangerous to be that deep in thought. 'The report is ready to send to Dublin.'

'I get the impression that you're not happy with it.'

'I would have preferred to have found some evidence that it was a planned disappearance. There's nothing missing from her room. Her clothes closet is scanty but intact and she never said a word to any of her *best friends*.'

'When my two daughters were teenagers, I never had a clue what they were up to.'

'But I'll bet Mrs Horgan did.'

Horgan put his hand on his heart. 'You got me there. That arrow stung.'

'Bad things can happen to naïve sixteen-year-old girls.' Fiona wasn't only thinking of Sarah Joyce.

'You think that something bad has happened?'

'I have no evidence to suppose that she's in danger. But it's an evil old world out there for someone who isn't yet prepared for it.'

'I hope you're prepared for tomorrow morning?'

'I checked my wardrobe and I didn't find a miniskirt so it'll have to be jeans.'

'I wouldn't be so flippant. I hear this Cooney is a bit of a hard arse. He's the one that'll make the recommendation as to whether disciplinary action will be necessary. He'll be here at ten and on the road back to Dublin by twelve according to the email. He'll interview you, Tracy, and me in that order.'

Tracy had been keeping his head down at his desk but looked up at the mention of his name.

Horgan continued. 'When Professional Services are involved, they like to spread the stink. You didn't think of that when you gave Molloy the beating.'

'I restrained him. For God's sake, don't call it a beating in front of Cooney.' She looked over at Tracy. 'And you stick to what you saw. Especially the fact that he threw the first punch.'

'I'm off home,' Horgan said. 'I left the patio furniture out and if this storm lives up to the warning and I don't put it away, it might end up in Clare or Mayo depending on the direction of the wind. Don't forget, Madden, try to limit the spread of the stink. I'd like to retire without a stain on my record and more importantly with my pension intact.'

'I thought it was traditional for the boss to offer a celebratory drink at the end of a case,' Tracy said when Horgan left the room.

'Have you ever had a drink with Horgan?'

'No.'

'Well be warned. He's never been known to stand his round. And I mean never.'

'What about you and me having a drink then?'

Fiona didn't think that a celebration was justified. But

aside from the arrest of Molloy, which wasn't really their case, it was Tracy's first outing as a detective so she supposed that could be recognised by a drink. 'As an exception, I'll stand a round in Taaffes. I'll give my partner a call and see if she can join us.'

# CHAPTER EIGHTEEN

Fiona and Tracy arrived early enough in Taaffes to snare the snug just inside the door. It was just as well they did because in the space of ten minutes an influx of after-work drinkers swamped the bar. Ashling arrived and pushed in beside them.

'Professor Ashling McGoldrick, meet Detective Garda Sean Tracy,' Fiona said. 'Be careful, Sean. She psychoanalyses people for a living.'

Ashling extended her hand and Tracy shook it. 'You didn't tell me he was so handsome.'

Tracy blushed, picked up his pint of Guinness, and used the glass to hide his face.

'Is it like the cop shows?' Ashling said. 'Do you call Sean your partner? Do I have to be jealous?'

Fiona ordered an orange juice, retrieved it from the bar, and put it in front of Ashling. 'Can't you see that you're embarrassing the poor man.' She touched her glass to Ashling's. 'Slainte.'

'What's the occasion?' Ashling said.

Fiona sipped her Guinness. 'Sean and I have successfully completed his first case as a detective.'

Ashling lifted her glass in a toast. 'Congratulations. You found the missing girl.'

'Chance would be a fine thing,' Fiona said. 'We completed our investigation and passed the file to the relevant specialist section at HQ like good civil servants.'

'You don't sound happy,' Ashling said.

'You're the second person who's said that this evening which means that either you and Inspector Horgan are incisive or I'm transparent. Take your pick.'

'So, you're not just unhappy, you're very unhappy.'

'There's a young girl wandering around out there. I think we should be concerned for her welfare.'

Ashling sighed and turned to face Tracy 'So how was your first case, Sean?'

'Working with Fiona is an experience. Are you from the west as well?'

Ashling burst out laughing. 'Good heavens, no, with an accent like mine I can only be from one place, the capital. I speak a bit of Irish, we must speak the language to qualify for a job at the university. But I'm not in Fiona's class.'

Fiona stood up, went to the bar, and paid. She drank the dregs of her pint standing up. 'The barman says the storm is about to break so we should head off before it hits properly.'

'I'll hang on a bit here,' Tracy said. 'I don't have far to go. Nice to have met you, Professor.' He looked at Fiona. 'I admire your courage.'

'Don't forget your lines for tomorrow,' Fiona said. 'The truth and nothing but the truth.'

'What was that last remark about?' Ashling asked when they left the pub.

'They're sending some arsehole down from HQ to look into the arrest of Molloy. He'll decide whether I should have to face a disciplinary board.'

'Are you worried?'

'Do I look worried?'

. . .

WAVES WERE CRASHING over the sea defences as they made their way from Salthill to Barna. Ashling's Mercedes was shuddering every time a blast of wind hit it and her knuckles were white from gripping the steering wheel. 'Looks like Met Eireann got it right for a change.'

Fiona didn't reply. She sat with her head against the passenger side window and her arms folded.

'What's up?'

'You mean other than a young man arriving at my home and telling me he's the child I sent for adoption eighteen years ago.'

'I know it's a shock but it's one that you can't run away from. And that's exactly what you're trying to do. Take the bloody DNA test and then find out exactly what Tim wants. He came here for a reason. Maybe it was simply to meet his biological mother but I have the feeling that there's something more complicated.'

'Thanks. I wasn't ready to be a mother eighteen years ago and I don't think I am now. I've spent the last few days wishing it never happened.'

'But it did. Now we have to deal with it.'

Fiona unfolded her arms and turned to look at Ashling. 'I wasn't aware that you were involved.'

'If it affects you, then it affects me.' The car wobbled and travelled to the opposite side of the road until Ashling jerked it back.

'Concentrate on driving. The Tim situation will resolve itself over time. A DNA test takes a while. Maybe he'll get restless and head back to the States.'

'Wishful thinking on your part. You have a son. You always had a son but he just didn't live with you. Your stable life has been knocked sideways and you're going to have to take steps to reach a new stability. Tim doesn't look like the type that's going to cut and run. Maybe he got that from his real mother.' Ashling steered the car through the gate and parked beside the cottage. 'Let's get the hell out of this storm.'

Fiona opened the car door and faced the rain that lashed against her driven by an Atlantic gale. She watched Ashling lock the car and rush to the cottage. In the distance towards the west, spumes of spray rose as the wild seas crashed against the rocks. She wanted to feel that spray on her face. She walked out the gate and down the narrow lane that led to the sea. She had covered half the distance when Ashling caught up with her.

'Ashling pulled at her arm. 'Are you mad?'

'I want to feel the spray on my face.'

Ashling held her tight. 'You'll be blown into the sea and some poor bugger with a wife and kids will have to risk his life to save you. Committing suicide will solve nothing.'

'I wasn't trying to kill myself. It just felt right to stand beside the sea.'

Ashling hugged her. 'You're already drenched. Let's get back to the cottage. Tim's gone to Galway. He left a note. Maybe your assessment of his patience was more accurate than mine.'

Fiona smiled. Rainwater was running down Ashling's face. 'You're right. We'll get pneumonia if we stay out here much longer.'

They held hands as they walked back to the cottage.


THEY SHOWERED each other and sat drinking hot whiskeys in front of a roaring fire in the log-burner.

'What possessed you to head off in the direction of the sea?' Ashling asked.

'It seemed like a good idea at the time.'

'This isn't you, Fiona. You're a strong woman who does a

difficult job very well. People like you don't fall to pieces easily.'

Fiona sat up straight. 'I'm not falling to pieces. There's a lot of things you don't know.'

'Then tell me.'

Fiona thought about the contents of the box beneath their bed. 'Maybe later, maybe never.'

'The more you hold it in the more it will gnaw at you.'

'Are you going to be the one that tells Tim that he wasn't a love child? There's a time to leave well enough alone. Unfortunately, that time has passed. When I had religion, I used to pray that my child was being well taken care of. My mother assured me that the adoption agency would find a good Catholic home for him. That assurance coupled with my prayers to a higher power allowed me to forget my own obligations.'

'What will you do?'

'I don't know. Your job is to help people like me. What should I do?' Fiona walked to the window and looked outside. The wind was howling through the reeds of the thatch and rain lashed across the garden. She was surprised to find that she was thinking of Tim and hoping that he was inside away from the tempest.

'If you were a client, and you are not a client, I would try to help you find the solution that you arrived at by yourself.' Ashling went to the kitchen and refilled their drinks.

'I always loved this cottage.' Fiona took the refilled glass and felt the heat on her hands. 'I like to think that my great grandparents were happy here. At least that was what my grandfather told me.' There was a picture of her grandfather on the wall above the fireplace. She turned and toasted him. 'The old man. He was everything to me. He was the safe haven that I could always depend on. My mother wasn't pleased that he left me this place. She wanted it for herself and threatened to go to court to get it.' She looked at Ashling and saw that she was appraising her. It was time to knock Ashling's psychologist's hat off. 'That's enough for tonight. Let's put on something soothing. The Danes have a word for it.'

'Hygge.'

'That's it. We can sit by the fire, listen to the wind howling and watch *Groundhog Day*.'

'How many times have we watched that damn film?'

'Not enough. Wouldn't it be wonderful to wake up in the morning and be able to put right all the wrongs from the previous day.'

Ashling fished out the DVD from the pile beside the TV. She put the disk in the player and pushed *Play* then hugged Fiona and brought her to the couch. 'Wonderful but impossible.'

# CHAPTER NINETEEN

Ashling flung her arm out and encountered nothing. She was famous for waking slowly and she rubbed her eyes several times before looking at the empty space beside her in the bed. She sat up and listened. Someone was speaking in the living room. She thought it was Fiona but who could she have been speaking with. It was three thirty in the morning. She climbed out of bed, put on her robe, and opened the bedroom door silently. The storm was raging outside and easily covered the noise of the creaking hinge. She slipped quietly out of the bedroom. Fiona was standing before the photograph of her grandfather and a stream of Gaelic was coming from her mouth. Ashling caught an odd word but Fiona was in full flow and speaking in her own accent. There was no way that she could understand the content but that didn't mean that she wouldn't like to know what was being said. Fiona stopped speaking and turned quickly. Ashling was certain that she hadn't made a sound but Fiona had sensed her presence. 'Does he answer you?'

'I only wish he could.'

'What were you saying? I didn't understand a word.'

'I was telling him how much I miss him.'

'You couldn't sleep?'

'The storm woke me. It's going crazy out there. Horgan was worried about his patio furniture and he had every right to be.'

'You're not a very convincing liar.'

'You haven't seen me in the interview room. It's on my annual evaluations: Madden can lie with the best of them.'

'It's not a joke, Fi.'

'I'm not laughing.'

'I'm not asking you to unburden yourself to me. Our relationship is more important than the knowledge I'd obtain. But I'd like to recommend someone to you.'

'It's always the same dream. I feel the tingle of fear as I hear the footsteps behind me. I want to wake but the God of dreams won't allow me. I must go on. He comes up behind me and grabs me by the throat. He's strong. Much stronger than me. He smells of stale cigarettes, sweat and musk. He bundles me into a field, pulls down my trousers and rips off my pants. He shoves him into my body. I try to scream but he has his hand over my mouth. I close my eyes and pray that it will end soon. But he continues to pound on me. When he's finished, he takes out the knife. My heart leaps. He's going to kill me. But instead he nicks my throat. If I speak, he'll be back and he'll kill me and my mother. Then I can wake. Usually covered in sweat and breathing heavily.'

Ashling hugged her. 'You poor darling. The experience was bad enough but being forced to relive it is a horror. I really think you should see someone. There are obviously some unresolved issues. If you talk it through, the dreams will stop.'

'Thanks, but no thanks. I have a busy day tomorrow and I've got to get some sleep.'

'The chickens have come home to roost. Running away isn't an option. I wish that you'd let me help you.'

Fiona took her by the hand. 'You can. Come back to bed and hold me. If I screw up my interview tomorrow morning, I might be looking for a new job.'

# CHAPTER TWENTY

Storm Rhodri lived up to its advanced billing. The Mercedes was covered in all types of garden debris including hedging that had been ripped from the ground and mountain ash saplings that had been planted a year ago. The clean-up would have to wait until the weekend. Fiona had taken Horgan's advice and wore a clean and pressed pair of blue cotton trousers. Her best flats replaced her biker boots and a cream blouse and blue jacket completed the ensemble.

'You look good,' Ashling said as she opened the car door. 'You should dress up more often.'

'Don't tease. You know that you're looking at my complete dress-up wardrobe.'

The drive into Galway was slower than usual. Trees were down in some places and the radio reported that more than ten thousand homes on the west coast were still without power. Atlantic storms were a way of life for Ireland's west coast inhabitants but in recent years their frequency and ferocity had increased.

'Good luck,' Ashling said as she dropped Fiona off at Mill Street.

'I hope I don't need it.'

Fiona drew some admiring glances as she entered the station. The officers involved must have been dyslexics. Fiona was reliably informed that the shithouse poets had spread the news of her sexuality far and wide in the Galway stations.

'DS Madden,' the duty sergeant said as she entered. 'The look suits you. Well wear.'

Fiona smiled and gave him the middle finger. She went directly to the squad room and had barely taken her seat when her phone rang.

'DS Madden?' The man's voice was local and strong.

'Speaking.'

'Sergeant Geraghty, I'm duty sergeant at Salthill.'

'What can I do for you, sergeant?'

'We're holding a fella here who claims to be your son, except his passport identifies him as Timothy Daly.'

'What's he done?' She felt her stomach lurch.

'Affray, him and another fella got into it in a pub last night. We had to bring them both in. I took the liberty of not writing him up on two grounds: one being his US passport and the other being his connection with you. What do you want me to do?'

'Was drink involved?'

'You can be certain it was.'

'I can't get out to Salthill now. I've a meeting with an inspector coming down from Dublin.'

'I'll let him out after his breakfast. The boys at the station were impressed by the way you handled the Molloy arrest. But young Timothy better keep his fists to himself in the future, because the next time his name appears on a sheet, he won't get off so easily.'

'Thanks, sergeant, it's appreciated. I owe you one.'

What the hell was that? She needed that phone call like she needed a hole in the head. Tim had told her and Ashling that he didn't drink alcohol and he's banged up for affray. That just didn't compute. She'd have it out with him when she saw him next but, in the meantime, she decided that when she had a few minutes she'd contact the arresting officers and get their side of the story. There was something fishy about this incident. She wasn't about to take Tim's word for whatever had happened. Getting Tim released had left her beholden to this Geraghty guy and she didn't like that. Unfortunately, for the moment she had bigger fish to fry.

Tracy's chair was still empty. Cooney was due at any minute. She was gripped with the sudden fear that Tracy was trying to duck the interview. That would not be at all helpful. She did some deep-breathing exercises and calmed her mind.

She was imagining a deep blue sky and a beautiful beach when the ringing of the phone interrupted her. 'Inspector Cooney has arrived,' the duty sergeant informed her. 'DI Horgan told me to show him to an interview room and supply him with a decent cup of tea. Maybe you'd be so kind as to come down immediately.'

'Thanks, I'm on my way.'

She stood up and straightened her clothes. She was walking out the door when Tracy almost ran into her. He had a large bandage on the side of his head. 'About bloody time, Cooney is downstairs. What the hell happened to you?'

'A light fitting detached from the wall outside my digs and cracked my skull. Well not exactly cracked but the cut's nasty. Five stitches in A and E and half the night spent waiting.'

'I'll see you later.'


FIONA KNOCKED on the door of the interview room and entered. Inspector Donal Cooney looked up from the file he was reading and closed it at the same time. He stood and extended his hand. Fiona took it and shook. He was what the Irish call a *fine man*. Fiona guessed he was in his early forties, over six feet tall, and unlike many of his age he hadn't turned to fat. He had a full head of silvery hair and his face was narrow and his cheekbones high. He had the look of a Viking about him.

Cooney sat. 'The famous or infamous DS Madden,' he said. 'Take a seat.'

The introduction did nothing to settle Fiona's nerves. She'd enjoyed restraining Molloy so much that she hadn't thought that there might be consequences.

'I suppose DCI Horgan has informed you of the purpose of my visit so we can get straight down to business.'

'Yes, sir.'

Cooney picked up his mobile, brought up the video of Molloy's arrest, and played it. 'I heard that the commissioner almost had a heart attack when he was shown the video. He asked was the young woman really a police officer or was the video part of a kung fu film being shot in Galway.'

'I know it doesn't look good, taken out of context,' Fiona began. 'There was a lot that proceeded the few seconds of action but unfortunately, nobody appears to have caught that on their mobiles.'

'Or they didn't upload it onto YouTube. Tell me your side of it.'

'There was a warrant out for the arrest of Patrick Molloy, and me and my partner discovered that he was working as a dishwasher in a pub in Shop Street.' She looked at the files on the table. 'Is one of those Patrick Molloy's file?'

Cooney nodded.

'I don't have to tell you that there are two facets of Molloy's character that are important. One is that he disappears easily and the other is that he is very violent. Nobody knew where he was living, so we couldn't organise a dawn raid. That was already tried before in Waterford and Molloy put two of the arresting officers in hospital. We decided to pick him up on his way to work. I waited for his approach, accosted him, and told him he was under arrest and that he should come quietly. He threw a punch and I defended myself. There was minimum fuss and if some tourist hadn't filmed the ten seconds of action the commissioner would never have known about the incident.'

'You have some martial arts training?'

'Yes.'

'What specifically?'

'Aikido 5th dan black belt, tae kwon do $3^{rd}$ dan black belt and ju-jitsu $5^{th}$ dan black belt.'

Cooney leaned back in his chair. 'Now that is impressive. I remember in the old days there was a joke that before a fight you should tell your opponent that your fists were registered as a weapon in the state of California. I don't suppose that you're required to tell people about your impressive qualifications in martial arts before you hit them?'

'Not by law.'

'How come this morbid interest is learning techniques to hurt and maim people?'

'I was raped at sixteen. I thought if I wanted to avoid a replay, I should learn how to defend myself.'

Cooney sat forward slowly. 'I'm sorry, that wasn't in your file.'

'Files only contain what people want them to contain. I wouldn't like to find what I just told you added to my file.'

'You have every right to defend yourself, but considering your level of expertise, you might have gone a little easier on Molloy.'

'I did go easy. I could have left him a quadriplegic like he tried to leave his wife. I didn't assault him. I was simply restraining what I knew to be a violent criminal.'

Cooney pushed a paper across the table. 'This is a letter from Molloy's solicitor. They intend to bring a case against the commissioner and you.'

'What does the Garda's solicitor say?'

'It could go either way.'

'Did he see the hospital report?'

Cooney smiled for the first time. 'You didn't leave a mark on him. How can you do that?'

'It's not about how hard you hit. It's important where you hit. I did the minimum to restrain the fugitive.'

Cooney wrote some notes on the front of the file. 'Our solicitor had only one question for me. He asked me to assess what kind of witness you'd make.'

'And?'

'I think you'll do fine if it goes that far. Okay, we're done.' He stood and offered his hand. 'You'll be informed of my decision in due course.'

Fiona shook. 'Thank you, sir.'

Cooney watched her walk to the door. 'And no more kung fu videos on the public street.'

'No, sir.'

Fiona passed Tracy on the stairs. 'Take the worried look off your face. You're not in the frame. Like I said, the truth, just as it happened.'

# CHAPTER TWENTY-ONE

Fiona grabbed a cup of coffee from the dispensing machine and went back to her desk. Thankfully, there was nothing in her urgent tray. Criminal activity had an annual pattern that followed the weather. Winter on the west coast of Ireland could be brutal. Rain pelted down and the thermometer hovered in the low degrees. The Irish began freezing at six degrees Centigrade, which would probably make Canadians burst out laughing. Atlantic storms, which had been a rarity when Fiona was a child, came in waves causing havoc through flooding along the coast. By May, the worst of the winter would be over and the sun, when it appeared, would feel warm. The muggers and burglars would dust off their tools and prepare, like the hotels and pubs, for their *season*. But for the moment, all was quiet on the western front. Sarah Joyce's disappearance flashed across her mind. Fiona sat back, sipped her coffee, and replayed her interview with Cooney. Overall she was satisfied with her performance though one could never be sure of the outcome. The commissioner was new in the post and he might want to make an example of her for the rank and file. She didn't like to think that she might have screwed up completely. Incarceration wasn't the answer for Patrick Molloy. He wasn't going to be rehabilitated. His record of beating up women was established and the inevitable conclusion would be that someone would die. But Horgan was right. It wasn't Fiona's job to dispense justice though when she'd looked into Molloy's eyes, she knew that the only way to stop a murder in the future was to turn Molloy into a quadriplegic. And she knew that she had the skills to do it. She finished her coffee and dumped the cup in the wastebasket. Then she picked up the phone and called Salthill Garda station. She gave her name and asked for Geraghty.

'DS Madden, he's already gone.'

'Thanks for that.' She winced and continued quickly. 'I'm going to give him a piece of my mind when I see him. Count on it. In the meantime, I'd like to have a word with the officers at the scene. I need to know what went down from their point of view.'

'They were both experienced coppers. Hold on and I'll see what time they're on. Garda Joe Nolan is on at eleven.'

Fiona looked at her watch it was a quarter to. It was one and a half kilometres station to station. She could just about get there. 'I'll leave here now. Will you ask him to wait a minute.'

'Of course, no problem.'


FIONA SPENT the fifteen-minute walk thinking about Tim. Her emotions were tangled. She was angry that Tim had used her name, disappointed that within a few days of arrival he had managed to get himself arrested and spent a night in jail, and confused that the issue appeared to be alcohol which Tim had said he didn't drink. She arrived at Salthill station with two minutes to spare.

'He's in the canteen,' Geraghty said. 'You can't miss him. He's got a head of the reddest hair you've ever seen.'

Fiona thanked him and followed the direction he indicated with his outstretched arm. The members of the next shift were sitting at the few tables set about a small room. When Fiona had joined the Garda, canteen facilities were provided that dispensed real food. Now, two dispensing machines stood at the end of the room. One supplied hot drinks and the other sandwiches and chocolate bars. There was only one red-headed man in the room and his mane was impressive. He was seated at a table with two other officers.

Fiona approached the table. 'Garda Nolan, I'm DS Madden, I'd like a word with you.'

'*The* DS Madden,' one of the officers said.

Fiona gave him her false smile.

Nolan looked up from his tea. His face was as pale as his hair was red. With skin that white, he would not be a candidate for a beach holiday. 'The sergeant told me you'd be around.'

'Maybe we could find somewhere more private.'

Nolan's companions stood together. 'We're off out anyway.' The one who had spoken said. 'By the way, we're all behind you.' They put on their caps and left the room.

Fiona took one of the chairs recently vacated.

She ran her hand through her hair as soon as she sat. 'First, let me apologise for whatever happened.'

'Why? It had nothing to do with you.' Nolan finished his tea and launched his cardboard cup at a waste bin. It was a direct hit. 'Practice makes perfect.'

'I'd be grateful for your view on what went down.'

'Nothing much to tell. We were called to an altercation at the Quays Bar. Several punches were thrown and both combatants sustained minor bruises. The bouncer had separated them by the time we arrived but they were still interested in continuing their altercation outside. We thought it best to give them a chance to cool off in the cells.'

'Sergeant Geraghty told me that alcohol was involved.'

'They both smelled of drink. In my opinion, lots of drinks. The origins of the row were a bit obscure. Could have been about a spilt drink or an attempt to chat up a girl. Take your pick. One thing for sure was that your boy was all up for the fight. A right little bantam cock he was. Typical American, all piss and wind. Shouted the odds all the way to the station.'

Fiona was stunned by the phrase "your boy". She was momentarily incapable of speech. 'When did he tell you he was my son?' She forced the words from her mouth.

'As soon as we arrived. It was one of those "do you know who I am?" things. We took no notice of him but he kept on at it when he arrived at the station.'

'And you're sure he was drunk?'

'Pissed as a newt. I'd keep an eye on that lad if I were you.'

'What do you mean?'

'I've been a guard for twenty-five years and I've seen all kinds. I might be wrong but he struck me as a vicious little bugger.' Nolan stood and picked up his cap from the table. 'The video of you arresting that guy has done the rounds. I don't hold with physical violence. Maybe your son was wound up trying to emulate his mother.'

Fiona blushed. 'It wasn't gratuitous. Molloy put two officers who tried to arrest him in hospital. He's a nasty piece of work.' She stood.

'My partner's waiting.' Nolan started towards the door.

'I owe you a pint.'

'No, you don't.' Nolan left the cafeteria.

Fiona watched Nolan's back as he disappeared and retook her seat. The experienced guard's rebuke stung. She took some deep breaths. He was entitled to his opinion but Fiona had no regrets about the way she had arrested Molloy. It might mean the end of her career or being demoted to the ranks but men like Molloy are hell-bent on inflicting pain on females. It was time to break the cycle. Nolan appeared to be a good cop and a decent man. The picture he painted of Tim wasn't very complimentary. Also, that picture didn't square with what she'd seen at the cottage. She'd let Tim have his say before she made up her mind.

# CHAPTER TWENTY-TWO

Most people dream of having a beach house. Gerry Higgins had been born and raised in a house set on the edge of a beach directly facing Mweenish Island. On his father's death, he had inherited the house. He sometimes wondered whether that had been a blessing or a curse. Whatever the weather, he took his morning constitutional along the beach. The daily walks allowed him to track the erosion that had taken place during his lifetime. That erosion appeared to be accelerating over the past few years. Gerry was no environmentalist but he was inclined to agree that changes in the weather patterns were responsible for the encroachment of the sea. He was not sure that his own son would have the pleasure of owning a beachside property that he had. He particularly enjoyed his walks after a storm. He was raised a beachcomber and over the years he had unearthed all manner of flotsam and jetsam on what he considered his beach. He found a use in the house for most of the driftwood. He wasn't sure that his wife appreciated the volume of what she considered as washed-up trash that he brought home. He sometimes felt like the cat the brings home a mouse for the delectation of its mistress only to receive a kick in the arse. Yesterday's storm had been one of the worst for some time. Wind speeds had touched a hundred plus kilometres an hour and given that his house faced west it had borne the full force of the wind. During his walk, he'd managed to pick up a few interesting pieces of driftwood. The tide was heading out as he made his way back towards his house along the last section of beach when he noticed a large black mass that had been exposed by the retreating water. He stood on the edge of the sea and waited while more of the mass was exposed. Eventually, it was clear that the mass consisted of black plastic bin bags. He'd watched a programme on television about the amount of plastic in the sea. The waters on his beach looked pristine but the tiny particles of plastic were there. He just couldn't see them. The ebbing tide revealed the full size of the mass. Whatever was in the bags was substantial. Finally, the water receded enough to allow him to approach the mass. He moved it with his foot. It was lodged in the sand and didn't budge. Whatever was inside was heavy. Gerry felt the beachcomber's tingle of excitement. He went to the rear of the beach and picked up a stick, returned to the bag, and used the stick to cut an opening. He pushed hard and then recoiled. A human hand fell out of the bag. He jumped back, his mind reeling at his discovery. He turned and ran back up the beach. He didn't own a mobile phone but he had a landline. He needed to call the Guards.


FIONA TOOK her time on the walk back to Mill Street. She needed to assimilate what was happening with her life. It felt like she'd been suddenly dropped into a maelstrom. The Molloy affair was totally down to her. She was ready to put her hand up for that. But the arrival of Tim on her doorstep was another matter. That had come out of the blue. The phrase "your boy" kept repeating in her mind. Perhaps she was in denial but she wouldn't accept that Tim was her son until she had a piece of paper showing that there was a ninety-nine-point nine per cent certainty. She didn't feel like returning to the station so she dropped into The Kitchen and ordered a coffee and blueberry muffin. If Tim were standing in front of her, she would ream him out. Where did he get off telling the world at large that she was his mother when that fact hadn't been established? Maybe she should do the DNA test today. The results would take three weeks. But the crux would remain. She tried to put the Tim issue to the back of her mind. She glanced at her watch. Cooney would have finished interviewing Tracy and would have moved on to Horgan. The die was cast. She looked at the other patrons in the café and then at herself in the mirror. For God's sake lighten up, she told herself. The disasters she envisioned might not happen. She finished her coffee and bun. As she exited the café the sun began to shine. She wondered was that an omen.

She went straight to the squad room when she arrived at Mill Street.

Tracy looked up from his desk. 'Where were you?'

'Out.' Her tone was sharper than she intended.

'Sorry I asked.' Tracy put on his hurt schoolboy look.

Fiona stood facing his desk. 'Let's get one thing straight. We're partners. That doesn't mean we have to be connected like Siamese twins. If you need to know where I am twenty-four seven, I'm afraid our partnership will be short-lived.'

Tracy returned to the open file on his desk. 'Testy,' he muttered under his breath.

Fiona heard and was tempted to continue the conversation but thought better of it. It had been a difficult morning and she didn't want to say something that she would later regret. It was time to build bridges. 'How did it go with Cooney?'

'I followed your instructions, the facts and nothing but the facts. He seemed like a nice man.'

'Was this your first experience with Professional Services?'

Tracy nodded.

'Don't be conned, they may try to act like nice people, but they're selected because they enjoy shafting their colleagues.'

Fiona went to her desk, switched on her computer, and brought up the daily report. She scanned it looking for Tim's name and saw that Geraghty had done her the ultimate favour of not including "her boy" in his report. She was settling into her daily routine when Horgan rushed into the room.

'Do you know a beach called Caladh Mweenish?' he asked Madden.

'Intimately, I spent my summers there.'

'Well, you and Tracy haul your arses over there double quick. Clifden received a report that a body had been washed up by the storm. The uniforms checked it out and sure enough, they found a body. The tide comes in four hours from now so get yourselves off. The technical bureau has been informed and they are already on the way. The local ambulance crew is standing by. We'll feed you any additional information on the way.'

Fiona and Tracy were on their feet and out the door without further comment.

# CHAPTER TWENTY-THREE

The west of Ireland contains some of the most beautiful sandy beaches in the world. It was unfortunate that Caladh Mweenish wasn't among them. The retreating ice had deposited an enormous number of boulders on the beach which spoiled the expense of sand that faced Mweenish Island.

Fiona was lost in thought. Dead bodies were part of the life of most police officers. Some were found dead in their homes, some in doorways, and some were the result of violence. It wouldn't be her first dead body that turned up on a beach. That was a common occurrence in those summers when the sun shone in Ireland.

'Maybe the death was natural,' Tracy said.

Fiona smiled. 'I don't think so. Horgan says the body had been contained in two black bin bags. That's a pretty clear indication that the body on the beach was a murder victim.'

'I suppose you've seen a lot of dead bodies.'

'Enough.' It was obvious from Tracy's tone that he hadn't. She hated viewing torn and bloodied bodies. It did things to you inside that changed you. They were police officers and it was part of the job. In Dublin, she'd been part of the team on a dozen murder cases. She'd been lucky, or unlucky, to have become a detective during a period when the drug lords of the city were jostling like rutting stags for the control of territory. That jostling had led to the violent deaths of gang members on both sides and more than a few innocent bystanders. A teenaged first-time hitman high on drugs was not a discriminating killer.

'I bet you saw some action when you were in Dublin.'

*So young and so naïve*, she thought. *Wait until your dreams are laden with the horrors you'll see daily*. 'My last drug feud case involved the murder of a young man and the dismembering of his body. His parents had had to suffer the pain of having his various body parts turning up at locations across the city. I can still see his bits lying on the autopsy table.'

'Mostly gangland stuff then?'

'Yes, mostly gangland interspersed with a couple of domestic murders. Husbands tired of wives and wives tired of husbands. The domestics were generally messy but easy to solve. The husband/wife/partner was generally in the cells in double quick time, whinging while explaining why the lover/partner/spouse just had to go. Meanwhile, the detectives would be in the boozer celebrating their brilliant collar. Turn on the radio.'

Tracy got the message and for the rest of the trip they listened to music.

As the car moved through the countryside there was a knot in Fiona's stomach that was telling her what was coming was not going to be pleasant.

She directed Tracy down a narrow lane. As soon as they entered the lane, they were confronted by a mass of vehicles. Tracy parked behind a van that had a large Garda Síochána logo on the side panel. They exited from the car and walked the final sixty metres to the edge of the beach, passing several police cars and an ambulance on the way. There were two houses on the right side of the lane, one in the middle and one just off the beach. Crime scene tape cut off access to the beach and a uniformed officer was posted at the point where the road ended and the sandy beach began.

Fiona signed the attendance sheet and passed the clipboard to Tracy. The uniform lifted the crime scene tape and she ducked under. She walked towards a group of uniformed officers and two Garda technical officers kitted out in snow white onesies. They were congregated around a black lump that had the appearance of a dead seal. One of the officers detached himself from the group and walked towards Fiona. He had three sergeant's stripes on his arm.

He extended his hand. 'Sergeant Rory Glennan, you'd be DS Madden.'

'Fiona.' She shook his hand and turned. Tracy had caught up with her. 'This is Detective Garda Sean Tracy.'

Tracy and Glennan shook.

'What have we got?' Fiona strode towards the black mass on the beach. She looked out to sea. The tide had already turned and was on the way in. Time was not on their side. They would soon have to move the body.

'The body is still covered by much of the bags but it looks like a young woman,' Glennan said. 'I'm no expert but I'd say that the body has been in the water for more than a couple of days. There's a bit of rope around the bags. Maybe it was weighed down but whoever dumped it didn't count on the storm. It wasn't a very professional disposal.'

Fiona reached the mass where the technical bureau officers were busy taking photographs and looking about for evidence. Good luck with that, she thought. They moved away as she approached. She bent and examined the bags. The uniforms had only carried out a perfunctory examination of the body and had been at pains not to contaminate the site. She looked up at Glennan. 'Has the local doctor been called?'

'He'll be here shortly.'

'In that case, we can look. We need to get the body out of

here before the water reaches it.' She approached the technical crew. 'Detective Sergeant Fiona Madden. I'm going to look at the body. This probably isn't the crime scene so we're safe enough.'

'Joe Foley.' There was no handshake. 'You're probably right. We're under the gun anyway. This place will be knee-deep in water in an hour or two. We'll do a quick scout of the area around the body but I wouldn't get my hopes up.'

Fiona took a pair of latex gloves from her pocket and put them on. She squatted beside the body. An arm and a leg were already exposed. Proceeding carefully, she prised open the bin bags exposing more of the corpse, making sure not to touch the body. A large stone had found its way into the bags; she removed it and indicated it to the CSIs. 'Bag it.' She continued peeling back pieces of plastic and gradually she revealed the bloated body of a young woman. The girl was lying face down but Fiona recognised the dress. 'Shit, shit, shit.' She stood up. She was sure she was looking at the body of Sarah Joyce.

Tracy bent, looked at the body, and gagged.

'If you're going to throw up, don't do it here.'

He rushed off before stopping to vomit.

'His first?' Glennan asked.

'I suppose.' There were going to be a lot of hard days ahead, Fiona thought. She looked into Glennan's eyes. 'It's the young Joyce girl. She's been missing for the past four or five days. For God's sake, she's only sixteen.'

'No way,' Glennan said.

'This is between you and me,' Fiona said. 'No one else is to know. You understand?'

Glennan nodded.

'I'm from here,' Fiona said. 'If I hear you blabbed, I'll make a complaint.'

Glennan turned away. 'I've heard about you, Madden. People say that you're a right hard case. Nobody will hear from me.'

'Sorry about that.' Tracy reappeared at her side wiping his mouth with a handkerchief.

'You're human. We all should be affected like that.' Fiona looked up the beach and saw the local doctor push his way through a group of onlookers who had gathered at the edge of the crime scene tape.

The doctor marched over to Tracy and Fiona. 'Fiona Madden, I heard you were in the neighbourhood.'

'Dr Ryan, you're still around?'

'They can't get rid of me. Any idea who the corpse is?'

'It's Sarah Joyce,' Fiona said.

'Oh God no,' Ryan said. 'It'll kill her poor mother.'

'Nobody is to know until the body has been formally identified.'

'That goes without saying.'

'We need to move her,' Fiona said. 'The tide will be in soon.'

'Then I better get on with it.' He went to the body and examined it.

Fiona turned to Tracy. 'The man who found her lives in the house at the edge of the beach. I don't suppose he has any relevant information, but we need a statement for the file. Why don't you go up there and talk to him, and while you're there cadge a cup of tea off him. It'll settle your stomach.'

The doctor returned to Fiona. 'She's been in the water a while. The body is bloated and partially decomposed. It's likely that the sea creatures have taken a nibble. You can move her as soon as you like. I'll write up a death certificate. There are some marks on the neck and my guess is that she was stran-gled before she was dumped.'

'Perfect,' Fiona said. 'Just what we needed, a murdered sixteen-year-old girl.'

'Has the coroner been informed?'

'Yes.'

'I have a feeling that the autopsy will be important.'

'Yeah, considering that she didn't fall off a boat. We're going to need every bit of evidence we can find. But I don't necessarily want that view known by the general public.'

'What about the man that found her?'

'I don't think he has a medical degree.'

'But he might have seen an episode of *Criminal Minds*. Her body was enclosed in two bin bags and wrapped up with ropes. Those facts are going to be on the bush telegraph by nightfall. And you don't need to be a brain surgeon to put two and two together and arrive at four.'

Fiona knew that in the context of a small village community keeping a lid on Sarah's death was going to be a problem. She called Glennan over. 'Get the ambulance down here and tell them to park so as to block the view of the onlookers.' Behind the crime scene tape, there were several bystanders videoing the scene. 'And move those people back to the main road.'

She took out her phone and gave Horgan the bad news. Sarah Joyce hadn't drowned, she'd been murdered.

# CHAPTER TWENTY-FOUR

Fiona and Glennan watched as the ambulance crew put Sarah into a body bag and loaded her into the rear of the ambulance. In an hour and a half, she would be on a slab at the mortuary in the regional hospital. The technical bureau guys were loading up and preparing to leave. They had collected the bin bags. With a bit of luck, there'd be some traces of the person who had murdered Sarah and dumped the body. However, the body had been immersed for days and then tossed around on the bottom by the storm. Running water was a perfect medium for stripping DNA.

'Who's going to do the nasty job?' Glennan asked as the ambulance pulled away.

'I'll do it,' Fiona said. She would have preferred to avoid it, but it came with the job.

Tracy joined them. 'The poor bugger who found the body is in shock. The doctor gave him a mild sedative, but I reckon he's going to have nightmares for a few months to come. So might I.'

The tide had almost reached them. Fiona led the two men up the beach. 'Don't worry, you'll get over it. It's time to give her mother the bad news.' She turned to Glennan. 'We'll be in touch.'

The detectives walked back to their car. 'The Joyce house I suppose?' Tracy asked.

Fiona nodded and climbed into the passenger seat.

Tracy had to continue along the narrow lane before there was enough space to do a three-point turn. Then they had to crawl back towards the main road. A uniformed officer was on duty at a strip of crime scene tape at the junction of the lane and the road. A crowd of onlookers was gathered on the roadside. Fiona saw Eileen Canavan at the edge of the group. Canavan looked sad and the man standing beside her had his arm around her shoulder. Fiona thought that she recognised him from school, but he was a few years younger than her. She hadn't taken notice of any of the boys in school. She was too in love with one of the girls in her class.

Canavan tried to flag down the car but when Tracy ignored her, she mouthed, 'Is it Sarah?' as the car passed. Fiona stared straight ahead.

They drove the short distance to the Joyce house and parked outside. Nora Joyce was standing in the doorway. Even from a distance, Fiona could see that she had already been crying. The bush telegraph had done her duty for her. The detectives were only there to formalise the information. She let out a deep sigh and exited the car. Tracy followed her up the short driveway.

'Is it true?' The words came through a fit of crying.

'I'm sorry, Nora,' Fiona said. 'You'll need to make the formal identification but it's Sarah.'

'God no, no!' Nora screamed and started to make a high-pitched wailing. She moved her body backwards and forwards. Then she collapsed in a heap. Fiona caught her as she fell and eased her to the ground.

She turned to Tracy. 'Help me get her inside.'

They lifted her, carried her into the small living room, and laid her on the couch. Fiona thought how innocent and naïve they'd been when they'd sat in this room just a few days ago. Little did they know that Nora Joyce's world was about to be turned upside down. She was in a dead faint, but she was breathing normally. It was the body's response to a situation it couldn't accept. There was no point in looking for smelling salts. People in this area had no need to be brought round on a regular basis. Fiona looked through the window and saw that Nora's neighbours were gathered at her gate. 'The clinic is back down the road. Get down there and tell Dr Ryan that he's needed here.' Tracy rushed out of the room. Fiona watched him brush the questions of the onlookers aside and take off in the car. She was still looking out the window when a battered old Ford Focus pulled up outside the house and the corpulent figure of the parish priest, Father Flanagan, exited. She despised the man and had assumed that the feeling was mutual but at that moment he was as welcome as a shaft of sunlight on a cold winter's day. He ignored the group of onlookers which was adding to its number by the minute and strode down the pathway to the front door.

'Aagh.' Nora began to stir.

Flanagan burst into the living room and his large body seemed to immediately take up most of the available space. 'I just heard.' He saw Nora prone on the couch and bent over her.

Fiona stood back. 'She hit the floor as soon as I confirmed the information that she'd already heard on the bush telegraph.'

'Come now, Nora.' Flanagan cradled her head. He turned to Fiona. 'Have you called the doctor?'

'My partner's gone to the clinic to get him.'

'We're lucky the shock didn't kill her.' Flanagan slapped Nora lightly on the cheeks.

She opened her eyes for a moment before closing them again.

'The poor creature, we'll leave her to the doctor.' Flanagan looked up and seemed to see Fiona for the first time. 'You... I heard you were in the parish this week.'

'Good to see you too, Father. When I saw how you responded to Nora, I didn't believe it was you. You're capable of displaying empathy. Are you still telling the locals that there's a special place in Heaven for the Gaelic-speaking Catholics? I envisioned your version of the Irish in Heaven as something like the Paddies in the third class of the Titanic playing their music and singing their songs just before they hit the iceberg. It sounds more fun than sitting around all day adoring God.'

Flanagan's mouth had taken on a rictus associated with the digestion of something unpalatable. 'You haven't changed. Why didn't you stay in Dublin? You'd be at home with the other heathens there. I'm surprised that you're brazen enough to show your face back here.'

'That's right, we don't want any scarlet women in Connemara. I'm a police officer now and a detective sergeant to boot. Given the current situation, I think we can set aside our bad impressions of each other. Sarah Joyce has been murdered and I don't think the perpetrator was a heathen from Dublin.'

Flanagan's bull neck was red. 'I don't suppose you called for the priest as soon as you found the body. That poor young girl should have received the last rites. You had no right to deny her the comfort of her religion. I'm going to speak to the bishop and ask him to complain to the commissioner.'

He'll have to join the queue, Fiona thought. But Flanagan was right, the thought of calling a priest hadn't crossed her mind.

Doctor Ryan and Tracy arrived on the scene and Fiona manoeuvred herself out of the room. She watched from the doorway as the doctor revived the stricken woman and gave her an injection.

Ryan joined Fiona and Tracy in the hallway. 'I've sedated her.'

'Is she out?' Fiona asked.

'No, but she'll be sleeping shortly.'

Father Flanagan joined them, and Fiona felt the hallway suddenly become claustrophobic. 'I'll get a neighbour to come in and take care of the kids.'

'We'll need her in Galway tomorrow,' Fiona said. 'She'll have to formally identify the body and I want to interview her at Mill Street afterwards. The autopsy will be carried out tomorrow morning so she should be at the regional hospital at three.'

'I'll arrange it,' Flanagan said.

'Thanks, Father,' Fiona said.

Flanagan returned to the living room.

Ryan moved to the door. 'You know where to find me.'

The detectives found themselves alone in the hallway. Fiona went to the door of the living room and saw that Nora was sleeping peacefully. She took out her mobile phone and called Ashling. She informed her about the body on the beach and told her that she would be home later than planned. Tim wasn't allowed to leave the cottage until she had spoken to him. When she finished the call, she looked at Tracy. 'Back to the station?' he asked.

# CHAPTER TWENTY-FIVE

A shling was about to leave her office when she received Fiona's call. She got the fact the Fiona was hyper about the girl that was found on the beach but there was a harshness in her voice that alerted Ashling. And it concerned Tim. Something had happened and whatever it was had made Fiona angry. Ashling wondered what the hell was going on. There were no secrets between her and Fiona. Or at least that was what she believed. Until now. Tim's arrival was a cataclysmic event and it was inevitable that it would create tension. Fiona's agitated voice on the phone indicated that the tension had been ratcheted up. She felt a shiver of fear that their well-ordered world was about to change forever. It was not a prospect that she welcomed. Before leaving the university, she decided to pass by the computer centre. She had abandoned her research into Tim. Fiona was the detective, not her. She had proven to be totally ineffective in looking into his background. There was no need to rush home. Fiona wouldn't be back until late and she didn't know where Tim was. She went to the Engineering Building and knocked on the office door of Dr Makara Sok and prayed that he hadn't left for the evening.

She breathed a sigh of relief when a voice inside asked her to enter.

As she entered, Sok's round Buddha-like face stared at her through a narrow gap in the three computer screens that sat on his desk. Sok was a Cambodian refugee who had made his way to Ireland after his studies in Canada. He was one of those people who connected perfectly with a computer. If anyone could track Tim Daly's social footprint, Ashling knew it would be him. Although they had never collaborated professionally, they had often shared a coffee, especially when Ashling was planning her trip to South-East Asia.

Sok hit a few keys before greeting her with a big smile. 'Ashling, long time no see.'

She moved two boxes from a chair and sat down. 'More's the pity.' She settled herself in the chair. 'I haven't seen you around lately. I was worried that you might not be in college.'

'Then you're lucky. I just came back from a consulting assignment in LA. How can I help you? Computer problem or travel planning?'

'Neither really.' Ashling didn't know how to begin. 'It's a bit of a story. My partner had a child when she was sixteen. The child was adopted out and a young man turned up at our door a couple of days ago. He claims that he's my partner's son and wants to reconnect with his mother. It sounds reasonable so far. But I have a feeling that's not all he has in mind.'

Sok's eyebrows raised into his shaven head.

'Okay, I know how it sounds. Professional psychologist looking for something that may not be there. Maybe that's true and I'm overthinking things.'

'So, where do I fit in?'

'This boy is eighteen years old and American. It's unthinkable that such a person wouldn't have a digital footprint, but he doesn't. At least not one that I can find. That's my predicament. I need to know more about this kid. I could psychoanalyse him if I had him on the couch, but I have the feeling that I'll never have that opportunity.'

'And you really think that you'll find what you want by looking at his social media profile?' Sok smiled making him look more like a Buddha than usual. 'The Internet is the perfect medium to project an image of yourself that might not be exactly accurate. You're aware of the dating sites where people submit old pictures of themselves or create profiles that are fictitious. This young man is probably social media savvy which means his footprint might be difficult to find. But I like a challenge. Give me the details.'

'I'm afraid the details are pretty scant. His name is Timothy Daly, Tim for short. I don't have his exact birthdate but the year was 2004.' She made a mental note to get the precise date from Fiona. 'Apparently, he was adopted by a couple living in Boston.' She stopped and looked at Sok.

He looked up from the pad he'd been writing on. 'That's it?'

'I'm afraid so.'

'You need to look up the definition of scant.' He sighed. 'It's not much to work on.'

'Even for a computer genius like you?'

Sok beamed. 'Flattery will get you everywhere. Get me the birthdate at least and I'll get back to you when I have something to report.'

'The next coffee is on me.' Ashling walked to the door.

Sok disappeared behind his screens. 'That goes without saying.'

## CHAPTER TWENTY-SIX

Fiona was grateful that neither she nor Tracy spoke until they were halfway back to Galway.

'I'm sorry about the vomiting business,' Tracy said.

'Get over it.'

'I let the team down in front of the guys from Clifden. I don't have to tell you that the body on the beach was my first dead one. My grandparents died when I was a young boy. I vaguely remember their funeral and the wakes mainly because so many adults wanted to shake my hand and I couldn't understand why. My mother's legs shielded the scene of the coffins being lowered into the earth.'

'You'll get used to it. I'd be willing to bet that a few of the boys from Clifden had already tossed their lunch before we arrived. I noticed that they were looking a little green about the gills. We're not all macho gung-ho Neanderthals.'

'You were right about the shithouse poet. On my last visit to the toilet at Mill Street, the first mention of *Dick* Tracy had appeared on the wall with the appropriate drawing. I'd be grateful if you'd keep my reaction to the corpse to yourself.'

'No problem.' She didn't bother to enlighten him on the remarks that had begun to appear in the ladies' toilet. She didn't want the poor bugger blushing all the way back to Galway.

Fiona closed her eyes signalling the end of the conversation. She had a perfect mental picture of Sarah Joyce's body wrapped up in bin bags. The young woman's death was an abomination but it had been compounded by the manner of disposal. Although the killer may not have intended it, the refuse bags had the connotation that the contents were trash. She was disappointed that her prayers vis-à-vis Sarah hadn't been answered. She'd long ago given up on prayer but every now and then her religious upbringing came to the fore and she begged the help of a supernatural being to solve a problem that was beyond her capacity. Though such attempts were the victory of desire over experience. Her thoughts moved to the investigation ahead. There was one damaged corpse on its way to the morgue. The investigation into the death would lead to more damaged lives. She had no idea what she was about to uncover but she knew it would be cataclysmic. The investigation into the murder of a young girl from a tight-knit community was likely to turn over stones that would best be left alone. It would be her job to root around beneath the stones and she would not be thanked for doing it. One of her mentors at Store Street had likened their job to the men employed at the beginning of the twentieth century who cleared horseshit from the streets overnight. Fiona had the feeling that her immediate future would involve a lot of shit shovelling.

They arrived at the station just after six o'clock and Fiona did a double-take when she saw Horgan seated in her chair. The Irish phrase *what's rare is wonderful* jumped into her mind. Horgan was famous in Mill Street, and possibly the rest of the Garda Síochána, for his OCD. He arrived at the station at exactly nine o'clock each morning and departed at five on the dot. His whole day from meetings to tea breaks occurred at specific times. He took tea at eleven with the same colleague every day. He deposited five spoons of sugar into that tea and consumed two biscuits. He wasn't just a creature of habit. He was a human clock. And the clock was showing the wrong time.

'Tell me.'

Fiona pulled up a chair and sat facing Horgan. 'The local doctor found ligature marks on her neck.' She took out her mobile phone, brought up the photos she'd taken on the beach, and handed the phone to Horgan.

Horgan flipped through the pictures. 'You're sure it's the missing girl?'

Fiona nodded.

He handed back the phone. 'You feel up to this?'

'I know the locality and I know the people.'

'That might be a positive or a negative in this kind of investigation. Communities out there tend to be tight-lipped. Maybe I should handle this myself.'

'The missing persons investigation has thrown up a couple of leads.' She couldn't think of one offhand but she wanted this investigation and she knew that Horgan didn't. What he wanted was to be convinced that she was the best person to be nominated as the senior investigating officer. 'We need to keep control of the investigation. I have experience in murder investigations and I can bring that experience to bear.'

'Where do we go from here?'

'The state pathologist has been informed and he'll be here tomorrow morning. He's due to start the post-mortem at ten. I'd like to attend.'

'I understand the *great man* doesn't like spectators.'

'I've met him before. I think he'll let me watch.'

'What about these leads?'

She nodded at Tracy. 'Sean and I will work up something for tomorrow. There'll be little or no evidence from the beach. She wasn't killed there. We'll have to start from scratch. The techs have the plastic bags and the rope. There was a large stone inside one of the bags intended to weigh the body down. There might be a print on either.'

'Chance would be a fine thing.' Horgan glanced at his watch. His dinner would be getting cold. 'Okay, Madden, you can have the case. But if it hits the shit, I might have to take it off you. Given your recent notoriety, I'll handle the media.'

'Thanks, boss. We won't let you down. It's kind of you to take on the difficult job of dealing with the media.'

'You're a cynical you-know-what, Madden.' Horgan stood up. 'You better not disappoint me. I'm putting myself out on a limb for you here. I'll have to give Cooney a bell. It wouldn't look good if you were hauled off the case by a disciplinary hearing.' He walked to the door. 'There's no overtime in the budget.'

'I didn't think there would be,' Fiona said.

'What's this about leads?' Tracy asked when Horgan had disappeared.

'I was bullshitting. We needed to keep this case. Go back over your notes. Strangling is up close and personal. It was someone who knew her.' Her mind had moved to her other problem. She was anxious to speak with Tim. 'Are you okay to hang in for an hour or two?'

'Alone?'

'There's somewhere I need to be.'

'This is my first murder case. I'm not afraid to admit that I don't know my arse from my elbow. Aren't you supposed to be mentoring me?'

'Part of what I have to teach you is personal responsibility. You can't go through life looking around for someone to wipe your arse. Go through the notes on the interviews and see if there's a lead we can follow. I still believe those kids were feeding us crap. There's going to be a lot of pressure to pull someone in post-haste.' She picked up her bag and made for the door. 'First thing in the morning.'

She arrived outside and remembered that she didn't have

transport home and Ashling had probably left over an hour ago. She saw a Garda Flying Squad car about to leave the compound and waved it down.

'You heading Barna way?' she asked.

The two uniforms looked at each other. 'Jump in,' the driver said.

# CHAPTER TWENTY-SEVEN

'Where is he?' Fiona dumped her bag on a chair and stared at Ashling.

'Don't you think we should have a chat first?'

'No, I don't. You don't figure in this drama. I don't mind you listening in but I need to talk to Tim, now.'

'You've had a tough day. Finding that young girl's body must have been traumatic. It's not the best time to conduct a heart to heart. Tim's in his bedroom. Maybe you should have a drink and relax before speaking with him.'

Fiona was on her way to the bedroom before Ashling had finished. She didn't bother to knock but opened the door and marched in.

Tim was lying on the bed and looked up from the novel he was reading.

'Get your behind out of that bed and come into the living room.'

'I will if you cool down. What's the problem?'

'Don't make out that you don't understand why I'm angry. In the living room, now.' Fiona returned to the living room. She wasn't going to play at being mother. She didn't have the practice. She wasn't mad at Tim because he might be her son.

She was mad because he had crossed a line. She would have been equally mad at Ashling if she had pulled a similar stunt.

Tim strolled into the living room and stood facing Fiona. 'What's your beef?'

'When were you going to tell us that you'd been in a fight in a pub in Galway that led to you spending the night in a cell in Salthill police station?'

'There was a misunderstanding. I was sorta hoping that you wouldn't hear about it.'

'Are you that naïve? Galway is nominally a city but in effect, it's a large village. Of course, I was going to hear about it. Especially when you told all and sundry that I was your mother. What gave you the right to pull a dodge like that? Were you really that drunk? I thought you said you didn't drink.'

'I don't and I wasn't drunk. The guy I had the beef with slipped something into my drink. That was why I went off on him. I don't know what it was or why he did it but I know he doctored the drink. Everything was cool and I was enjoying the music when I came over real strange.'

'I've spoken to the sergeant and the officers who broke up the fight so don't give me any bullshit. They claim that you smelled like a brewery and that you were the aggressor.'

'Sure thing I was. That guy set me up. I swear. I was drinking a soda and he put something in it. If they'd taken a blood sample, they would have found some drug or other.'

'This doesn't gel with what the officers reported. Your stories are too different. Why did you bring up the fact that I was your mother? That hasn't been established.'

'It will be when you take a DNA test.'

Touché, Fiona thought. 'In the meantime, you've put me in the shit with my colleagues. You have no right to use my job to get you off the hook.'

'I was high on whatever that guy slipped into my drink. I didn't know what I was saying.'

'Don't do it again.' Fiona was bothered by the discrepancy between Tim's story and the reports of the officers. His explanation seemed logical but it all hinged on the fact that some random guy slipped a drug into his drink. Why would someone do something like that? 'We need to set some ground rules here. Until we find out whether there is a relationship between us, we don't go around telling people that we're mother and son. And you keep yourself out of trouble. You're here a wet week and you've already seen the inside of a police cell. It doesn't bode well.'

'Why are you breaking my balls? I'm a victim here. I did nothing wrong. Some guy decided to have a bit of fun with the Yank.'

The storm that had been raging inside Fiona since the early morning had blown itself out. She suddenly felt very tired.


ASHLING HAD BEEN OBSERVING the exchange with interest. Although she hadn't been briefed by Fiona, she had picked up the bones of the story and she understood Fiona's preoccupations. The young Tim had presented himself as a calm pleasant teenager but on his first outing had got into a brawl that had been serious enough to require the intervention of the police. An experienced police officer had smelled alcohol on Tim but he had told her and Fiona that he didn't drink. The explanation that he'd given for the brawl appeared believable. Her students kept her aware of current events on the club scene in Galway and she knew that drugs such as Rohypnol were in regular use. She could understand Fiona's distress at Tim declaring her to be his mother and using that fact to influence the police's reaction. Putting Tim's behaviour together as a package, it was incompatible with the picture that he had painted of himself. She may never be able to get Tim on the couch but she was in the process of compiling a picture from his actions that was giving her cause for concern. Fiona and Tim looked to have blown themselves out and they stood in the centre of the room staring at each other so she said, 'I stopped at the pizza place in Spiddal,' she said. 'I'll pop them in the oven.'

'I'm not hungry,' Tim said. 'I had a big lunch in Galway.' He stared at Fiona. 'Anyone mind if I go to my room and read.'

Fiona shook her head.

Tim stalked off in the direction of his room.

'You look bushed, Fiona.' Ashling hugged her. 'I'll heat up a couple of pizzas and open a bottle of red.'

'I think I'll turn in.'

'Not until you've had something to eat and a glass of wine to help you wind down. You can tell me about the young girl you found on the beach.' She led Fiona into the kitchen and closed the door behind them. She was glad that she had Sok working on researching Tim's background. Events seemed to be accelerating around them. What appeared like a simple case of an adoptee searching for his birth mother was possibly more sinister. She decided to push Sok to find information on young Tim. There was a lot more to the boy than she had initially thought.

# CHAPTER TWENTY-EIGHT

Fiona smiled at the surprise on Tracy's face as she placed a cardboard cup containing a takeaway coffee and a Danish pastry on a Styrofoam tray on his desk.

'What's the occasion?' Tracy asked. 'It's not your birthday by any chance?'

'No occasion, I missed breakfast myself and I thought that a young guy like you might have been on the town last night and that a coffee might go down well.' In fact, she was feeling bad about the way she had treated her new partner the previous day. In the evening, she'd discussed the finding of the body with Ashling and had come to realise that the event would have been traumatic for Tracy. It was his first murder case. It would get easier but there was always a psychological impact. It wasn't normal to find human beings who have been maltreated to the extent of murder. Anyone who can pass off violent death needs psychological help themselves. Tracy had acquitted himself well and she should have recognised that. Unfortunately, sometimes her level of empathy was not a high as it could have been.

'There was no night on the town. I had a hamburger and chips followed by a quiet pint and a movie on Netflix. I couldn't get the picture of Sarah Joyce out of my mind. I keep wondering what kind of person dumps a young girl's body at sea.'

'The kind of person who doesn't want to be nabbed for her murder.'

'I caught the end of the news on TV last night. They had a short piece on the finding of the body.'

'That means we're going to be asked a lot of questions soon. And we better have answers.'

Tracy bit into his Danish. 'I didn't get out of here until just on eight o'clock.'

'Did you come up with anything from the notes?' She took a bite of her Danish and washed it down with a slug of coffee.

'I think we should concentrate on the boys at the school and this older kid who is in college in Sligo. She was a good-looking lass.'

Fiona picked up her phone and called the morgue at the hospital. Professor George Kenny hadn't arrived yet but he had called and was on the way. He was expected to do the post-mortem on time. 'I'm off to the morgue. Kenny is suppos-edly on time. That'll be a first. I've attended post-mortems in Dublin and he's never been on time.'


MILL STREET to Galway University Hospital was a ten-minute walk. Fiona had half an hour and she therefore strolled slowly. There was nothing she could do to speed up the pace of the investigation. There were a couple of preliminary steps that had to be followed. The post-mortem and the identifica-tion of the body were two things that could be neither skipped nor sped through even though she wanted to get back to Glen-more because that's where the murderer would be found. It was a fine morning and she sauntered through the city streets. Coming back to Galway had been a risk. The first half of her life had been spent in the county and it had been a happy life for the most part. The event that changed her life also changed her desire to spend the rest of her life there. She knew that her rapist was an aberration. Over the past few days, she had passed the spot where she had been dragged into a field and the direction of her life had been altered. Reliving the trauma of rape wasn't pleasant. She remembered the pain after he entered her. She could still hear the animal rutting noises and she would never be able to get his smell out of her nostrils. She could still remember the elation of realising that she was going to survive. If she had only known what was ahead. Her religion wouldn't allow her to abort the child. She only vaguely remembered the birth. At the time, she was so out of it that it appeared to be happening to someone else. After the pain and the pushing, what looked like an alien creature was planted on her chest. And now he was living in her house. She passed the Quays Bar. The doors were closed. She looked up and saw that the area was covered by CCTV. There would also be CCTV inside. The bar would be open later in the morning and she decided to test the veracity of Tim's version of events.

# CHAPTER TWENTY-NINE

Fiona didn't envy members of the pathology profession. It wasn't that she didn't like the sight of blood; with her it was the question of smells. And it wasn't just the antiseptic odours. In Fiona's opinion, there was nothing to match the smell of decomposing flesh. She waited until a minute to ten before entering the morgue and she went directly to the room in which the post-mortem would be held. She often tried to describe the smell of death to Ashling but she never got it quite right. It wasn't just sickly sweet mixed with incipient decay. There was something profoundly intimidating for her olfactory senses. Perhaps she was oversensitive, but no police officer that she had spoken to enjoyed attending a post-mortem. Fiona would have chosen to skip the experience but she wanted the result of the procedure immediately. As soon as she arrived. she removed a tube of Vicks from her pocket and spread a smear just beneath her nose to cut through the odour. Professor Kenny hadn't yet arrived but would be present shortly. He was enjoying a cup of coffee with his old friend, the head of the pathology department. Fiona was about to take a turn in the fresh air when she almost bumped into the impressive figure of the *great man* himself. Kenny stood six feet four and weighed in at a hundred and twenty kilos. In his youth, he had been a Gaelic football star for the county of his birth, Kerry. Whether because of his job or his physique Kenny exuded gravitas.

'Excuse me, young lady.' Kenny's voice was deep and he had a strong Kerry accent.

'Detective Sergeant Madden.' Fiona thrust out her hand.

Kenny looked at the hand and then ignored it.

'I'm the SIO on the case of the young woman you're about to carry out the post-mortem on.'

'Please tell me that you do not wish to attend.' Kenny walked towards the post-mortem room.

Fiona fell into step beside him. 'I would prefer not to but I think I should.'

Kenny looked at the smear of opaque paste under Fiona's nose. 'I see you've already attended a post-mortem.'

'I've attended several. Even one with you.'

Kenny stopped. 'Where?'

'Dublin. I worked on several murder cases where you autopsied the bodies.'

Kenny stared at her for a moment before striding on. 'Get gowned up. Keep your mouth shut while I work and make sure any question you wish to ask has a point. Otherwise, you won't get an answer.'

They entered the autopsy room together. The young doctor who would assist Kenny almost genuflected at the sight of the *great man*.

Kenny ignored the display of obsequiousness as though it was par for the course. He dispensed with his jacket and began to scrub up. Kenny turned and held his hands out straight. The assistant slipped a gown on.

Fiona picked up a gown and put it on.

Kenny moved to the table and removed the sheet that covered Sarah Joyce's body. He stood for a moment staring at the young woman's corpse.

Fiona wondered if he was praying.

'Turn on the recorder.' Kenny picked up a scalpel from the tray of instruments and made the first incision. 'The body is that of a young woman approximately sixteen years of age.' His bass voice rebounded from the tiled walls.

FIONA STOOD SLIGHTLY behind Kenny as they both looked down on Sarah Joyce's naked body. She might have been wrong but she thought Kenny looked sad. The immersion in saltwater had already created a significant amount of crinkling of the skin. Sarah didn't look as young and beautiful as in her Facebook photo. There were signs of decomposition and Fiona was aware of a smell despite the dollop of Vicks clinging to her upper lip. She heard Kenny sigh as he picked up a scalpel. The man might be an arrogant bugger but it appeared he had a heart. She watched him as he worked. His movements were smooth and gentle, contrasting with his physical size. Viewing a post-mortem was never a pleasant task. There were parts of the human body that were not designed to be viewed. However, Kenny went through his work in such a fashion that the feeling of desecration was totally absent. Although it was unsaid, Fiona recognised that the pathologist treated the young girl's body with respect. The whole procedure was like an artfully crafted piece of theatre.

Kenny stopped dead and turned to face Fiona. 'Our young friend was pregnant.'

'What!' Fiona felt the shock from the top of her head to the soles of her feet. She looked down at the body and almost cried. It wasn't empathy. It was pity. She'd been there. The feelings were eighteen years old but she remembered the shock when she discovered that she was pregnant at sixteen. It wasn't supposed to happen like that. She had been raped and she would now have to consider the possibility that Sarah had also been defiled.

Kenny took a dish from the table at his side and deposited a small blob into it. He showed the dish to Fiona. 'I'd estimate that she was in the first trimester. The embryo has approximately three months' development.'

The embryo was tiny, no more than an inch in length but Fiona could see the outline of the baby that would never be born. As a veteran police officer, she didn't shock easily but she was speechless.

Kenny put the dish aside and continued his work.

Fiona's mind was racing. This put a totally different complexion on the murder. She stared at the embryo in the dish and realised that she was probably looking at the motive for murder.

When he finished, Kenny turned from the table. He left the closing up to the young doctor who had assisted him. Without speaking, he tore his gown off, tossed it into a plastic bin in the corner of the room, and went to the sink.

Fiona followed suit and stood beside the pathologist as he washed up.

'There you have it.' Kenny dried his hands and threw the towel into a bin at his feet 'She was strangled with some form of ligature. I'm sure someone in the technical bureau will have an idea about what the medium might have been. She ate a meal and had sex shortly before she died. The state of maceration on the exposed skin of the hands and feet is well established. I would say that she has been in the water for four to five days and was probably murdered just prior to immersion. She was three months pregnant. Otherwise, she was a perfectly healthy young woman who had her full life in front of her. Any questions?'

'What is maceration?'

'The softening of the skin due to immersion in liquid. You probably noticed the looseness of the skin around the hands and feet, and unfortunately, also about the face.'

'The crinkling of the skin.'

'Yes.'

'Will we be able to obtain the father's DNA from the embryo?' Fiona asked. She supposed that she should have considered that Sarah might have been pregnant.

'I assume so. I've taken a sample for analysis. We'll check the mother's DNA and the lab should be able to come up with the father's DNA.'

'Was she alive when she was put in the water?'

'There was no water in the lungs. So, no, she was dead.'

'No skin under the fingernails?'

'They were chewed to the quick.'

'She was attacked from behind?'

'I think so. By someone that was bigger and stronger.'

'A man?'

'It would be speculation.'

'Can you think of another question I should ask?'

'No.'

'Not much in the way of forensic evidence then.'

'You have what there is on the table.' Kenny reached for his jacket and put it on. 'You'll have a copy of my report through the official channels. I'm sorry but I must leave. I'm due back in Dublin early this afternoon. You will catch the bastard that did this, won't you?'

'I don't like to make promises but I'm certainly going to try my best.'

Kenny held out his hand. 'Good luck, Detective Sergeant Madden.'

Fiona's hand was enveloped by what looked like a baseball mitt. Then Kenny was gone and Fiona was left in the room alone with the assistant who came forward and handed Fiona three sealed clear plastic evidence bags.

'You'll have to sign for these,' he said as he handed the bags over.

Fiona was holding a bag containing the black dress and another containing underwear. Sarah Joyce travelled light.

The third bag contained a glass vial which Fiona assumed contained the sample that had been taken from the embryo. She signed the form on the clipboard which affirmed the chain of custody. 'I don't fancy walking through the streets with these. Do you have something I can put them into?'

The assistant went into a connecting room and returned with a supermarket shopping bag that he handed over without comment.

Fiona deposited the evidence into the shopping bag. Before leaving the morgue, she made the arrangements for the identification of the body at three o'clock and made sure that Sarah's unborn child was safely stored away.

# CHAPTER THIRTY

Fiona phoned Tracy as she left the hospital and filled him in on the results of the post-mortem. Tracy and Horgan had been working on a press release that they had thankfully managed to keep to the bare bones. Fiona was aware that the news of the body's finding had already been broadcast on Radio na Gaeltachta, the Irish language radio station which most of the people in the Connemara region listened to. That broadcast wouldn't make things easier for Fiona and Tracy. The locals were naturally tight-lipped but nobody wanted to be involved in a murder investigation. The fact that Sarah had been pregnant would have to be kept from the general public. It was something that Fiona hadn't expected and it was a complicating factor. It was also a strong lead. She decided that finding the father was going to be her first objective. She would get the father's DNA from the embryo but how would she get the match? She couldn't see the man who had impregnated a fifteen-year-old rushing forward to give his DNA. That would be the equivalent of admitting rape. She'd been there. Only she hadn't ended up on a slab in the morgue. The arrangements for the identification took a little longer than she'd anticipated and she needed to get back immediately to Mill Street to see the evidence safely deposited. Then she called Ashling and arranged to meet in Quays Bar for lunch.

The lunch crowd had not yet arrived when Fiona entered the bar. She noticed the man who had presented himself as the manager the day she had arrested Molloy and remembered his name was Peadar.

'You again,' he said when he looked up and saw her. 'I hope you haven't been up to mischief outside.'

'Not today.'

'The video went viral. The boss was over the moon. Better than an ad on the TV. What can I get you? On the house.'

'Nothing thanks, I'm meeting a friend for lunch.' She glanced around the bar area which was extensive and on several levels. There were several CCTV cameras visible. 'However, you can do me a favour.'

'Name it.'

'There was a row in here two nights ago.'

'There's a bit of a row in here every night.'

'The police were called for this one.'

'I was on two nights ago. This row involved two blokes?'

'That's the one. You wouldn't have CCTV of the event?'

He nodded to a young woman behind the bar. 'Bridget, take over here for a minute.' He turned to Fiona. 'Come through to the office.' He started walking towards the rear of the bar.

Fiona followed him into a small office area.

Peadar sat behind a computer. On the screen were twelve images of different areas of the bar. 'All the images are uploaded to the cloud.' He brought up a screen with a form in the centre. 'Two nights ago.' He inserted a date. 'It was about eleven o'clock and in the back bar.' He typed the information slowly. A picture of the back bar appeared on the screen. He scrolled forwards.

Fiona saw Tim standing at the bar. He was holding a pint of Guinness in his right hand and he looked to be staring in the direction of a group of girls. 'Move it forward to the altercation.'

The picture moved forward until Tim and the young man standing beside him started to wrestle each other.

Fiona leaned close to the screen. 'Reverse it and go slow over the start of the argument.'

The picture returned to a scene of relative calm. During this period, Tim was holding his drink in his right hand. At no time, did he put the drink on the bar. The fight broke out between Tim and the young man on his left.

'Can you focus on the young man on the left and play the start of the altercation again?'

Peadar obliged.

At no point did Fiona see Tim's drink being interfered with. 'Can you make me a copy of that footage? Just the start of the fight.'

Peadar fished around in a drawer and pulled out a USB, inserted it, and made a copy. 'It's an MP4 file so it should play easily on your computer.' He handed her the USB. 'It was just a bit of a barney. Handbags at ten paces. You want to be around when the fists really fly.' He turned and looked at Fiona. 'On second thoughts, I don't suppose a bit of flying fists would bother you.'

Fiona held up the USB. 'Thanks for this. You can get back to work now.'

Peadar stood up. 'The offer of a drink still stands.'

'Not in the middle of the day and I prefer to pay for my own.'

'If the boss turns up, he won't take no for an answer.'

They made their way back towards the entrance and Fiona saw Ashling outside the door glancing at her watch.


'He lied.'

They had found a table and ordered a sandwich and coffee.

'You're sure?' Ashling shivered as though hit by a blast from a cold wind. 'That would not be good.'.

Fiona took out the USB. 'It's all on here.' She handed the USB over. 'Play it this afternoon on your computer and tell me what you think. But I'll tell you nobody interfered with Tim's drink and he had a Guinness in his hand. So, he lied on two counts.'

Their lunch arrived and they started to eat.

Ashling put down her sandwich. 'It's quite difficult to discuss Tim at home when he's in the next room. I told you I had already tried to look at his social media footprint but I found nothing. That was strange. He's eighteen. At that age, they live on the phone. We have this computer genius at college. I've asked him to research Tim for me.'

'This is crazy shit and I don't need it right now.'

'Maybe we should ask him to leave.'

The idea appealed to Fiona but throwing her son out of the house for lying seemed a bit extreme. She had no experience to fall back on but she assumed that every teenager lied to their parents and possibly more than once. 'I don't know. So he lied about the cause of the fight. It's not such a big deal. What sort of Irish mother would turf her son out?'

'Are you serious or is this a joke? It wouldn't be such a big deal on its own but there's also the issue of no social media footprint. What do we really know about Tim? He arrived out of the blue and announced himself to be your son and we instantly took him in. But what do we really know about him? Maybe we should contact his adoptive parents. If he was applying for a job, he'd have to provide references.'

'I don't think presenting himself as my son and applying for a job are in the same category. I'll ask him this evening about his adoptive parents.'

'I already did. He gave me the vaguest answer possible. I

got the impression that he was holding back on the information.'

Fiona had finished her lunch. 'I feel that to. But maybe both of us are mistaken. Every now and then you should stop thinking like a psychologist. Everyone you meet doesn't have deep and dark motivations. He did his research and he found me. The only issue outstanding is the DNA test to confirm the relationship.'

'My God, you're talking like his mother. You're defending him. You're sure that he's your son.'

Fiona nodded.

'Why?'

'Because he's the spitting image of the man that raped me.'

## CHAPTER THIRTY-ONE

Fiona removed the shopping bag from her desk drawer and sat down.

Tracy looked up. 'Horgan is going to be on the box this evening. RTE are sending someone out from the local office to take some shots of the beach and interview a couple of the locals.'

'It's already a big story and I think it's going to get bigger. It isn't every day that a sixteen-year-old murder victim washes up on a local beach. I hope a make-up person is going to add some colour to Horgan's face. Otherwise, he might frighten some of the children.'

'What's in the bag?'

Fiona withdrew the two evidence bags containing Sarah's clothes and tossed them on Tracy's desk. 'Get these over to the technical bureau. I doubt that a forensic investigation will turn up much but let's try it anyway.' She put the vial containing the sample from the embryo into her desk drawer. She wanted to deliver it herself to the lab.

Tracy examined the bags containing the dress and the underwear. 'I doubt she left the house wearing those clothes.

Which poses the question: what was she wearing when she went out and where are those clothes now?'

'It's time to set up the whiteboard.' Fiona picked up the picture of Sarah, walked to the whiteboard in the centre of the room, and stuck the picture on the top. She wrote what they knew about Sarah beneath the picture. It wasn't a lot. There was her date of birth and the time that she'd been missing. Beneath she wrote strangled and pregnant.

Tracy put the evidence bags aside. 'I'll get these over to the Lab. How did the post-mortem go?'

'An hour and a half of watching a young girl being sliced and diced before being sewed back together again. It was the highlight of my day. She was a healthy sixteen-year-old with another three score years ahead of her.'

'Being pregnant, that could be important.'

'Your powers of detection are impressive. I think it is of the utmost importance. It could be the reason that she's lying on a slab in the morgue.'

'Where do we go from here?'

Fiona looked at her watch. It was a quarter past two. 'You and I are going to the morgue. Sarah's mother is due at three to identify the body. We'll take a car and when we're finished, we'll bring Nora back here for an interview.'

'Horgan told me to contact Clifden and get them to talk to the locals.'

'Good luck with that. Sarah left her house five days ago in the evening. Somewhere along the line she changed her clothes and got herself killed. We know that she had a mobile phone. But there's no sign of it. We need to start working on that timeline and we need to locate those clothes and the mobile phone. If the uniforms in Clifden turn up something, so much the better but I think you and I stand a much better chance of getting someone to talk. You've been back over the interviews with the kids in her class. What did you conclude?'

'They didn't give us much. She wasn't interested in boys of her own age.'

Fiona wrote *missing clothes and mobile phone* on the whiteboard. 'After the interview with Nora we'll start establishing the timeline.'

# CHAPTER THIRTY-TWO

Nora Joyce and Father Flanagan were standing in the vestibule of the morgue when Fiona and Tracy arrived. Nora's eyes were surrounded by dark circles.

'I'm sorry you have to go through this,' Fiona said. She had arranged for the body to be ready for viewing. She wanted to get the process over as quickly as possible. The viewing would take place through a window. Fiona nodded at Tracy and he stayed behind in the vestibule. She led Joyce and Flanagan into the viewing area and looked at them. 'Ready?'

They nodded in unison.

She drew back the curtain that covered the viewing window. The morgue assistant stood impassively behind a trolley on which Sarah Joyce's body lay. Fiona nodded and the assistant pulled back the sheet exposing only the face.

'Oh God!' Nora buckled at the knees but Flanagan was ready and caught her and held her upright.

'Is that your daughter Sarah?' Fiona asked.

'Yes.' It was almost inaudible. She turned to Fiona. 'Can I hold her hand?'

'Not now. The body will be released to you soon and you can wake her properly.' She drew the curtains. 'Nora, I know this is a difficult time for you but it's important that we get the murder investigation underway as quickly as possible. I don't want to impose on your grief but I wonder, would it be possible for you to come to Mill Street station so that we can ask you a couple of questions?'

'Is that really necessary?' Flanagan said. 'Hasn't the poor woman been through enough the past week?'

'I'm sure that Nora is as anxious as we are to catch the person responsible for Sarah's death. The first few days are vitally important in a murder investigation. We have little forensic evidence to go on and any that does exist will probably degrade over time. So, unfortunately, it is necessary that we ask Nora some questions.' She turned to Nora. 'I would prefer to speak to you alone if that's alright. Father Flanagan can wait for you at the station if he wishes.' She looked at Flanagan who didn't look pleased. 'I hate morgues.' She took Nora by the hand. 'Let's get out of here.'

'How long are we talking about?' Flanagan asked as they walked to the entrance.

'Come by the station in an hour,' Fiona said. 'We should be nearly finished by then.'

'I need to get Nora home. She's needs rest and recuperation for what lies ahead.'

'I understand.' Fiona took Nora's arm and led her to their car. 'You sit in the back and young Tracy here promises to drive carefully on the way to the station.' She opened the rear door and assisted Nora into the back seat.

Tracy had already climbed into the driver's seat. Fiona sat in the passenger seat and they joined the cars heading for the hospital exit.

FIONA HAD BOOKED the only *soft* interview room available at the station. Interview rooms at Garda stations were just as they were shown in police TV shows. They are universally small, windowless, and sparsely furnished with a below IKEA grade table and four uncomfortable chairs. Recent advances in community policing had led to the creation of *soft* interview rooms which were furnished with a couch and armchairs at IKEA grade. Fiona led Nora into the interview room and sat her on the couch. 'Will I ask young Tracy to get us a cup of tea?' she asked as soon as Nora was seated.

'Do whatever you want. I couldn't care less.'

Fiona turned to Tracy. 'And try to rustle up a couple of biscuits. I'll sort you out later.'

Tracy didn't look pleased to be saddled with the job of teaboy but nevertheless left the room.

Fiona wanted to get on with the investigation but there was no point in running around like a chicken with its head chopped off. They were already more than twenty-four hours into the investigation and the only evidence that gave a clue as to the motive for Sarah's murder was the result of the post-mortem 'Are you okay now?' she asked.

'I still don't believe it.' Nora suppressed a sniffle. 'I keep expecting her to walk in the door. She was only sixteen a month ago.' She broke down crying.

There was a box of tissues on the coffee table that sat between them and Fiona pushed it in Nora's direction.

Tracy entered the room carrying two cardboard cups containing tea and put one in front of Fiona and the other in front of Nora. He'd already added milk, and he produced four sachets of sugar from his jacket pocket and dropped them on the table. He took a small packet of chocolate wafers from another pocket and added them to the sachets. He looked at Fiona.

'Thanks, what about yourself?'

'I'm okay.' He took an armchair, moved it beside Fiona, and took out his notebook and pen.

Nora's crying fit had subsided and she helped herself to two of the sachets.

Fiona looked at the anaemic liquid in her cup and decided to ignore it. 'I'm sorry to impose on your grief but we need to get moving on finding the person who did this dreadful thing to Sarah. Let's start with the evening she left the house and never came back.'

Nora had another attack of the sniffles.

'You said she was wearing a white shirt, brown pullover, and blue jeans.'

Nora nodded.

'You remember the photo we showed you of Sarah that was posted on Facebook.'

Nora blew her nose and pulled another paper handkerchief from the box. 'Yes.'

'She was wearing that dress when she was murdered.'

'I wouldn't let her out of the house in a dress like that.'

'We haven't located the clothes she left in. Have you any idea where she might have changed?'

Nora shook her head.

'She left the house at about a quarter past six. How are you so sure of the time?'

'I watch the news on RTE every evening at six. The second segment had just started when I saw her slip out of the front door.'

'And she didn't say where she was going?'

'She never did. Like most teenagers, she was feeling her oats. Her business was her business.'

Fiona watched the older woman as she sipped her tea. She reckoned it was time to drop the hammer. 'When did you realise that Sarah was pregnant?'

The cup wavered in Nora's hand but she didn't drop it. Fiona took that as a sign that the news wasn't a surprise.

'I heard her getting sick in the bathroom about six weeks ago. When it happened regularly, I put two and two together.'

'Did you talk to her about it?'

'Lord no, when she was younger, we were as thick as

thieves. Lately, we'd grown apart. I thought it was the normal progression of being a teenager. It would have worked itself out over time.' She put down the cup and began to cry.

Fiona waited until Nora had composed herself. 'Have you any idea who the father was?'

Nora shook her head.

'How did Sarah seem?'

'Sometimes I saw a look of fear on her face and sometimes she looked happier than I'd seen her in a long time.'

'She was in love?'

Nora shrugged.

'She never talked about a boy she might have been seeing?'

'Not to me. You'll have to speak to her friends. Maybe she told one of them.'

'That's possible. Why didn't you tell us that she was pregnant when we interviewed you earlier?'

'It was none of your business.'

'It's not up to you to decide what's not our business. By holding back you could have impeded our investigation. The pregnancy could have been pertinent to her disappearance.'

Nora broke off eye contact with Fiona.

There was a knock on the door and Tracy rose and went to the door. He returned and whispered in Fiona's ear. 'Father Flanagan is in reception and the desk sergeant says he doesn't have the look of a man who likes to twiddle his thumbs.'

'We're going to be active around the village over the next few days.' Fiona noticed the look of fear on Nora's face. 'Don't worry. We're not going to say anything about Sarah's condition but we're going to actively investigate her love life. There's a distinct lack of evidence so we probably won't be wearing our kid gloves. We'll be turning over rocks and that might expose secrets that people would prefer weren't revealed. Normally, they'll take their spleen out on us but there may be times when they'll turn on you.'

'I want you to find the bastard that killed my daughter and my grandchild.'

'Father Flanagan is waiting for you in reception so we'll let you get back home. We will most likely want to talk to you again and I'll want to take a more detailed look at Sarah's room.'

Nora picked up her bag from the floor and stood. 'I don't want to keep the reverend father waiting. He's been good to me and I'm sure he has other business to attend to.'

'Yes, let's not keep the parish priest waiting.' Fiona stood and extended her hand. 'I'm deeply sorry for your trouble and you can be assured that we're going to do our best for both you and Sarah.'

Nora took her hand. 'I might have been a little short with you the other day and I'm sorry for that. Whatever is between you and your mother is no affair of mine.'

'We'll be around tomorrow and we'll drop in to look at Sarah's room. I'd be grateful if you wouldn't touch anything.'

Nora nodded and allowed Tracy to lead her to the door.

Fiona gathered the cups. The wafers were untouched and she put them in her pocket. Outside the door, she dumped the cups in a waste bin and walked back towards the CID office. As she passed the reception area, Flanagan looked over his shoulder and caught her eye. He was wearing his hellfire-and-brimstone look. She gave him a smile and watched while he turned away quickly.

Tracy slumped in his chair when he returned to the squad room. 'She didn't give us much.'

Fiona was reading her emails. 'She gave us all she had. If she'd known who the father was, she would have told us.'

'You owe me four euros for the tea and biscuits.'

Fiona took a five euro note from her purse, balled it up, and threw it at Tracy. 'Keep the change.'

He caught it in mid-air, laid it on his desk, and flattened it before depositing it in his pocket.

'Why do I get the impression that you think being sent to fetch the tea and biscuits was beneath you?'

Tracy's face flushed.

'I hope that's the worst task that's going to be demanded of you during your time working for this august organisation. You probably thought that being a uniform was the bottom of the tree and it is. But like the clever monkey that you are, you've jumped to a bigger tree and you find that you're only entitled to sit on the bottom branch of the new tree. So, get used to it.' She was about to return to her emails when Horgan entered. She reckoned it must be close to five o'clock.

'What's the story?' Horgan stood between Fiona's and Tracy's desks.

Fiona gave him a rundown on the day's events.

'The mother had no idea who the father might be?' Horgan asked when she'd finished.

'So it appears.' Fiona had stolen a look at her watch. It was five minutes to five which meant that Horgan would disappear in exactly five minutes.

'What's your plan of action?' It was Horgan's turn to take a sneaky look at the watch.

'The pregnancy is the only lead we have for the moment. Tomorrow Detective Garda Tracy and I will head out to Connemara and begin our investigation into who might possibly be the father.' She opened her drawer and held up a plastic evidence bag containing a small vial. 'Kenny took this sample from the embryo. We'll need to run a DNA test on it. Any potential father will have to be measured against the embryo's DNA profile.'

'DNA testing costs money,' Horgan said, beginning to fidget.

Fiona assumed that the little hand was on the five and the big hand had passed the twelve. 'It'll catch the killer.'

'We'll hold back on the information concerning the baby,' Horgan said. 'The press is all over this already but that will give them the opportunity to add sex to the cocktail they're mixing.'

'How did your piece to camera go?'

'Okay, I think. At least the super and Phoenix Park seemed happy.' He started moving to the door. 'Keep me informed.' He opened the door, exited, and closed the door in one smooth movement.

'Have a nice evening, sir,' Fiona called after him. She burst out laughing.

'It's not funny,' Tracy said. 'It's obsessive-compulsive behaviour. You should have your friend Ashling have a couple of sessions with him. My mother was adopted and my adoptive grandmother is obsessed with cleanliness. As a child, I hated visiting her. Every time I dropped a crumb on the floor, she rushed off to get the vacuum cleaner to pick it up. He's more to be pitied than laughed at.'

'It's been a tough day. I think you owe me a drink. I'll give Ashling a call and ask her to meet us in Taaffes.'

# CHAPTER THIRTY-THREE

Summer was coming. For some people that was signalled by the sun rising at six thirty, for others it was the arrival of the swallows and for yet more it was the appearance of the barbeque on the patio deck. Fiona knew that summer had arrived when she couldn't find a seat in Taaffes for her after-work drink. She looked ruefully at the masses of American, French, and German tourists filling the seats that she normally occupied. The barman saw her distress and signalled her to move further into the bar where he found room for Fiona and her party of Ashling and Tracy.

'This place is getting a little busy,' Tracy remarked as he took his seat.

'You think this is busy,' Fiona said. 'Just wait for high summer. You won't be able to move for the knapsacks, fiddles, and bouzoukis.' Fiona made a sign to the barman for two pints of Guinness and a soft drink for Ashling. Several of the usual musicians arrived but since they couldn't find seats, the music would be on hold.

'We'll have to find another watering hole,' Tracy said.

Fiona and Ashling looked at him sharply.

'What?' he said.

'Heresy,' Fiona said. 'This is our pub and we'll stick with it through thick and thin.'

'I suppose we're out in the sticks again tomorrow?' Tracy wanted to get away from committing heresy.

'First, we'll send off the sample for DNA testing. Then you and I will head west. It promises to be a fine day.'

'I saw the piece with Horgan on the RTE website,' Ashling said. 'How is the investigation going?'

'She was three months pregnant,' Fiona said.

'Cherchez le boyfriend,' Ashling said.

'That's one of our problems. No one is aware that she had a boyfriend.'

'Have you spoken to her friends?'

'We interviewed a couple on the missing persons investigation. Sarah was popular but I got the impression that she was maturing faster than her friends and was leaving them behind. Personally, I think they were selling us a pup.'

'Teenagers can be very secretive,' Ashling said.

'You don't say. Do you need a PhD in clinical psychology to come to that conclusion?'

'Don't be touchy. Did you speak to a male friend?' Ashling asked.

'Yes, and he had the same feeling.'

'That might mean that the boyfriend is an older boy. I'd look at the class above hers or maybe even the one above that.'

The drinks arrived and Fiona looked at Tracy. 'I think this is your round.'

Tracy handed over a twenty euro note. 'I knew there was some reason you invited me along. The two of you have been nattering away and treating me like a piece of sculpture.'

'You'd look good as a statue,' Fiona said.

'You'd be perfect as the beautiful Greek shepherd,' Ashling added.

Tracy picked up his pint. 'I'm sorry I spoke.'

'Slainte.' Fiona touched her glass to his. He was growing on her.

Ashling sipped her orange juice. 'Remember that case in Dublin recently. Those two boys lured that poor Eastern European teenager into a derelict building, had sex with her, and then murdered her.'

'Her name was Ana Kriegel,' Fiona said. 'I worked on the case. She was fourteen and so were the boys. A right pair of toerags. I don't think we're looking at a similar scenario. Sarah left the house dressed like a tomboy and wound up on a beach looking like a sophisticated siren. My guess is that she went to meet some boy or other who had already made her pregnant. They had a row about whether she should keep the baby or not and it got out of hand.'

'Were there signs of violence on the body?' Ashling asked.

'Only the ligature mark, that's the problem with my ideal scenario. Maybe they didn't argue and he'd already decided to kill her. The pathologist found evidence that she had sex sometime before she died.'

'So the pregnancy was the motive?' Ashling asked.

'That's our jumping-off point for the investigation.' Fiona had finished her drink and signalled to the barman for a round of refills.

'I hope we're not in for a session,' Tracy said.

'What's the problem?' Fiona said. 'You have a hot date?'

'I have a dinner date with a young lady.'

'Oh, how super.' Fiona put on an upper-class English accent. 'We shouldn't detain you from going home to change into your tuxedo.'

Ashling slapped Fiona's hand. 'Someday Sean is going to be your boss and he's going to remember the way you treated him on his way up.'

'Maybe I'll always be Sean's boss.'

'Don't worry, Sean,' Ashling said. 'We're going home as

soon as we finish the next drink.' She looked at Fiona and saw that it wasn't part of her plan.

'I thought we might eat in town,' Fiona said. The drinks arrived and she paid.

'We need to go home.'

Tracy looked from one to the other. 'Is there something here that I'm missing?'

'You'll make an ace detective yet.' Fiona raised her glass. 'Goodnight and peace be with you all.'


'I LIKE THAT YOUNG MAN,' Ashling said as soon as they were seated in her car. 'You'll have to cut him a bit of slack. You're supposed to mentor him not haze him.'

'Someday when you're bored, I'll tell you about the way I was treated.'

'Are you sure you're not letting your problem with Tim transfer to Sean? In Taaffes I had the impression that you didn't want to go home.'

'Did you look at the CCTV from the Quays?

Ashling nodded.

'And?'

'His drink wasn't spiked.'

'So he lied, twice.'

'What do you intend to do?'

'I'm going to show it to him and expose the lie.'

'You think that's the best approach.'

'It'll get the drinking and the lie out in the open.'

'Maybe it'll just lead to an argument. And if so, Tim will trump you again by asking about the DNA test. I'm assuming that you haven't proceeded with that.'

'No.'

'You're going to have to do it. It's the right thing to do.'

'I don't care if it's right. I was never meant to be a mother. There isn't a mothering bone in my body.'

'You know I told you I was married.'

'Yes, and then you discovered that you preferred women.'

'I always knew I preferred women. I never told you that I had a child; a little girl.' Ashling stared at the road ahead. The tears were welling up in her eyes.

'Where is she now?'

'She was born with a rare heart defect. They tried to fix it but she didn't last. She was three months old when she died. I didn't think that I could love any human as much as I loved that child and I didn't even know her. Don't tell me there isn't some stirring within you when you look at Tim.'

'Nothing. He's a total stranger. Yes, we share some DNA but I think perhaps we're finding out that he has more in common with his father.'

'He's part of you, Fiona. It isn't just about strings of DNA. If I were you, I would keep the USB to myself. From the day he arrived, I've been trying to find what Tim wants here. If it's just to have a relationship with his birth mother, I think you'd be silly if you didn't accommodate him. Play his game. Take the DNA test.'

'I'll take it after we put the Sarah Joyce investigation to bed.'

'By then there'll be something else that's stopping you. Either take the test or tell him that you think that he's your son.'

'I said I'll take the test when the investigation is over.'

They were approaching the cottage. 'What are you going to do with the USB?' Ashling asked.

'I'm going to listen to the psychology professor.'

# CHAPTER THIRTY-FOUR

Fiona stuck her tongue out at the mirror. The white coating that obliterated the normal red colour didn't look healthy. She knew why it was there: two pints of Guinness in Taaffes, followed by a stiff gin and tonic at the cottage and a half bottle of red with dinner. Tim wasn't home when they arrived but had left a note indicating that he was spending the night in Galway. Fiona wasn't sure whether she was happy or sad. Although she had told Ashling that she was going to follow her advice, in effect she hadn't made up her mind. Ashling and her had a drunken discussion on the way forward. Luckily, Fiona had no memory of what they had concluded and from the state of Ashling neither did she. Fiona sent Tracy a text instructing him to send the specimen from Sarah's embryo to the lab for a DNA profile of the father and to pick her up on his way west. She took a shower, running the water as hot as she could bear then as cold as she could manage. The business with Tim was having an adverse effect on her drinking and she vowed that it was stopping immediately. The Tim genie was out of the bottle and would have to be faced head-on. The solution would not be found at the bottom of a bottle. Ashling was right on one point: they needed to find out exactly what Tim wanted from this new relationship. It could be as simple as confirming that he was her son and they would stay in long-distance contact. Although any eighteen-year-old might expect to continue living with their parents, Fiona could not imagine a future with Tim living under her roof. And what about his adoptive parents? She could imagine that they would be climbing the walls at this point. Tim hadn't mentioned that he had contacted them. But why hadn't they contacted him? Ashling was right. There were holes in Tim's story that would need to be filled. After completing her toilet, she made her way to the kitchen and made a breakfast of fruit juice, tea, toast and marmalade. She managed to haul Ashling into the land of the living despite her protestations that she didn't have a lecture until midday. They ate silently.

'That was an interesting conversation we had last night.' Ashling was putting the dishes in the dishwasher.

'Was it? I can't remember what we were talking about.'

'There's only one subject of conversation these days: your son.'

'I wish you wouldn't keep calling him that.'

'What else would you like me to call him?'

'Anything except *your son.*'

'Are you ready to move things along? We can't go on like this. He's supposed to be getting ready for college but he seems content to hang around here.'

'Like a bad smell.'

'I didn't say that.'

'But you want him gone.'

'He has an agenda and I think we should find out what it is. There's something going on behind those deep blue eyes of his and I'd love to know what it is. Unfortunately, my skills don't extend to divining a person's thoughts from the look on their face.'

'I'm a police detective and you're a clinical psychologist.

Wouldn't you think that between us we could manage to elicit what he's up to.'

'There's a distinct lack of information. What's the address, phone number, and email of his adoptive parents? Is he in contact with them? What do they think of this little adventure of his? Does he have friends? Is there anyone on the planet we can contact who can tell us anything about him? I'm beginning to think of him as a phantom. I'd love to sit him down and get answers to all those questions and others. My only sit-down with him produced more questions than answers. Which leads me to believe that he doesn't want us to know too much about him. The last question is why? You would think that a young man presenting himself to his mother would want to talk more about himself. I understand reticence and someone being taciturn but I can't understand having to drag words out of someone.'

'My mind is totally occupied with finding who murdered Sarah Joyce. Tim will have to stay on the back-burner until the investigation is complete.'

'That might be an error.'

'It's the way things are. Tracy will be coming by here soon to pick me up. I must get myself ready. It's going to be a long and difficult day.'


'I SEE you carried on where we left off.' Tracy got back on the coast road and headed west.

'Is this weather the result of global warming?' Fiona was wearing a pair of Ray-Bans which thankfully were cutting most of the glare from the sun that was streaming into the car. 'Someone should tell the man up above that July and August are the summer months. They said on the radio that today might be the hottest day of the year.'

'Changing the subject?'

'Yesterday was stressful and booze destresses me. The

police aren't known for being teetotallers. Show me a policeman who doesn't drink and I'll show you someone who works for Professional Services. I heard that one of the drug gangs have a mole in the Garda that they pay off in cocaine. Years ago, the ordinary decent criminals would give a Garda mole a good night out on the town.'

'The cocaine amounts to the same thing.'

'Is that the voice of experience speaking?'

'I did the college thing and that's all I'll say on that subject. What's the plan for today?'

'A quick visit to the Joyce house to have a more detailed look at Sarah's room. Then I want another word with the kids we spoke to the last time. I have a feeling that we were only told what they wanted us to hear.'

'We're not going to be popular.'

'That's not part of the job description.' She turned on the radio.

Tracy took the hint and they continued in silence.


THERE WERE two cars parked directly in front of the Joyce house in Glenmore when they arrived. Although Sarah's body wouldn't be released until the post-mortem report was approved, it was inevitable that Nora Joyce's friends and neighbours would be dropping by to express their condolences. A secondary objective of their visits would be to glean some salacious details of the murder that could be fed into the local rumour mill. In a small village, information was power. Fiona and Tracy knocked on the door which was answered by Nora.

'We'd like to look at Sarah's room,' Fiona said. 'We'll be as quick as we can.'

'I have visitors.' Nora Joyce opened the door to permit their entry.

Fiona pushed past her and glanced into the living room.

There were three ladies staring back at her and tea and biscuits were on the coffee table. 'We won't bother you.'

Nora touched her on the arm. 'Everyone is asking when the body will be available for viewing and I have to make the arrangements with the funeral home and Father Flanagan.'

'I'll let you know when the pathologist signs off on the post-mortem.' Fiona and Tracy pushed ahead down the short corridor and turned right into the bedroom area. They went straight to Sarah's room.

'What are we looking for?' Tracy pulled on a pair of latex gloves.

'Anything that'll give us a lead to who the father might be.' Fiona took her gloves from her pocket. 'Ideally, I'd like to find her mobile phone but I have a feeling it might be at the bottom of the Atlantic. There was no sign of a diary the last time we were here. I'm not even sure people keep diaries anymore. Certainly, young people don't. But if Sarah was in love there might be some letters hanging around. Who am I kidding? Everything would be in the mobile phone.' She tipped the mattress up exposing the wooden slates underneath. Nothing.

Tracy went to the bookshelf. There was a selection of modern novels. He picked up a copy of *Normal People* and flicked through the pages. 'She's read this book from cover to cover. Not my taste. But I suppose it would appeal to a young girl in love.' He flicked through the rest of the books before replacing them on the shelf.

Fiona picked up a stack of papers from the small table that acted as a desk. She leafed through them. They related to homework and the only handwritten additions consisted of doodles. Young Sarah wasn't much of a writer. She took another look at the wardrobe, feeling around inside for a secret hiding place. There was nothing. There was a Lady Gaga poster on the wall above Sarah's bed. Fiona ran her hand behind it and felt only a plastered wall.

Tracy was flicking through a small pack of photos. They

showed a younger Sarah clowning around on a beach with other children who might have been her friends or relations. He replaced the photos and turned. 'Anything?'

'Zilch.' Fiona took off her gloves and returned them to her pocket. She'd had a bedroom just like Sarah's. But she didn't remember it being so bare. She knew the Joyces lived on whatever the state provided, as did her mother, but the signs of poverty were apparent in the bedroom.

They retraced their steps to the hall door and Nora came to meet them.

'We'll try not to bother you again,' Fiona said. 'But I can't promise. Did Sarah have a computer or a tablet?'

Nora's eyes cast down. 'Money is a little tight. I was going to buy her one for Christmas.'

Fiona opened the door, aware of the stares from the living room. 'No worries, I'll be in touch about the release of the body.'

'Where next?' Tracy asked.

Fiona looked across the street at Tigh Jimmy. 'I fancy a cup of coffee and a bun.'

Tracy looked her up and down. 'How do you stay so trim?'

'I work out like a bitch in the dojo.'


'Bad business.' Jimmy had just opened and was ready to serve an empty pub.

'You mean the lack of customers.' Fiona planked herself on a bar stool.

'Don't be a smartarse. You know exactly what I mean.'

'We'll have two Americanos and I'll have a bun if you have such an item. Young Tracy here is on a diet.'

Jimmy stared at Tracy. 'He doesn't look like he needs to be on a diet.'

'Nora seems to be bearing up,' Fiona said.

'Wait until the wee girl is lying in the front room in a

coffin.' He moved to the coffee machine and set the coffee on the way. 'The village is in shock. Nobody has ever been murdered around here.'

'That we know of,' Fiona said.

Jimmy made the coffees and put them on the bar. 'What do you mean by that?'

'Don't mind me. You know I talk a load of shite.'

Jimmy smiled. 'That's something that'll never be said about you.'

'What about the bun?'

'You'll have to go next door to the shop.'

Fiona turned to Tracy. 'A Danish if they have one.'

Tracy sipped his coffee and stood up slowly.

Fiona and Jimmy burst out laughing as the door closed behind him.

She put her dark glasses on her head.

'Looks like you had a bit of a night of it,' Jimmy said.

'Bad day at the office.'

'I bet.' He took down an unmarked bottle. 'A drop of the cratur.'

'Poitín at this hour of the morning is the last thing I need.'

He held up the bottle. 'Are you sure? It'll cure or kill.'

She shook her head. 'There are two people in any village out here who know what's going on: the publican and the parish priest. The parish priest is constrained by the confidentiality of the confessional. I don't think the publican has the same constraints.'

'I already told you what I know.'

Fiona looked around the empty pub. 'I think we're alone. Nobody will ever know.'

'Somebody always knows. You're the living proof of that.'

'My dirty little secret is old news.'

'They should have given this case to someone else.'

'I do what I'm told.'

The door opened and Tracy retook his place. He put a small bag in front of Fiona.

She removed a Danish pastry from the bag and smiled. 'Jimmy was about to tell us what we should know about Sarah's sex life.'

'I already told you.'

'You snowed us. But that was all right when we were investigating a missing teenager. This is a murder inquiry. Someone strangled Sarah and tried to sink her in the Atlantic. Lucky for us nature intervened because otherwise, they might have succeeded.' Fiona put the Facebook picture on the bar. 'These were the clothes that Sarah was found in. Nora swears that she left the house wearing a pullover and jeans. Sarah was meeting someone. The question is who?'

While Jimmy looked away into space, Fiona took a bite of her bun and sipped her coffee.

'I honestly don't know who she was meeting,' Jimmy said when he looked at her again. 'Given the pain her murder has caused Nora, if I knew, I'd probably tell you. I've seen the way a couple of the lads looked at her. I wasn't happy with it but there's no harm in looking.'

'She was sixteen.'

'That doesn't stop them.'

'Maybe it should.'

'I have a bad feeling this village will never be the same when you're finished here.'

She bit into her pastry and finished her coffee. 'When I was a little girl, I loved going to the beach and lifting up the rocks to see what was hiding under them. The creepy crawlies would scamper in all directions when the light hit them. Remind you of anything? It was a habit that served me well in the police.'

'You might find something that you didn't bargain for.'

Fiona slipped off the stool and Tracy followed suit. 'It is what it is.' She took some money out of her pocket.

'The coffee was on the house.'

Fiona moved further into the pub. 'The little girls' room still at the rear? Coffee always does this to me.' She opened the toilet door. The room was small, containing only a toilet bowl and a handbasin. She saw that there was no place to stash clothes. Then she flushed the toilet, washed her hands, and exited.

'Take care, Fiona,' Jimmy said as she passed on her way to the front door.

'Always, Jimmy, always.'

'Not very productive,' Tracy said as they crossed the road to the car.

'I wouldn't exactly say that.'

'Where to next?'

'We're going to reinterview Sarah's three friends. And this time I didn't bring my kid gloves.'

# CHAPTER THIRTY-FIVE

Fiona told Tracy to park the car just outside the gate to the school. There was a group of the younger children playing in the yard as she and Tracy made their way to the front entrance.

The teacher supervising the children intercepted them before they reached the door. 'Can I help you?' she asked.

Fiona didn't recognise her which meant that she wasn't a local. She was young, pretty, and bubbly. Fiona assumed that she was only just out of college and a job in a remote school in the wilds of Connemara was the only option. 'We'd like to speak to Miss Canavan.' It was strange that once a woman became a teacher, she was immediately regulated to a *miss* again even though she might be married.

'Who shall I say wants to speak to her?'

'Detective Sergeant Madden and Detective Garda Tracy.' Fiona looked at Tracy. He was staring at the teacher.

'I suppose you're here about the poor young girl who was found on the beach. The school is upside down today. We're trying to find someone locally who is trained as a counsellor. The students in Sarah's year are terribly upset.' She withdrew a key from her pocket and opened the front door of the school.

'Would you keep an eye of the children while I get Miss Canavan?'

Fiona looked at Tracy. 'Detective Garda Tracy would be delighted. He loves children.'

Tracy sighed.

The teacher looked at Tracy. 'Don't let any of the children go outside the gate.' She went inside.

Fiona stopped before following her. She turned to Tracy. 'You could do worse.'

Fiona waited in the vestibule until the young teacher returned with Canavan in tow. She knew that she looked a sight but she was nothing like Eileen Canavan. The dark circles underneath her eyes indicated that she was having trouble sleeping.

'What an appalling business.' Canavan extended her arms.

Fiona could feel a hug coming on and stepped back. 'Yes, it is. The last time I was here we were dealing with a missing person. It's now a murder investigation and I'm leading it.'

'The children in Sarah's class are traumatised. Some have stayed home and we're hoping to counsel anyone who feels they need help to assimilate what happened.'

'I need to speak to the children again, more specifically Alicia Egan. I think that young lady led us up the garden path.'

'Alicia didn't come to school today.'

'Why am I not surprised. Where does she live?'

'Just outside the village on the right, there is a group of four newly built houses. The Egans live in the last one. Shouldn't Alicia receive counselling before you interview her? I get the impression that you think she lied. I hope you're not going to be too harsh.'

'She will have an adult present during questioning and it'll be up to her whether that questioning takes place at the Egan house or in Mill Street.'

'Would you like me to be present? I can get someone to supervise my class. I could be a positive influence.'

'Thanks for the offer but I think her grandmother will choose to be the responsible adult.'

'What other children will you want to speak to?'

'That depends on what Miss Egan has to tell us. We'll do our best not to bother you too much.'

'You will get the person that murdered Sarah?'

'Detective Garda Tracy and I will do our best.'

Fiona noticed the relief on Tracy's face when she and the young teacher exited.

Fiona turned to the teacher. 'I didn't catch your name.'

'Emma Griffin.'

'Is this your first school?'

'Yes, how did you know?'

'Lucky guess. You don't come from around here.'

Emma appeared to be looking over her shoulder in Tracy's direction. 'No, I'm from Wicklow.'

'I think my partner has taken a shine to you. Do you have a boyfriend?'

Emma blushed and went to gather up the children.

Fiona and Tracy went back to the car. 'Her name is Emma; she doesn't have a boyfriend and she fancies you.'

'I don't need you to matchmake for me.'

'Sorry, why don't you grab her before she disappears into the school and ask her for a date.'

'God, but you're bossy.' Tracy turned and hastened to catch Griffin before she entered the school.

Fiona watched the mating ritual and smiled when she saw the young teacher nod. Tracy was certainly growing on her. Perhaps there was a mothering nature somewhere deep inside but she doubted it.

FROM THE OUTSIDE, the Egan house appeared newer but a carbon copy of the Joyce house in the village. Obviously, the local council maintained their faith in the architect who had drafted the original plans. Tracy did the necessary with the doorbell.

Fiona hid her disappointment when the door was opened by Grandmother Egan. She was sure that the interview with Alicia would be difficult and was hoping that another less-engaged relative might be caring for the traumatised teenager. 'We'd like a word with Alicia.' Fiona could hear loud modern music coming from inside the house. It indicated that Alicia might not be as traumatised as reported.

Grandmother Egan blocked the entrance. 'She hasn't left her room since that poor girl was found on the beach. They were closer than sisters.'

'In that case, she'll be as interested in finding the murderer as Detective Garda Tracy and myself.'

'She's already told you all she knows.'

'No, she's already told us everything she wants us to know. This is a murder investigation. We'll talk to Alicia here or Detective Garda Tracy will take her into police custody and bring her to Mill Street. It's your decision.'

'Once a bitch, always a bitch. You've not changed much over the years.'

'Neither have you.'

Grandmother Egan paused for a moment before moving aside and allowing the two police officers to enter. Fiona led Tracy into the living room. The television was on in the corner and Fiona recognised a bald American host famous for psychobabbling his audience.

'I'll get Alicia.' Egan disappeared down the corridor.

Fiona and Tracy looked around the room which had the obligatory framed photograph of Pope John the twenty-third, a faded JFK photo, and a modern framed photo of Pope Francis. There were smaller family portraits on the shelf above the fire-place. But the dominant feature of the room was the fifty-five-inch smart TV.

When she appeared at the door, Alicia was wearing a grey

hoody over a pair of black training pants. It was more chill-out than trauma. There wasn't a trace of a tear on her pasty face. Fiona thought that she was doing trauma rather well.

'Sergeant Madden,' Alicia said. 'Granny says you want to speak with me again.'

'Do you mind if we sit?' Fiona said.

Granny Egan nodded.

Fiona chose a battered-looking couch. 'Sit down here beside me, Alicia.'

The teenager looked at Granny Egan before complying.

'When we spoke with you at the school, we were investigating Sarah's disappearance. That was a serious enough matter but a lot less serious than a murder investigation. We took notes of our conversation at the time but since you were Sarah's best friend, we may require you to make a statement this time. That means that you would have to sign the statement as proof that it represented exactly what you said.' Fiona noted that Alicia's pasty face had taken on a whiter shade of pale.

Alicia looked at her grandmother.

Fiona followed the look. It said *Help Me*.

Fiona stared at Granny Egan. 'Is that alright?'

'Alicia's a good girl' Granny Egan said. 'She hasn't done anything wrong.'

'Then she has nothing to worry about.' Fiona returned her gaze to Alicia and smiled. 'You know that I was born out here. I even went to the same school you go to. My mother lives not a mile from here.'

'Granny told me.' Alicia's voice was soft and her eyes were downcast.

'What do you kids do for fun around here?'

'What do you mean?'

'Don't tell me that you spend every evening looking at that box in the corner. What do you and your friends get up to of an evening?'

Alicia shuffled uneasily. 'At the weekends there are dances.'

'I'm sure there are. But on a fine evening where do you and your friends go? When I was your age we sometimes went to the beach.'

'We hang out there sometimes.'

'Boys and girls?'

Alicia shot a look at her grandmother who stared back at her. 'Yes, boys and girls.'

'And Sarah?'

'Yes, Sarah hung out there sometimes.'

'So, what do you get up to?'

'We build a fire and sit around and chat.'

'That seems pretty tame. Does anyone bring something to drink with them?'

'Yeah, Coke and lemonade.'

'Things have changed since I was a girl. Nothing stronger than soft drinks?'

'I don't want to have my granny here, please.'

'I think that your granny knows what you're going to say.' She looked at Granny Egan. 'Don't you?'

If looks could kill, Fiona thought as she stared into Granny Egan's eyes. 'Don't you?'

'Yes.'

Fiona turned back to Alicia. 'You think that what happens on the beach is a secret between you and your friends but others have been there before you. Someone brings alcohol, right?'

'Yes.'

'What?'

'Cider, beer, sometimes a bottle of vodka.'

'Who brings it?'

'Sometimes one of the boys, sometimes a girl.'

'Sarah?'

'Yes.'

'You have cider parties, big deal,' Fiona said.

Alicia remained silent. She stared at her grandmother.

Fiona noticed that whereas earlier in the interview Alicia had been tense she had now begun to relax. She seemed comfortable that the interview was concentrating on the drink parties. Fiona wondered whether she might go further. 'Where did Sarah get the booze? I doubt that her mother gave her the money to buy cider and beer.'

Alicia shrugged. 'Maybe she took it from Tigh Jimmy.'

Fiona looked at Granny Egan. 'Jimmy must have changed since I knew him. He valued his licence and he knew that if he was caught serving alcohol to children, his licence would be revoked.'

Granny Egan looked at her granddaughter. 'Where did she get the alcohol?'

'She had a new boyfriend and he got it for her.'

'Is that all he got for her?'

Alicia began to fidget.

Granny Egan looked at Fiona. 'What do you mean?'

'Alicia, is that all he got for her? You have to realise that because this is a murder investigation, you're going to have to tell us everything.'

Alicia started crying and put her face in her hands. 'I'm sorry, Granny,' she wailed.

'Sorry about what?' Granny Egan looked at a loss.

'What else did Sarah's new boyfriend supply?'

Alicia pulled in gulps of air. 'Weed and pills.'

'What kind of pills?'

'Ecstasy mainly, sometimes uppers.'

'Who was this boyfriend?'

'She didn't say.'

'But you paid for the drugs.'

'Yes. Sarah collected the money.'

'And the drinks?'

'They were free.'

'But you have an idea who the boyfriend was?'

'I don't know and she didn't say.'

'But you have an idea.'

'I know that she was keen on Michael Canavan.'

Fiona looked at Granny Egan. She was pale and she didn't look Fiona in the eye.

'The Canavans live on the other side of the village. They do a bit of fishing. Michael is the youngest. He must be about nineteen or twenty. He's studying something or other at Sligo Regional Tech.'

Fiona turned to Alicia. 'Was Michael Canavan supplying Sarah with drugs?'

'I don't know. Sarah never said.'

'Are you telling us everything?'

'That's all I know.'

Fiona was inclined to believe the young girl. 'We're finished for today but we'll need you to come into Mill Street to give us an official statement.'

'Will I be put in prison?'

'No, you've done nothing wrong. And what you've told us today will be a big help.'

Fiona stood and Tracy closed his notebook and joined her.

'I hope this will be kept private,' Granny Egan said.

'If we do our job properly, there'll be a court case at the end of this investigation. A lot of things will come out but we won't be giving anything to the press.'

As they exited the living room, Alicia was lying in the foetal position on the couch. Fiona turned to Granny Egan. 'Don't be too harsh on Alicia. She's just being young. The alcohol and drugs are a rite of passage. You'll need to keep a better eye on her.'

The older woman nodded. All the fight had gone out of her. She was no longer the feisty defender of her grand-daughter she had been at the school.

'It's all our fault,' she said.

'Nonsense, it would have happened whether you supervised her or not. It's a combination of raging teenage hormones and peer pressure.' Fiona put her hand on Granny Egan's shoulder before exiting the house.

'Sex and drugs and rock and roll,' Tracy said as they headed back to the car. 'I didn't see it heading in that direction. Not here in sleepy, remote Glenmore.'

'The newspapers say that drugs are in every town and village in Ireland, and maybe they're right.'

'What now?'

'The plan was a pub lunch but that's on hold until we pay a visit to the Canavan residence.'

# CHAPTER THIRTY-SIX

Tracy found the small group of houses easily enough. They were similar in construction to most of the dwellings in and around Glenmore. Each was on its own plot of land and the last in the group was the closest to the sea and was approached by a fifty-metre gravel driveway.

Fiona saw a thin line of smoke rising from the rear of the property.

As it reached the house, the gravel driveway expanded into a parking area where a battered white van sat on the left side. Tracy parked their car beside the van.

He was about to exit the car when Fiona put her hand on his arm.

'There something burning at the rear of the house. Trash collections in this area are few and far between and the locals have the habit of burning their trash. But that usually happens on a Saturday or Sunday when the environmental officer isn't working. I'll go to the house. You skip around behind and see what they're burning.'

Tracy nodded and they exited the car together.

The door was opened by a woman in her fifties wearing a housecoat. She was short and stout and her dark hair was sprinkled with grey. Her face was crisscrossed with worry lines and was what people would call lived in. However, she still possessed clear eyes and pleasant features and Fiona guessed that she would have been a good-looking woman in her youth. She took out her warrant card and showed it. 'Detective Sergeant Madden, I wonder if I could have a word.'

'I know who you are.' The woman didn't look pleased. 'The whole village knows who you are. Where's the young fellah that you drove up with.'

'That's Detective Garda Tracy. He's from somewhere in Kildare where they never see the sea. So, when he gets a chance to enjoy a view like yours, he wanders off.'

'What do you want a word about?'

'It might be more comfortable if we talked inside. You're Mrs Canavan?'

'Yes, Mary Canavan.' She moved aside reluctantly and allowed Fiona to enter.

TRACY MOVED around the back of the house and spotted the source of the smoke immediately. An old rusty barrel, which might once have contained fuel, sat at the bottom of a back garden that was littered with rubbish that consisted mainly of car parts and empty cans. He approached the barrel and saw that it was more than half full of smouldering clothes. He put his hand on the edge of the barrel and got a burn for his trouble. Looking about the garden, he saw a circular piece of wood that looked like a broken brush handle. He picked it up and prodded the barrel's contents. As far as he could make out, there were the remnants of a jacket, trousers, and pullover. He also recognised what had once been a pair of Nike trainers. He used the stick to tip the contents onto the ground and tried to stamp out the fire. He was only partially successful. The clothes were severely burned and the trainers had begun to disintegrate. He rolled the barrel aside. The clothes were too badly charred to discern whether they were male or female. It looked like they'd arrived a little too late. Nevertheless, he took out his mobile phone.

FIONA SETTLED herself on the settee in Mary Canavan's living room. 'I suppose you heard about Sarah Joyce's body being found on the beach at Caladh Mweenish.'

'I'd want to be blind, deaf, and dumb not to have heard. It's the main subject of talk and gossip.'

'We were looking into Sarah's disappearance before the body was found. Everyone was hoping that she'd just turn up. Now I'm leading a murder inquiry.'

'What do you want with me?'

'I'm talking to a lot of people in the village and picking up leads as I'm going along. I don't mind admitting that we're stumped. We don't really know exactly when or where she was murdered. That means we don't have a lot of forensic evidence so we must be more concentrated on questioning people. Did you know Sarah?'

'Only as much as I know any of the young people in the village.'

'She worked part-time in Tigh Jimmy. Did you ever run across her there?'

'Maybe she served me once or twice. She seemed to be a nice quiet young girl.'

There was a knock on the front door.

'That will be Detective Garda Tracy.'

Canavan got up to answer the door and Fiona took the opportunity to look at the photos in the living room. There appeared to be four Canavan children, two boys separated by two girls and all bunched together. They all had curly black hair and were a handsome group. There were good genes somewhere in the Canavan family.

Canavan returned accompanied by Tracy who had a

worried look on his face. He took his place beside Fiona. There were no individual photos of the children in the room. In the family photo, Mikey Canavan was probably sixteen years old and he had a big grin on his face. He looked like a happy young boy.

'Did any of your children know Sarah?'

'My daughters are nurses. One lives in Sydney and hasn't been home for three years. The other lives in London. My oldest boy lives in the village and is married with three children and my youngest boy is studying at Sligo Regional Tech. The short answer is no. Sarah was sixteen and my children are much older.'

'What about your youngest, Michael isn't it? How much older than Sarah is he?'

'Mikey is nineteen going on twenty.'

'He's likely run across Sarah then.'

'I suppose so.'

Fiona was aware of Tracy fidgeting beside her. 'My colleague has a few questions.'

'What were you burning in your back garden?'

'That's none of your business. You have no right to go poking around on my property. Aren't you supposed to have a search warrant?'

'I tipped out your burning barrel and it looks to me like you were burning items of clothing.'

'Just some old clothes that were stained.' Canavan's hands were clenched on her knees.

'I fished out a pair of Nike trainers that looked pretty new.'

'They were ruined by paint stains. I'm not answering any more questions. I want the two of you out of here and I don't want either of you poking around here without a warrant. I know my rights.'

'I'll have to inform the environmental officer that you've been burning without approval,' Fiona said. She was wondering how long it would take them to get a warrant. The answer was probably too long. Whatever had been in the barrel would be long gone by the time they came back with the requisite papers. 'You are aware that it is an offence to destroy evidence.'

'Who says it's evidence? The clothes were old and stained. They were no use to anyone and I was getting rid of them. Now get out.' She started to herd them towards the front door. 'Get off my property.'

'Before we go,' Fiona said. 'We need an address and a phone number for your son Michael.'

'Find it yourself.'

'I suppose a spare photo of Michael would be out of the question.'

'Get out.' Canavan pushed them outside and closed the door behind them.

'Five will get you a lot more than ten that she's on the phone right now to her precious son in Sligo.'

'What are we going to do about the burned clothes?'

'What condition were they in?'

'Barely recognisable. There was a strong smell of petrol in the air. The fire had died down but it must have been an inferno. It looked like there was a jacket, pullover, and trousers, and beneath that was a charred mass that could have been anything. Are we going to get a warrant?'

'There's no point. As soon as we're off the premises, she'll get rid of the detritus. Look around, there's a lot of space to disappear what you saw.'

Tracy took out his mobile phone. 'I took photos.' He switched it on and handed it to Fiona.

'Good man, we'll make a detective of you yet.' She flicked through the photos. There was no doubt in her mind that Mary Canavan had destroyed evidence that her son Mikey probably had traces of Sarah Joyce on his clothes. But that didn't mean that he had killed her. They would need more evidence than a few pictures of burned clothing.

'Where do we go from here?' Tracy asked.

'We need some sustenance. I'm going to stand you a pub lunch and we're going to contact our colleagues in Sligo. We need to contact young Mikey and arrange an interview. If his mother won't play ball, we'll have to apply a little pressure.'

# CHAPTER THIRTY-SEVEN

Lunching possibilities in Glenmore were limited and a return visit to Tigh Jimmy was out of the question. Fiona directed Tracy to follow the road towards Clifden and they pulled in at a small hotel/B&B that had a sign offering *Bar Food All Day*. They sat in the corner of the large dining room and ordered two portions of the daily special: bacon and cabbage. It was time to reflect on what they had learned during the morning.

'This Mikey Canavan guy is the prime suspect.' Tracy forked some cabbage into his mouth.

'So it would appear.' Fiona couldn't believe that they had made so much progress in the investigation. Alicia Egan had cracked like an overripe pomegranate and set them on the trail of Mikey Canavan. But Fiona knew that a murder investigation was prone to make detectives rush off in the most likely direction while ignoring facts that later prove to be more important. 'Get out that phone of yours and google Glenmore Rangers. They're a big enough team, and they might have individual photos of the players.'

Tracy did as he was told. He smiled and turned his mobile towards Fiona. 'Meet Mikey Canavan as he is today.'

Fiona took the phone. There was no smile on Canavan's face which had grown harder with the years. He was handsome in a mature way and there was a twinkle in his eyes. She could well believe that he would cause a flutter in a young girl's breast. Fiona handed back the phone. 'He's almost as handsome as you.'

Tracy looked away as he put the phone back in his pocket. 'We can do Sligo in a couple of hours. I've never been there and I hear it's nice.'

There was a light in Tracy's eyes that Fiona recognised. She'd seen it in the mirror often enough. It was the look of the hunter. Arthur Conan Doyle had it right when Sherlock Holmes used the phrase the *game is afoot*. A police investigation was a hunt and the excitement rises when the game is in sight. Tracy might be new but she could already see that he had the instincts for the business. He was feeling the momentum and he wanted to get on with the chase. So did she, but there was no point in wasting time. The sooner they had Mikey Canavan in Mill Street with a swab in his mouth the better. 'I want a blown-up copy of that photo on the whiteboard as soon as we get back to Galway.'

Tracy nodded while he shovelled bacon, cabbage, and potatoes into his mouth at a rate of knots. He was either a fast eater or he was anxious to get on the road.

'We need to talk to Horgan first.' The owner of the hotel came by and asked if they were enjoying their meal. Tracy nodded enthusiastically while Fiona told her in Gaelic that it reminded her of her mother's bacon and cabbage. It was a remark that was taken as a high compliment. Fiona's phone rang and she took the call.

'Sligo,' she mouthed to Tracy as she pushed her half-finished plate aside. She listened without speaking, then terminated the call. 'They've an address for Canavan and a phone number. They've been ringing the number but there's no answer. Not surprising since his mother will have told him that we're going to be looking for him.'

'No point in going to Sligo then.'

The investigation had built up considerable momentum. From virtually nowhere they had a prime suspect. It was important to keep that momentum up. And that meant getting to interview Canavan. She phoned Horgan and brought him up to date.

'Sounds like an arrest is imminent,' Horgan said.

'There's many a slip twixt cup and lip.'

'I think the mother burning his clothes is indicative.'

'I think so too. But with no forensic evidence, we're probably going to be depending on someone breaking and confessing. You haven't met Mrs Canavan but she didn't look like the kind that breaks easily.'

'What do you have in mind?'

'We could drive up to Sligo and try to see Canavan but I have a feeling he's been forewarned and he might be difficult to find. We could ask our colleagues to find him for us. If we go to that trouble, we'll have to pick him up and ferry him back to Mill Street. The only evidence we have is the foetus. If we can link Canavan to Sarah as the father of her child, we'll have him. If we get him back to Mill Street, we can swab and interview him. I don't want to lose the momentum we've built up.'

'You want me to ring the chief super in Sligo?'

'The thought crossed my mind. It might save Tracy and me a drive and a possible fruitless search.'

'Let me see what I can do. The chief super is talking about having a press conference. He thinks that an appeal by Mrs Joyce might induce someone to come forward.'

'It might also induce the public to think that we're not up to the job. Let's follow the Canavan lead and see where it goes. If that turns out to be a dead end, we can always consider the chief super's suggestion.'

'I'll make the point to him. But we need to show him that we're progressing.'

'We are.'

'I'll take your word for it.'

The line went dead. Fiona terminated the call and put the phone on the table.

Tracy dropped his knife and fork onto his empty plate. 'We're not going to Sligo.' There was a hint of disappointment in his voice.

'We're not going to Sligo now, but I think we'll be taking a trip soon. My guess is that Canavan is shitting a brick. He's hunkering down somewhere with one of his mates or a girlfriend while the rhythm of his heart returns to normal and he considers how he can get himself out of the shit. The local uniforms know the area. We'll leave it to them to pick him up.' Fiona had been thinking about Sarah's missing clothes and the burned clothing at the Canavan house. 'Let me have another look at the photos.'

Tracy took out his phone, brought up the photos, and handed the phone to Fiona

Fiona zoomed in on each of the photos. Mrs Canavan had been thorough. The clothes had been reduced to a mass of charred remains. Individual items couldn't be identified. The Nike trainers were severely burned but recognisable. They could well have been female. Whether it was Sarah's clothing would remain a mystery. She passed the phone back. 'I want those photos printed and blown up when we get back to Mill Street.' Fiona walked to the bar and paid the lunch bill.

Tracy joined her at the exit. 'Where to?'

'Galway.'

FIONA HAD MOVED ON MENTALLY. There was no way to maintain the momentum of the investigation until Sligo called back with news that Canavan had been picked up. She thought of what they could usefully do around Glenmore and drew a blank. Problem number two, Tim, was occupying her brain. 'There's nothing more for us here. Let's get back to Galway but we'll take the scenic route.'

They drove slowly through the village of Glenmore in order to give the inhabitants the message that they were there for the duration of the investigation. Beyond the village, Fiona averted her eyes from the house where she knew her mother was sitting in the living room watching television. She and her mother hadn't spoken in sixteen years. They had parted in Dublin after the birth of her son and his adoption. Her mother was happy that the scandal could be buried and didn't understand that she was grieving for her lost child. That last misreading of each other was the root cause of the schism. There had been several attempts at reconciliation mostly mediated by Father Flanagan but harsh words only led to more entrenched positions. She closed her eyes and wished that they had been more understanding of each other.

The scenic route took them from Glenmore to Screebe where they turned right and headed for Costello. The road ran through one of the most sparsely populated areas of Connemara. There were precious few houses and nothing that could be called a village. Both sides of the road had narrow lanes that led, at first sight, into a void of scrub bogs.

Fiona watched the landscape go by. She wondered how many times she had travelled this road. During the past year, she'd had multiple opportunities to visit the scenes of her youth but she had clung to Galway city like a comfort blanket. Connemara and Glenmore were her past and she wanted to escape from it. But life had pushed her in the opposite direction. First her promotion to detective sergeant and her consequent posting to Galway. Secondly, meeting Ashling and the exposure to events from her past that she had tried to bury. And now the Sarah Joyce murder in the very village she'd sworn never to return to. And Tim. His arrival had been the last straw. The past was catching up with her at a pace that she found uncomfortable. Fiona was thankful that her new partner wasn't a chatterbox. They generally drove in silence. Their relationship was new and would undoubtedly develop but for the moment Tracy seemed, like her, to be happy to keep it on a superficial level. They were busy learning 'facts' about each other. They hadn't yet started to wonder what made the other one tick. Maybe they would go there. She envied the cops shows where the partners knew what each other were thinking. That was a load of tosh. What woman will admit that she knows what her husband of forty years is thinking? We are all a mystery to each other. Only people in Ashling's profession had the arrogance to claim that they know what is going on in their clients' minds. The human being is the most devious animal. All the thoughts running through her head had their origins in the return of her son. She had no idea what he wanted from her. Their lives had coalesced for a short period and then had deviated widely. Could they ever be mother and son? Did she want to be a mother to a son who was already an adult? Was she ready to have the life she was building with Ashling disrupted more than it was at present? Ashling was right. She would have to discover Tim's agenda. But that would only happen when he agreed to tell her. At that point, they could decide what the future held for them both.

At Costello, they passed Costello Lodge, the house to which J Bruce Ismay, chairman of the White Star Line, retired after the debacle of the *Titanic*. Just before the next crossroads, Fiona told Tracy to turn right in the direction of Rossaveel. Beyond the port, they took a small road that ran along the seaside of a small peninsula. At the end of the road was a stout round tower built to protect Britain's westerly colony from French invaders. She told him to stop fifty metres before the tower.

'What are we doing?' Tracy asked.

Fiona was already out of the car and had only half heard

Tracy's question so she decided to ignore it. She went to a dilapidated wooden gate, heaved it open, and entered a field that was more rocks and stones than grass and earth. Around the field, generations of the same family had spent years digging and removing rocks that had been deposited by the retreating ice. However, the field in which she stood was untouched. It would never bear a crop and never be grazed by a beast. It was to all intents and purposes useless.

Tracy looked out to sea. 'Nice view.'

The Atlantic was slate grey under the heavy clouds.

'My grandfather left me three things in his will,' Fiona said. 'A rundown cottage outside Barna, a Vincent Black Shadow motorcycle, and this field.'

Tracy looked around. 'It's not exactly the Garden of Eden. Although I suppose there are patches of earth between the rocks.'

'I don't think he left it to me because it was valuable. I don't think anyone would buy it.'

'He wasn't doing you a favour then.'

'He had his reasons. He brought me here just before I left to go to Dublin. He told me he was leaving it to me and that I should hold on to it.' She turned and walked back to the gate. She looked at her phone. Nothing from Sligo. 'Let's head back to Galway.'

# CHAPTER THIRTY-EIGHT

Fiona had delayed their arrival in Galway to coincide with quitting time. She knew that Horgan would be anxious to leave and, in any case, they had nothing new to report. She'd texted Ashling and arranged a drink in Taaffes before heading home. It had been a productive day and she was tired but enthused. She looked at the clock when she entered the squad room: eight minutes to five. The timing had been perfect. She had no idea why she had made the diversion to Rossaveel. She hadn't thought about that piece of land in donkey's years. She should probably sell it but her grandfather had made her promise that she would never do so. She loved the cottage and the Black Shadow and would never think of parting with either but the promise only pertained to the field. As she anticipated, Horgan strode into the squad room shortly after they arrived.

'Anything new?' he asked.

She shook her head. 'We're waiting on Sligo.'

'Did he do it?'

'I don't know but he's a good candidate.'

'I've had a call from the Phoenix Park. The commissioner

wants to be kept up to date on the inquiry. I told them we were making good progress. The chief super will brief the press tomorrow morning. The tone will be upbeat and my neck will be on the line.'

'You didn't lie.'

'Good.' Horgan had one foot out the door. 'Have a good evening.'

'Same to you, boss,' Fiona and Tracy intoned together.

Fiona turned to Tracy. 'Get the whiteboard up to date. Print the photo of Canavan from the phone and stick it under Sarah's photo. You can write prime suspect beside it.'

'What about getting on to the drugs boys,' Tracy said. 'Maybe they know who the dealer in the local area is. It might be a clincher if it turned out to be Canavan.'

'It's worth following up. I wouldn't hold out much hope but give them a bell.' Fiona looked at her desk. In her absence, Horgan had deposited a stack of files in her in-tray. They'd just have to wait. 'What time did you arrange to meet Emma?'

'How did you know that she agreed to go out with me?'

'I don't know. Maybe it was that silly smile on your face when you came back to the car. I'd watch out there if I were you. You've managed to escape so far but I get the impression that Emma might be a keeper so be prepared.'

'I'll get the whiteboard up to date but I'm out of here at six.'

'Don't put in for overtime. It's looked on as a lack of commitment. And it's also a waste of time since they don't have any funding, so you won't be paid anyway.' Fiona sat at her desk. Ashling replied that she would be in a meeting until six. Fiona needed a quiet place in order to discuss the Tim situation. She could try to clear a few files or she could get a head start on Ashling. She sifted through the files and her eyes lit on an advance copy of the post-mortem report. She opened it and saw that Kenny had added the photos to the report.

They didn't make a pretty sight. Sarah Joyce was a young woman with a long life before her. Somebody had taken that life. She examined the section on the stomach contents. Sarah had drunk alcohol within two hours of her death. The alcohol was vodka but the report was light on the quantity. She'd eaten a meal that had consisted of a meat sandwich and some tomatoes. Fiona castigated herself for not asking for a tox screen. Maybe Sarah had some drugs running around her system. It wasn't too late. She wrote a note on the cover of the file. The lab would be closed at five but she would contact them first thing in the morning. She closed the file and left it in the centre of her desk. It was five thirty and there was still time to get a drink before Ashling arrived. She wasn't usually a procrastinator but she found herself thinking of ways that she could postpone a confrontation with Tim. Maybe he wouldn't be at the cottage when they got home. If they stayed for a few extra drinks in Taaffes, he might have passed them on the road on his way into Galway. She rooted around in the other files looking for something that might pique her interest and banish the thought of sitting in a pub cradling a pint. Nothing. Administrative crap. She signed her name on the cover of the files and tossed them into the out-tray. The large hand on the wall clock was moving in slow motion. She looked at the whiteboard and saw that Tracy was almost finished. She stood and joined him in front of the board. 'It seems too easy,' she said almost to herself. 'What was the motive?'

'He didn't want to become a father.'

'If that was a valid motive for murder, this country would be overflowing with murdered girls. He could be like thousands of other *would-be fathers* who simply walk away. He had no obligation to her.'

'Maybe they had an argument.'

'Look at him. He's a strapping twenty-year-old footballer. The post-mortem report is on my desk. Sarah was strangled from behind with a ligature. If there had been an argument, they would most likely have been facing each other and his first reaction would have been to hit her or grab her by the throat with his bare hands. So, why did he pick up something to use as a ligature and come from behind?'

'It was premeditated murder. He knew that she had to go.'

'But she didn't need to go. All he had to do was walk away and leave her to solve the problem on her own.'

'It's a small village.'

'With lots of secrets; one more wouldn't make any difference. Especially to a young man.'

Tracy looked up at the clock. 'It's almost six. I'm off home.'

'A shower, a shave, and a new set of clothes. Emma won't be able to resist.'

ASHLING WAS late and Fiona had a head-start whether she liked it or not. She'd found a quiet corner and kept a seat for Ashling. There was a group of guys at the bar and one had taken a fancy to her. If she had been like the women who rate themselves by the quality of the men they attract, she would have been pleased. He was fit and good-looking and a little younger than her. His stare was becoming more intense and she was glad when she saw Ashling coming through the front door. She made a point of hugging Ashling and kissing her on the lips. Her admirer didn't miss the message and turned his back on the two of them.

'What was that about?' Ashling sat and ordered an orange juice.

'Lots of eye contact from a guy at the bar. I often thought of having the word *lesbian* tattooed on my forehead.'

'Give the poor man a break. An attractive young woman sitting alone in a bar. He drew the obvious conclusion.'

'The meeting ran late?'

'Faculty meetings always run late. Academics are verbose as a rule. This after-work drink business is becoming a bit regular. I'm beginning to think that it's an avoidance mechanism.' Her orange juice arrived and she paid. 'Personally, I've had a rough day and what I'd really like would be to head home, shower, and change into something more comfortable and get started on a bottle of Chardonnay. Instead, I'm in a jam-packed pub bathed in the smell of sweat and testosterone. I don't suppose you had the time to organise your DNA test.'

Fiona concentrated on sipping her pint.

'I didn't think so. He's not going away and we're not going to find out what he has in mind until his parentage is established. Since you keep insisting that his father is dead, that means you.'

'I know I'm dodging the issue. I'm thinking of forgetting about the DNA test and agreeing that I'm his mother.'

'Are you ready for what that means?'

'As in?'

'It's not like admitting that you've pilfered the petty cash and you'll replace the fifty quid you took. You'll have a son, with all that implies. Your life will never be the same again. There will always be someone out there that you'll be thinking about and wondering what's happening to him. There's more to being a mother than dropping the word into polite conversation like you just did. There will be consequences.'

Fiona drained her glass and ordered another. 'You don't pull your punches.'

'I just want you to be prepared. Once you openly admit you're his mother, the genie will be out of the bottle and it won't be going back.'

'Any news from your computer guys?'

'It may come as a surprise, Fiona, but other people do have a life. He'll be back when he's back. I can't get him to put a priority on our research because you're in a hurry.'

'You're giving me a little too much of a reality check. If I was dealing with a break-in on Shop Street, I'd take it on the chin. But a murder investigation tends to not leave too much in the emotional tank.'

'I don't arrange the sequence of events to fit your work schedule. Life does that.' Ashling finished her juice. 'Skull that pint and let's get out of here. I need to get started on that bottle of Chardonnay.'

## CHAPTER THIRTY-NINE

Fiona tried not to show her disappointment when she and Ashling entered the cottage and she saw Tim sitting on the couch reading a book.

Ashling tossed her messenger bag on a chair. 'I need a shower and a change of clothes.'

Fiona found herself alone in the room with Tim. 'How did you spend the day?'

Tim marked his page and put down the book. 'I walked into Barna and had lunch. Then I went down to the end of the pier and read. The weather was great.'

'Aren't you bored?'

'Not really, it's all new to me.'

'Any news from your adoptive parents?'

'Are you joking? I thought I told you. They're on a three-month world cruise. I'm probably the last thing that they're thinking about.'

'Did they not offer you the chance to join them?'

Tim laughed. 'You've got to be kidding. You think I'd spend three months in the company of geriatrics. Cruises are for old people. If I'd agreed, it would be the worst forty thousand dollars they'd ever spent.'

'When did they leave?'

'Two weeks ago. I'd already decided to come over here and look you up. It was the perfect way to spend the gap between college and university. I'm not just an Irish-American, I'm a hundred per cent Irish so I should visit the old sod.'

'It's still your plan to go back to university?'

'That's the plan, but things could change. Did you take the DNA test?'

'I'm in the middle of a murder investigation. During the day, I hardly have time to go to the loo. I'll arrange it as soon as there's a lull in the activity.'

Tim looked disappointed. 'I'd sure like to get things cleared up as soon as possible but I've watched crime shows on TV. I know the first forty-eight hours are important in any murder investigation.'

'We're way beyond forty-eight hours. But we've got a lead and we're running with it.'

'Tell me about your case.'

She told him how the Sarah Joyce missing persons case had morphed into a murder investigation and a difficult one at that.

'You like your job. I can tell by the way you talk about it.'

'It's what I do.'

'I think it's more than that. You care about what you do.'

Fiona let out a sigh of relief as Ashling returned to the room dressed in tee shirt and harem pants.

'That feels so good. Drinks?' Ashling made for the kitchen without waiting for a reply.

Fiona and Tim looked at each other and laughed. She thought that maybe being his mother mightn't be such a bad thing after all.

Ashling returned with two glasses and an open bottle of white wine. 'Steak and salad for dinner. Tim, there's a barbeque out back and a bag of charcoal. Do the man thing and get it lit. Fiona and I will enjoy a sundowner in your absence.'

Tim saluted and headed for the rear garden.

'You guys getting on?' Ashling asked.

'His adoptive parents are on a world cruise. They left just before he arrived here.'

Ashling handed over a glass of wine. 'And?'

'It's a coincidence. They're away on a ship somewhere and I bet they can't be contacted. I thought that you were playing psychologist and that your research into Tim's background was just you disappearing down the rabbit hole. But I don't like coincidences and particularly when they close an avenue of inquiry.'

Ashling clinked glasses with Fiona. 'What do you intend to do?'

'Take this shit a whole lot more seriously.'

# CHAPTER FORTY

Fiona smiled as she listened to Tracy humming happily as he steered their car around the final roundabout outside Galway onto the N17 in the direction of Sligo. He was getting his wish to travel through Yeats Country but she didn't think that was the only reason for his lightness of spirit.

The phone call from Sligo station had come just as she was preparing for bed. Michael Canavan had been picked up and was currently in their care. It would be up to Galway to transfer him as soon as possible. He had been arrested and cautioned and would be kept in a cell overnight. Fiona thought about calling Tracy and heading to Sligo immediately but she had been drinking and she guessed that Tracy might be in the same situation. So, it would have to be first thing in the morning. Before hitting the road, she had phoned the lab about a tox screen on Sarah.

'You're happy this morning,' Fiona said. 'The date was obviously successful.'

'Need to know.'

'Emma's a nice girl. I hope the two of you are going to be happy.'

'For God's sake, it was only a first date. I wouldn't pencil in a wedding day in your calendar yet.'

'Young man like you at the start of a glittering career in the Garda Síochána should be thinking of a wife and family.'

'Have you ever looked at the statistics about the effect of police work on family life?'

While working in Dublin, Fiona had had two of her long-term relationships go down the drain. She was one of those statistics. Ashling was more understanding of Fiona's job description but there was ample proof that the demands of the job-imposed stresses on personal relationships. 'What's the next step?'

'We're having dinner at the weekend and the subject is now closed. Why the change of plan with Canavan? I thought we'd drag him back to Gal;way.'

'In chains no doubt, I didn't see why we have to ferry him back to Galway.' She removed a packet from her bag. 'I picked this up at the lab this morning. We can interview him in Sligo and take his DNA. If he proves to be the father, we'll have him brought to Mill Street.'

'It's a suck it and see situation.'

Fiona turned and looked at him. 'I'm glad Emma is on the scene because you've definitely been watching too much TV.'

'I thought I said the subject of Emma was closed.'

'Did she mention anything interesting about Sarah?'

'It was a date, not a police interview. The murder has caused a bit of an upset at the school. The pupils and teachers can't get their heads around it. They've been in contact with the Department of Education about getting the children coun-selling. Emma thinks that some of the teachers would benefit from counselling as well.'

Fiona remembered the group of teachers outside the school. Some of them looked haggard. 'No insights as to who might be involved?'

'It's her first job and she's only been there a wet week. She tries to get out of Glenmore as much as she can. Apparently, the nightlife is rather limited: Tigh Jimmy or nothing.'

'See what you can get from her next time.'

'No.' Tracy turned on the car radio and found a music station.

TRACY HAD no difficulty in locating the Sligo Garda station in an open area of Pearse Street close to the centre of town. The building, with a large blue GARDA sign at the front, was a dated, grey, stone-faced, three-storey building with an extension at the rear.

They parked the car fifty metres down the road and walked back to the building.

The entrance hallway was small with a bank teller-like glass panel separating the rear of the station from the public. As soon as they entered, a young policeman came forward to the reception. Fiona and Tracy showed their warrant cards and the officer pressed a buzzer which opened a door and they entered the rear of the station.

'Inspector O'Brien is expecting you.' He waved his right hand in a circular motion. 'His office is around to the right.'

Fiona and Tracy followed the direction indicated and attached to the door of the first office was a small black plastic rectangle with the name Inspector James O'Brien inscribed on it. Tracy did the honours and knocked on the door.

'Come in.' O'Brien looked up from a file he was reading.

'Detective Sergeant Madden and Detective Garda Tracy from Galway,' Fiona said. 'Good morning, sir.'

'Good morning.' O'Brien was a large man with a bull neck that required the top two buttons of his light blue shirt to be open. He had a head of grey hair and wore reading spectacles that he removed as soon as Madden and Tracy entered. Fiona guessed he was somewhere in his fifties. He smiled showing two rows of tobacco-stained teeth. 'The famous Detective

Sergeant Madden. We've all seen the video. It was just like old times.' He stood and extended his hand.

Fiona gave him her fake smile and took his hand. 'Molloy put two male officers in hospital the last time he was arrested. Neither my partner nor I were going to hospital.'

'You did what you had to do. I might have done the same in your place.' O'Brien flopped back into his seat and it creaked loudly in complaint. 'What's the story with the young man in the cells?'

Fiona gave him the outline of the Sarah Joyce investigation. So far, he's our prime suspect.'

'We only have one interview room,' O'Brien said. 'We picked him up in one of his friend's apartments. They'd been drinking and he made a bit of a fuss. We held him on a drunk and disorderly charge but it won't stick and we'll have to let him go when you're finished with him. I'll have him brought up.' He picked up his phone and made the arrangements. 'We don't have a cafeteria but I can offer you a cup of tea.'

'Thanks,' Fiona said. 'We'll pass, I'd like to get on with the interview.'

'You're the boss,' O'Brien said. 'The interview room is at the end of the corridor. I had the recording equipment set up.'

'We'll be as quick as we can and we'll be out of your hair. And thanks for the cooperation.'

'You'd do the same for us.'

Fiona nodded to Tracy. They left the room and made their way to the end of the corridor where an officer was opening a door and pushing a young man inside.

Tracy caught the door before it closed. He looked at the uniform. 'It's okay. We've got this.'

'I'll be outside,' the uniform said and left the room.

The interview room architect had been at work in Sligo. The room contained a wooden table and four wooden chairs. The only upside was the window set into the outside wall which flooded the room with natural light.

Michael Canavan was standing in the middle of the room, immediately recognisable from the photo they'd seen, dark curly hair, blue eyes, regular features, full lips. He was a couple of inches over six feet, broad-shouldered and narrow-hipped. Fiona decided that Canavan took his sport seriously.

'Let's sit down,' Fiona said. She and Tracy sat on one side of the table.

Tracy laid the small folder that constituted the Murder Book on the table.

Canavan sat facing them.

'I'm Detective Sergeant Madden and my colleague is Detective Garda Tracy. We're from CID in Galway. I think you already know why we're here.'

'No, I don't.' Canavan tried a surprised look.

'What are you studying?'

'I'm doing a higher certificate in building construction.'

'There'll be a good job at the end of that.'

'The police picked me up last night and said I was drunk and disorderly. What's that got to do with Galway?'

'Our colleagues tried to contact you yesterday but you weren't answering your phone.'

'My battery was flat.'

'What do you bet that if we examined your mobile phone, we'd find a call from your mother yesterday morning? I'll bet you that your battery went dead immediately after that phone call.'

Canavan's shoulders slumped and he cast his eyes down. 'Okay, my mother told me that you were looking for me. But I've done nothing wrong.'

'That may well be.' Fiona took a photo of the body encased in a mass of black plastic on the beach and put it in front of Canavan. 'Three days ago, the body of Sarah Joyce washed up on Caladh Mweenish. Sarah was strangled and her body dumped at sea like a piece of trash. If it hadn't been for the storm, we might never have found her. I'm the senior investigating officer looking into her death.'

Canavan had taken one glance at the photo and then looked away. 'What's this got to do with me?

'You knew Sarah, didn't you?' Fiona said.

'To see.'

'Nothing more than that? We have information from one of her friends that Sarah fancied you.'

'That was her problem. I never came on to her. She's four years younger than me.'

'Four years isn't so much. She was a good-looking girl. She showed that she was interested in you. Why wouldn't you respond to that?'

'I go out with girls my own age here at college.'

'You never even fancied a one-night stand?'

'No.'

'But you did supply alcohol to the younger kids for their beach parties?'

'Everybody does. They can't buy it in the shops and it's traditional for the older kids to buy it for them. It happened when I was their age.'

'But you supplied it to Sarah and she passed it on to the other kids.'

'I also bought cider for other kids.'

'No scruples about leading children into alcohol then,' Tracy said.

'Come on, you've never been to a cider party when you were fifteen? There was no harm in it.'

'You supplied alcohol specifically to Sarah. Did you ever supply anything else?'

'Where are you going with this? I think I need to speak to a solicitor.'

'If you wish,' Fiona said. 'Detective Garda Tracy and I are prepared to take you back to Galway with us for further interview. You can walk out of here today if you cooperate fully with us or we can take this whole circus to Mill Street. If you have nothing to hide, there's no problem in talking to us. On the other hand...'

'Okay, ask your questions.'

'Did you ever supply Sarah Joyce with anything other than alcohol?'

'No, I didn't.'

'Did Sarah confide in you that she was pregnant?'

She could see the shock on his face.

'No.'

'Was the baby yours?'

'I told you I never had sex with Sarah. I had no idea that she was pregnant.'

'Three months,' Tracy rummaged about in the file. 'There's a photo of the foetus here somewhere.'

Canavan closed his eyes. 'I don't want to see it.'

'Is there anything you'd like to tell us, Michael?' Fiona asked.

'I don't know anything about what happened and I had nothing to do with her pregnancy.'

'When we were at your mother's yesterday, she was burning some clothes and what looked like a fairly new pair of trainers. Do you know why she was doing that?'

'No, did you ask her?'

'Yes, but the answer she gave us wasn't very satisfactory. We get nervous when someone burns what might be considered evidence in a murder case.'

Fiona took out the plastic envelope. 'I have a DNA test here and I'd like to take a swab if you're agreeable.'

'Don't you have to have a warrant or something like that?'

'We can take you to Mill Street and arrest you for the murder of Sarah. Then we can take your fingerprints and DNA. Your fingerprints and DNA will stay in the system. If you give us a swab today and you have no connection to

Sarah's murder, your sample will be destroyed. The choice is yours.'

'Go ahead.'

Fiona tore open the bag, removed the glass container and the swab, and handed it to Tracy who asked Canavan to open his mouth. When the process was completed, Tracy had Canavan initial the label on the glass vial.

'Okay, Michael, we're finished for the moment. I'd like you to think about where you were about five or six days ago and who might be able to verify your movements. Also, please don't leave the west of Ireland and make sure to have the battery of your mobile phone charged. Off home with you now.'

'They took my phone and what I had in my pockets when they arrested me.'

'The duty sergeant will return them to you.'

Canavan stood. 'What about the drunk and disorderly change?'

'It'll disappear.'

'Don't forget, Michael, we may need to speak with you again.'

Tracy opened the door and let Canavan out. The uniform was waiting and led Canavan away in the direction of the reception.

Fiona stowed the DNA sample in a pocket of her bag.

'What do you think?' Tracy asked.

'I don't know. He was prepped by his mother. The version we got of his relationship with Sarah was the narrative they put together and they want us to swallow. We're going to have to take a closer look at the Canavan family. I'm sure that Sarah was murdered by someone local.'

'You don't look happy.'

'I'm not. I'd pencilled in Mikey as the potential father of Sarah's baby. I thought that there would be more resistance to giving the swab. But he appeared quite happy to have his DNA compared with that of the child's.'

'Maybe he's not up on his biology. He might not believe that we can extract the embryo's DNA to the extent that the father can be identified.'

'Could be, but it's a situation that doesn't gel with our overall hypothesis. And that bothers me. This investigation has a full house of everything that pisses me off. There's no crime scene, no forensics, no witnesses to the crime, I don't suppose that there's a single CCTV camera in Glenmore, and now it looks like our prime suspect may not be in the frame after all. Maybe I should have kept my big mouth shut with Horgan. The commissioner is about to make an ass of himself with the press and guess who'll be blamed for that. I had visions of Mikey breaking down in tears when confronted with the blue bloated body of the mother of his child. I don't think that either Mrs Canavan or Mikey are going to break easily.'

'But you're sure that they're involved?'

'I was when I heard that the mother was burning perfectly serviceable clothes.'

'But you're not so sure now.'

Fiona walked to the door. 'Let's say goodbye to the boss man. We can grab a cup of coffee before we head back to Galway. I want to get this sample to the lab. Matching Mikey to the embryo is the only thing that'll save my bacon.'

## CHAPTER FORTY-ONE

Ashling finished her lecture at ten o'clock and made a beeline for the cafeteria. She'd hung on in bed until the last possible moment after Fiona had left the cottage at the crack of dawn. It meant that she didn't have time to both shower and have breakfast. She decided to shower. By the time she reached the cafeteria, she was ravenous. She selected a breakfast roll which consisted of a fried egg, streaky bacon, a pork sausage, and a piece of black pudding somehow crammed into a six-inch buttered bread roll. She was seated alone at a table when Sok entered and walked to the counter. She waved and motioned him to her table.

'Morning, Mak.' Ashling brushed breadcrumbs from the corner of her mouth.

Sok put a tray containing a Danish pastry and a cup of coffee on the table and sat. He looked at the remnants of the breakfast roll on Ashling's plate. 'How can you eat something like that? It's an invitation to a heart attack.'

'I could say the same about some of the dishes that were put in front of me in Cambodia. Any progress on researching Tim Daly?'

'That's what I like about the Irish, you get straight to the point.'

'Most people say the opposite. We like to waffle.'

'The provision of his date of birth was helpful.' Sok dumped two sachets of sugar into his coffee. 'Like you, I struck out in terms of social media. There's no footprint on Facebook, Twitter or Instagram. A Google search turned up several hundred Tim Dalys, but none with the same birthdate as your man. The conclusion I drew is that Tim wants to live under the radar and that he is computer savvy. I had a misspent youth as a hacker but I learned that it was better to stay on the right side of the law. There are places that are safe to hack into computer systems and others that I wouldn't go near with a bargepole. Every US government site fell into the latter group. The Americans have a nasty habit of extraditing the miscreants and slapping a heavy jail sentence on them. My guess is that while Tim Daly might be his real name, he's been operating under another name for some time. We call it a ghost in the computer game. You'll need to find that name or names. Saying that, this is a guess because I have no idea what you're dealing with.'

Ashling realised that she hadn't touched her sandwich or coffee since Sok had started speaking. What the hell were they dealing with? There was a man in their cottage about whom they knew absolutely nothing. Was he really Fiona's son? She had confirmed that he was the image of the man that had raped her, but was that enough? Why would a young man use a different name to hide his identity? She tried to remember whether there was any mention of the adoptive parents on the documents he'd shown them. She didn't think so. They had been more than a little naïve. She could understand herself but Fiona was an experienced law officer.

'I'm sorry,' Sok said. 'I feel I've let you down on this one.'

'On the contrary, Mak, you've opened my eyes.' She needed to get into that messenger bag that Tim guarded so jealously. Too many things about Tim didn't gel, but she would have a great deal of egg on her face if she confronted him and there was a reasonable answer for all the questions she had developed. She needed information but how was she going to get it? She pushed the coffee away. Half the breakfast roll was still on her plate but it had congealed and she was no longer hungry. She stood up. 'Thanks, I've got to get back to the office.'

Sok bit into his Danish. 'Get me another name and I might be able to do something. I hate coming up empty.'

'Thanks, you're an angel.'

Back in her office, Ashling found there was a slight tremor in her hand as she wrote what she knew about Tim in her notebook. She would have to discuss Mak's findings with Fiona. She took out her schedule. She had a tutorial at three o'clock. She could go back to the cottage for lunch. If Tim were out, she might get a chance to look in his bag.

# CHAPTER FORTY-TWO

Ashling contemplated calling Fiona and discussing her plan. But she was afraid that she would be talked out of it. She pulled up before the cottage and looked around before leaving the car and inserting the key in the door. There was no sign of Tim outside. It was the kind of fine day that invited people to take a walk. She pushed the door in making the maximum amount of noise. If Tim was in the cottage, she wanted to know. She stood in the living room before going into the kitchen and putting on the kettle to make a cup of tea. There was still no sign of Tim but the door to his room was closed. Here goes, she said to herself as she approached the door. She knocked but there was no reply. 'Tim,' she called. 'Any interest in a cup of tea.' Silence. She opened the door and peered inside. There was no sign of Tim but the kitbag was hanging over the back of a chair beside his bed. It was now or never. She went in and made straight for the backpack. The straps were already undone and she opened the bag and looked inside. The first thing she saw was the file of papers that she and Fiona had examined. There was a second file in a buff-coloured cover. She picked it out and started to examine the contents. There were bank statements in the name of Tim

Daly as well as Internal Revenue Service annual tax returns. It appeared that Tim had something approaching nineteen thousand dollars in his account. She put the second file aside and delved deeper into the bag. She came up with two US passports. She opened the first and saw that it was in the name of Timothy Eugene Daly. So far everything was kosher. She opened the second passport. The picture was Tim's but the name on the passport was Michael Patrick Power. She put the passports back in the bag and hung it back on the chair. Her heart was pounding like the engine of an express train. Tim could walk in on her at any moment. She thought she heard a noise outside and rushed from the room. The kettle was singing on the hob and she arrived in the kitchen just as the front door of the cottage opened and Tim walked in.

'Is that you, Tim,' Ashling called. 'You're just in time for a cup of tea.'

Tim walked into the kitchen. 'You don't usually come home in the middle of the morning.'

Ashling turned. 'That sounds like you're questioning me being here. For your information, I live here. Now do you want a cup of tea or not.'

Tim did a double-take. 'Sorry, it's just that I wasn't expecting to hear someone when I came in. Yeah, I'd love a cup of tea.'

Ashling put some teabags into the teapot. 'You could set the table.' She poured hot water into the pot. 'I left in such a hurry this morning that I forgot some books that I need for a tutorial this afternoon.'

Tim put two cups, milk, and sugar on the table.

'Dig out a few biscuits,' Ashling said. 'I missed breakfast.'

Tim emptied a sleeve of biscuits onto a plate. 'Have you been here long?'

'No, I just walked in. Why do you ask?'

'No reason, I went for a walk to the sea.'

Ashling's heartbeat was returning to normal. She was

beginning to get a read on Tim that she hadn't had before. The young man thought he could handle a professional psychologist. He'd have to get up earlier in the morning, as her mother used to say. 'You chose a fine day for it.' She sat down and poured two teas. 'Fiona left for Sligo at the crack of dawn and I stupidly had a lie in. Since then I've been running around like a blue-assed fly trying to catch up on my day. Aside from the trip to the sea, what have you been up to?'

'Nothing much.'

'You don't find it boring out here in the sticks?'

'Kinda. Did Fiona say anything about the DNA test?'

'She's up to her neck in the murder investigation. I'm sure she'll get around to it. Are you thinking about your college plans?' Ashling selected a biscuit, dunked it in her tea, and bit into it.

'Yeah, but I'd like to clear things up here before I head back to the States.'

'What's the hurry? You and Fiona have a lifetime ahead.'

'I need to know for sure. If Fiona is my mother, then she knows who my father is.'

'If he's dead, does it really matter.'

'Maybe he's not dead.'

Ashling stared into Tim's eyes and the stare was returned.

'What kind of books did you forget?' Tim asked.

Ashling stood up, left the kitchen, and returned with a book in her hand. She laid it on the table. It was entitled *Puzzling People: The Labyrinth of the Psychopath*. 'We're discussing psychopathy.'

'If you're dealing with psychopaths, you're in a dangerous business.'

'They're easy enough to identify.' Ashling could feel the skin on her face tighten. 'They're often narcissists with no empathy for anyone else.' She finished her tea.

'When I left, I closed the door of my room, it was open when I returned. Did you go into my room?'

'No, I knocked on your door when I came in to see if you wanted to join me for tea.'

Tim picked up the teacups, took them to the sink, and washed them. He turned around as Ashling stood up. 'It's part of your job to look into people's lives.'

'Not their lives, their minds.'

'But their minds dictate their lives.'

'To an extent.'

'Say someone doesn't like you looking into their mind.'

'They shouldn't present themselves as a client. Thanks for cleaning up. I need to get back to the university.' She started to move to the living room.

Tim nodded at the table. 'Don't forget your book, again.'

Ashling turned and picked the book up. 'It's an interesting book. You should read it sometime.'

'I might take you up on that.'

Ashling took in a deep breath of ozone-filled air when she left the cottage. Her heart had begun to race again. She let the breath out and inhaled, then opened the car door, sat in the driver's seat, and looked back at the cottage. She loved that little house and she loved her life there with Fiona. It was always so welcoming. For the first time, it looked forbidding. The curtain moved and she shivered. Tim's message was clear. Would she listen to it?

# CHAPTER FORTY-THREE

F iona and Tracy arrived back in Galway just before three o'clock. They grabbed a quick sandwich and coffee in the cafeteria before making their way to the squad room. The note on Fiona's computer keyboard was terse – *My office soonest.* It was unsigned but she recognised Horgan's scrawl. She tossed the plastic bag containing Canavan's swab to Tracy. 'I'm wanted. Get that to the lab and use that pretty face of yours to get a rush put on the DNA profile.'

Tracy caught the bag and smiled. 'It's a pity you're a lesbian, you've got good taste in men.'

Fiona was smiling as she left the office. The rapport with Tracy was coming along nicely.

Horgan's office was next door. Fiona didn't bother to knock and walked straight in.

'Holy God, Fiona, don't you ever bother to knock. I could have been doing something private.'

'That conjures up a mental picture I'd rather not have. What's the problem?'

'The problem as you put it is that I'm being squeezed like a lemon by the chief super and the commissioner's office. The head man went on the box at lunchtime and the local media are ramping up the interest in the Sarah Joyce case.'

'Quite right too.' Fiona sat in Horgan's visitor chair.

'Do you have anything new to report?'

Fiona knew that Horgan wanted to hear something positive. 'I think that young Canavan knows more than he was telling us. Tracy is getting the DNA swab to the lab and hopefully, we'll be able to put a rush on it. If Canavan shows as the father, we'll have him down here for a formal interview.'

'*If* Canavan shows as the father?' Horgan put an emphasis on the first word. 'I thought he was the only one in the frame.'

Fiona looked out the window, then turned to face Horgan.

He was leaning forward expectantly.

She was about to make him unhappy. 'He gave us the sample a little too willingly. He didn't know about the baby and he denied that he'd ever had sex with Sarah. I got the impression that he was happy to have his DNA taken because he knew he'd be cleared.'

Horgan put his head in his hands. 'An arrest is not as imminent as you led me to believe and I passed a positive message to the chief super and the commissioner's assistant. You've probably ruined my career.'

'Don't be overdramatic. You've only got a couple of years to go and you're going to hand me the shit end of the stick if things go pear-shaped. I'm the one going under the bus.'

'What about his mother burning the clothes?'

'I didn't say that Canavan is out of the frame. But I'm bothered by the ease of getting the swab.'

'Where do we go now?'

'We focus on the Canavans. They're involved somehow. Tracy struck gold when he found the burn barrel. That wasn't supposed to happen. This investigation has been about coincidences and both were in our favour. If there hadn't been a storm, the sea creatures would have had a feast and Sarah would have been a bag of bones within a few months. There was already a finger pointing at Mikey Canavan but not a shred of proof. Then his mother decided to burn some clothes the very day we went to interview her. Let's be honest, we'd be nowhere without the coincidences. Sarah Joyce would have been a missing person, end of story. It would have been the perfect murder.'

'There's no such thing as a perfect murder.'

'It would have been close: no body, no crime scene, no forensics, no witnesses. We would have been flailing around in the dark. Sarah Joyce would have been a cold case. Except for those coincidences.'

'You're sure about the Canavans?'

'They're involved. I feel it in my gut. We're going to shine a light into the Canavan family's life. The girls are out of it. It'll be the boys we'll have to investigate and the mother. Tracy is going to give the drugs lads a call and see if either Canavan is active.'

'What do I tell the chief super?'

'The investigation is progressing.'

Horgan massaged his forehead with his hand. 'Get out, Madden, just get out.'


Fiona returned to the squad room and saw that Tracy had been at work bringing the whiteboard up to date. The photos from the burn barrel and Sarah's autopsy had been added. Yesterday, the investigation had received a jolt of momentum. They were stalled but the case was building slowly. 'How long for the DNA profile?'

'Two days, our lab is still working on the embryo. That'll be available this evening.'

Fiona stared at the photos from the burn barrel. So far, the fates had been kind to her. Maybe it was time to push her luck. She'd been tempted to ask for a warrant to search the Canavan house but had thought it would prove fruitless. If there had been incriminating evidence there, it had been collected and burned. The remnants would be buried somewhere on the Canavan's land. Now, she had changed her mind. Mikey Canavan had been cocky and his mother scornful. Maybe a warrant would shake the tree a bit and they'd see what fell out. She picked up the phone and dialled Horgan's number.

# CHAPTER FORTY-FOUR

The evening drink in Taaffes was becoming a habit except this time it was Ashling who had insisted that they meet there after work.

Fiona arrived at five thirty and found Ashling already installed. 'I thought we decided we had to give this pub a break. I'm on the Black Shadow so it's non-alcoholic beer for me this evening.' Ashling wasn't smiling. 'What's the urgency?'

'Michael Patrick Power.'

'Who is he when he's at home?'

'I met with Professor Sok this morning and found that he'd also drawn a blank on finding Tim's footprint. That shook me. Mak has a reputation as a hacker. The rumour is that he's banned from the US for five years because he hacked a bank. If he couldn't find Tim's footprint, nobody could.'

'And?' Fiona didn't like the direction this was going in.

'I had some free time this morning so I thought I'd return unannounced to the cottage and look in the bag that Tim guards so carefully.'

'Tim wasn't home.'

Ashling nodded.

'You shouldn't have done that.'

'I know. I couldn't believe the way my heart was beating. I made straight for the bag. It contained the file of his research into you and at the bottom, there were two US passports. One in the name of Timothy Daly and the other Michael Patrick Power. They both looked genuine to me.'

'Did he find you rifling through his belongings?'

'No, I heard a noise outside and I got out of his room and into the kitchen. I'd already set the kettle going so I was making tea when he came in. But I left the door to his room ajar.'

'He knows you were in his room.'

'It's our damn house.'

'But he can't be sure you saw the second passport.'

'I don't think so.'

'You look shaken. What happened?'

'We had one of those conversations that was loaded with subtext. The upshot was that he threatened me indirectly and I accused him of being a psychopath.'

'Thank you, Ashling. It was already a stressful situation and you've probably managed to ratchet up the tension.'

'That's not all. I passed on the Power name to Mak. Maybe Michael Patrick Power has left a footprint.'

'I thought I was supposed to be the detective. You think Tim is a psychopath?'

'I spent the best part of the afternoon working on a profile. I tried to rewind the tape of our first meeting and plug in what we've learned up to now.'

'And what have you come up with?'

'Given the level of his research, I'd say that he has some abandonment issues. His single-minded pursuit of his biolog-ical mother displays a high level of need. He managed to find you and he's anxious to find his father. It all points to the fact that he blames you and his biological father for abandoning him. I looked up the research and in many cases of a person who feels abandoned, there are some PTSD issues. Also, there's a tendency to depression. None of this is good.'

A short time ago, Fiona had believed that the son she had given up had a better life than a sixteen-year-old rape victim could have given him. Now, she wasn't so sure. What the hell had she done? Life with her was not going to be easy, but if Ashling was right, the decision she'd been forced to accept might be a lot worse. 'But you might be wrong.'

'Of course, I might be wrong. I'm not infallible. But I'm just as likely to be right.'

'Then Tim is a psychopath.'

'Possibly. I know you don't want to hear this.'

'But that doesn't mean that he's dangerous.'

'Not all psychopaths are serial killers and not all serial killers are psychopaths. It appears that the highest number of psychopaths can be found among business leaders. But I don't think that Tim's agenda is benign.'

'So, he is dangerous?'

'I think we should start locking our bedroom door at night.'

Fiona finished her beer and left the money on the bar. She stood. 'I left the Shadow in Mill Street. I don't want to leave it there overnight. You go ahead and I'll follow.'

'I'll pull in after Barna village and we'll travel home together.'

'Don't be ridiculous.'

'I'd prefer to go home together. If that's alright with you.'

Fiona hugged her. This wasn't like Ashling. One of the attributes that had drawn Fiona to her was her strength. 'I'll look out for you. Drive carefully.'

Fiona left the bar and headed back to Mill Street station. A life that a few weeks ago appeared simple had suddenly become complex. She walked along the street replaying what Ashling had said. Her son had a bundle of mental issues that she and her mother were responsible for. He needed help and she was going to make sure that he got it. She was his mother even if she hadn't behaved like it. And that had to mean something, didn't it?

# CHAPTER FORTY-FIVE

Fiona arrived at the station an hour early. She'd needed to get out of the cottage. The tension between Ashling and Tim was so apparent that it could be cut with a knife. A neighbour had been out fishing and dropped off two fat pollock which Fiona had filleted and pan fried. Ashling had made a salad and they'd had the making of a pleasant meal except that it was eaten in silence. It was a situation that couldn't be allowed to continue. Both Ashling and Tim were looking to her for a solution. After dinner, she and Ashling had watched a rom-com on Netflix while Tim went for a walk. Although she didn't make a production of it, Ashling had locked the bedroom door before retiring. At the station, Fiona flopped into her chair and was grateful that she wouldn't have to think about the war at home for another ten hours. She desperately wanted to return their lives to their former status quo but she agreed with Ashling that Tim's arrival should have been anticipated. Nothing would ever be the same again. As soon as she had cleared the Sarah Joyce case, she'd face up to Tim and whatever he had in mind. She reckoned that she owed him something for abandoning him at birth. The trips to Glenmore and Sligo meant that administrative tasks were building up.

Tracy wouldn't arrive for another hour and she decided to attack the files in her in-tray. She was lost in notes from Dublin covering such exciting topics as budgets, overtime, training, and health insurance when she finally found a file that interested her; the chief super had signed her request for a search warrant for the Canavan house and the surrounding land. It would be presented to the local peace commissioner as soon as he opened for business.

Tracy entered carrying a cardboard tray with two coffee cups. He put one cup of coffee on the desk beside her. 'The early bird catches the worm.' He sat at his desk, opened the lid of his own coffee, and blew on the contents.

Fiona sipped the coffee and got a scalded tongue for her trouble. 'We're off to Glenmore.' She tossed the file containing the request for the search warrant to Tracy. 'We'll get Clifden to loan us a few uniforms to make it look more like a Garda operation than a personal vendetta by DS Madden.'

'I thought you said it'd be a waste of time.'

'It probably will be but it's what we do. The peace commissioner's office is open at nine. Haul your arse over there and get it signed, then we're on our way to Glenmore.'

Tracy looked at his coffee.

'Drink it on the way.'


It was fifteen minutes past eleven when Tracy rapped on the door of the Canavan house. The two detectives had been joined by two stout uniforms from the local flying squad. Fiona and Tracy would do the searching and the two uniforms would act as props.

'What do you want?' Mary Canavan struck an aggressive pose as she blocked the entrance to the house. The sneer on her face indicated her displeasure at seeing the group of police officers assembled on her doorstep.

Tracy waved the search warrant in the air. 'We have a

warrant to search this residence and any outlying buildings.'
He handed the paper to Canavan.

'What's up?' a male voice called from inside the house.

'It's the police. They want to search the house.'

'The hell they do!' Two men came from the rear of the
house. One was similar in age to the woman at the door and
the second was a younger version. The older man was blocky
with long black hair, a purple whiskey nose in the centre of a
ruddy face, and a black beard flecked with grey. The younger
man was in his late twenties or early thirties, handsome but
already running to fat. Both men strode forward towards the
door.

Fiona recognised the father. Con Canavan had a reputation as a belligerent alcoholic who had been arrested several
times for brewing the local illicit whiskey known as poitín.
Fiona didn't recognise the young man. On their previous visit
to the house, she'd seen him in the family photo and assumed
he was Mikey Canavan's older brother. He would have been
two or three classes below her in school eighteen years before
which meant that she would have taken little or no notice
of him.

The older Canavan pulled the paper from his wife's hand.
'This is fucking harassment.'

'It's okay, Dad.' The younger man held his father back.
'Remember we've nothing to hide.'

'What's your name?' Fiona asked.

'Thomas.'

'Well, Thomas, you keep your dad in check. He has a
reputation and I don't want to take anyone back to Mill Street
with me.'

'There's been nothing but trouble since this skinny bitch
came back,' Canavan senior said. 'We all know about you,
Madden. Everybody in this village and everybody in
Connemara knows about the chip you carry on your shoulder.'

Tracy pushed past the two men and glared at them as he

entered the house. 'Any more bad language or vocal abuse will be construed as impeding the police in the course of their duty and I'll ask the uniformed officers to remove you.'

Fiona asked one of the officers to search behind the house with an emphasis on the burn barrel. She was sure that he'd find nothing but you never knew.

Tracy had entered the house and was behind the three Canavans. 'You may leave the house or stay inside while we conduct the search. But you must remain seated so as not to impede the search and do not use your mobile phones.'

The Canavans joined Fiona on the doorstep.

'We'll be as quick as we can,' Fiona said. 'And we'll try to make as little mess as possible.' She entered the house and left them in the care of the second uniform.

The house had started life as a cottage much like Fiona's own but had been added to by two or three generations of Canavans with money from America. It was built on one level with a large extension at the rear and another at the side. Tracy and Fiona split up. Tracy took the kitchen, living room, and bathroom while Fiona concentrated on the bedrooms. She ignored the master bedroom that was occupied by the elders and started on what had been the children's bedrooms. The first room she entered was easily identified as the boys' room by the football posters that adorned the walls. There were two made-up single beds, a bedside locker set between them, and a small chest of drawers. This would be Mikey's room when he was at home and would be the focus of her search. She examined the beds first. The sheets smelled of fresh lavender which made her believe they had been recently laundered. She wondered whether this room had been Mikey and Sarah's love nest. She lifted her head from the bed and sniffed at the air: bleach. The room had been cleaned to within an inch of its life. Mary Canavan had been at work. Fiona wondered whether there was any point in asking forensics to look. She thought not. Sarah had been strangled. There would be no blood. The bleach would have eradicated every morsel of DNA. Sarah may have been in this room but there would be no evidence to confirm it. Mikey might be the father of her child but there was no proof that he had strangled her. She examined the contents of the bedside locker. There were football magazines and football medals but precious little else. The Canavan boys were turning out to be aesthetics, except for football. The chest of drawers contained the clothes Mikey left at home. One drawer contained underwear and socks, one had shirts and Ts, and the final drawer contained shorts and jeans. Everything was freshly laundered and folded neatly. She had expected as much. She moved on to what she assumed was the girls' room. There was no smell of bleach and the bed linen didn't smell of lavender. There was little or nothing in the chest of drawers, a few knickers and blouses that were years out of date. She was leaving the room when she bumped into Tracy.

'The bathroom looks like it's been gone over with something that smells like it removes skin,' he said. 'The kitchen is just what it says on the tin, same for the living room. The living room has the smell of wet dog in it.'

'The boys' room's been thoroughly cleaned as well. If Sarah had been bludgeoned, I bet they would have torched the house.'

'It's a bust.' There was disappointment in Tracy's voice.

'It's what we expected. We're not going to be handed anything on a plate by the Canavans. We're going to have to work for our grain on this one.'

'You're still sure that they're involved?'

'I always hated that programme, *Columbo*. He'd zero in on the culprit from the very start of the investigation and he was always right. I find myself in the same position. I know the Canavans are involved. I just can't prove it. But we'll get there.'

They walked back to the front of the house and exited.

'It's all yours,' Fiona said. The smug look on the faces of

the trio making their way into the house told her all she needed to know. They had won another round and they didn't care that she knew it. The old man turned as he entered the house and gave her the middle finger.

'You come back here again,' Thomas Canavan said, 'and we'll take a case against you for harassment.'

Fiona thanked the uniforms and sent them back to Clifden. It was another setback but not an unexpected one.

'Where to?' Tracy asked.

'Let's take a drive through the village. We need to show the locals that we're serious about bringing someone down for Sarah's murder. It's not going to be another of those village scandals that everyone whispers about behind cupped hands. Mikey knows Sarah and buys alcohol for the younger kids' cider parties. He swears that he's never had sex with her and gives his DNA willingly. He also refutes the idea that he would supply drugs. But his mother burns his, or possibly Sarah's, clothing and his room has been cleaned with bleach and his bedding is fresh.'

'Mrs Canavan could be a cleaning freak.'

'Maybe, but her focus was on Mikey's room and the bathroom.'

'But Mikey's no longer in the frame?'

'He is until the DNA results come in... and he provides us with an alibi for the approximate time of death.'

'You have a hard-on for Mikey.'

'I have a hard-on for the Canavans plural.'

Fiona would have loved to have a plan of action already worked out but she wasn't a planner. That didn't hinder her ability as a detective. Murder investigations were organic. New leads were constantly cropping up and evidence was out there to be found. All she needed to crack the case was to stumble over a piece of evidence that would point straight to Mikey Canavan.

It was possible to drive through the village of Glenmore in

five minutes and that's precisely how long it took their police car.

Fiona saw Father Flanagan's banger parked outside the church on the outskirts of the village. 'Stop and pull in behind that piece of shit.'

The church was set in a large open area off the main road. A winding path led to the entrance. To the side of the church there was a small bungalow which had housed several generations of priests. It was eighteen years since Fiona had put her foot beyond the church gate. She pushed the gate open and she and Tracy took the side path that led away from the church and towards the priest's house.

Tracy did the honours by knocking.

Father Flanagan opened the door himself. He saw Fiona on the doorstep and looked theatrically at the sky.

'I get it,' Fiona said. 'I was expecting a bolt of lightning myself.'

'I'm about to have a cup of tea, would you like to join me?'

Fiona recognised the declaration of a truce when she saw one. 'We'd be delighted. Detecting is thirsty work.'

Flanagan looked at Tracy. 'I suppose you're a good Catholic lad?'

'That I am.'

Flanagan led them into a comfortable living room. 'Take a seat. It's my housekeeper's day off. But don't worry I'm a dab hand at making tea and she left a lemon drizzle cake.'

Fiona and Tracy sat together on a couch. There was a copy of a police procedural on the coffee table.

'You guys friends now?' Tracy asked.

'Temporary truce, I think.'

Flanagan returned with a tray containing a teapot, three mugs, a jug of milk, a bowl of sugar, and a plate with three thick wedges of cake. 'I'll play mother.' He filled the cups, milk and sugared them to requirements, and passed them out. When he finished, he sat facing them. 'Sarah is coming home this afternoon. She'll be at the house at four and she'll be brought to the church at seven. The funeral is ten o'clock mass tomorrow. I suppose you'll be there.'

'We will.' Fiona selected a piece of cake and bit into it.

'You think that whoever murdered her will turn up?' Flanagan said.

'They do in the cop shows on television,' Tracy said.

'The good Father knows the murderer will turn up,' Fiona said.

'How so?' Flanagan said.

'Because you know who it is.'

The only sound in the room was that of Tracy masticating lemon drizzle cake.

'You know who the father of Sarah's child is,' Fiona said after a pause. 'She would have confessed.'

'And if she did, you know that I would never be able to tell. It's my absolute duty under the Seal of the Confessional not to disclose anything I learn from penitents during the Sacrament of Penance.'

'And you'd allow a murderer to go free.' Fiona finished her tea.

'I would never break a sacred vow.'

Fiona opened her bag, took out an autopsy picture of Sarah Joyce, and laid it on the coffee table beside the tray and facing Flanagan. 'The killing of a sixteen-year-old pregnant girl is an abomination and you would let the person that did this go free.'

'Whoever did this will never be free in their mind.'

'Is that the church's concept of justice? Mine is a little different. I want the bastard that did this to be hauled before the court, convicted, and put in jail for as long as possible.'

'That sounds like vengeance to me.'

Tracy's phone rang. He looked at the caller ID. 'I have to take this.' He stood and went out into the hall.

Flanagan lifted the teapot. 'A refill?'

'No thanks.'

Tracy returned and whispered in Fiona's ear.

'My colleague has just had a call from the lab. A tox screen shows that Sarah had taken ecstasy on the day she was killed.'

'God in Heaven.' Flanagan made the sign of the cross.

'You know about the cider parties on the beach,' Fiona said. 'Of course, you do. You know all the little secrets of the village. Do you know that Sarah has been pushing drugs on the younger children?'

'I knew that drugs were circulating but I didn't know that Sarah was the pusher.'

'The father of her child is the most likely source of the drugs. This person is infecting the children of this village with poison and you still refuse to name him.'

'If I did, I would no longer be a priest.'

Flanagan was a large man but as Fiona looked at him, he seemed diminished in size. She was sure it was a fantasy. People didn't shrink suddenly. She stood and Tracy followed.

Flanagan didn't rise.

'We'll see ourselves out,' Fiona said.

The two detectives went into the hall. 'Thanks for the tea and cake,' Fiona called over her shoulder. 'And keep up the good work.' The truce was over.

# CHAPTER FORTY-SIX

Fiona would not like to admit it but the investigation was losing momentum. They still had a prime suspect but if she was being honest with herself, she would discount Mikey Canavan on the grounds that he'd agreed to the DNA test too easily. Flanagan thought that he'd given nothing away, but Fiona was sure that the father of Sarah's child was a local. And he was possibly the supplier of the drugs that were being sold to the village's young people.

'Did you ever follow up that idea you had of contacting the drug squad?' Fiona said when they were back in the car.

'Yeah, I spoke to one of the undercover guys. They have a line on the locals involved in supplying in big towns like Tuam, Loughrea, Ballinasloe, and Clifden. But they can't concentrate on every small village in the west of Ireland. It's likely that whoever is supplying in Glenmore is buying in Clifden in small quantities and passing the drugs along. He's small-time but he could lead to someone further up the ladder.'

'That works both ways. If our friends in Galway have the name of someone in Clifden, he might be willing to say who from Glenmore is buying drugs.'

'We've no proof that the drugs in Glenmore are coming from Clifden.'

'It's a shot in the dark. But we're running out of leads.'

Tracy's phone beeped. He looked at the screen. 'Message from the Forensic Science Lab on the Dublin Road. They want a word but we have to go there.'

'Okay, back to Galway. But I want the name of a drug pusher in Clifden. We're back out here for the funeral tomorrow. We could hit Clifden afterwards.'

The Forensic Science Lab was located on the campus of the Galway Mayo Institute of Technology. Fiona and Tracy grabbed a quick lunch at a pub in Oughterard and arrived at the lab at half past three. They were requested to wait at the reception where they were picked up by one of the scientists.

'Dr Eva Van Espen.' A thirty-something blonde woman wearing a white coat held out her hand to Fiona. She had blue eyes, her hair was tied back and her face was attractive rather than good-looking.

'Detective Sergeant Fiona Madden and my colleague Detective Garda Sean Tracy.' Fiona took the outstretched hand,

Van Espen shook hands with Tracy.

'You're Dutch,' Fiona said.

'No, Irish, my parents are Belgian.' Her accent was pure Galway.

'Sorry,' Fiona said. 'In the past twenty years, we've become an ethnically diverse country. I should have known better considering that one of our premier actors is called Fassbender.'

Van Espen smiled. 'I'm looking at the DNA samples that you sent us. My lab is upstairs.' She led them along a corridor and up a set of stairs before arriving at a door with her name on a plaque at eye level. She opened the door with a key and stood back while they entered. 'Sorry for dragging you over here in person. I could have written a report I suppose but I felt it necessary to present the results in person in case you had questions. Please sit down.'

Fiona and Tracy sat before her desk on which there were two large computer monitors.

Van Espen took her seat and swivelled one of the monitors around to face the detectives. 'You sent us three samples for DNA analysis: a sample from the embryo, a sample from the mother, and a sample from the potential father. This is a comparison of the sample from the embryo and the mother.'

Fiona stared at the monitor. There was a document on the screen set out in columns. The first column had the title *Locus* and the second *Allele Sizes*. There were a series of what looked like codes in the first column and two columns of figures in the second column. A set of columns on the left had the heading *Embryo* and, on the right, the series was entitled, *Mother*. 'This is like looking into a bush. We're police officers and speaking for myself I was never much good at physics or maths. Can you give it to us in layman's terms?'

'Sorry,' Van Espen said. 'The whole field of DNA is complex but I'll try to be as clear as possible. The column on the left is the DNA profile of the embryo and that on the right is the mother. The profiles are not exactly the same. No DNA profile is exactly like another even for a mother and child. The numbers circled in red show the comparison between the profiles. You'll note that not all the numbers are circled. But the upshot of the analysis is that the possibility of maternity is ninety-nine point nine-nine per cent.' Van Espen hit some keys and the first sheet was replaced by a second. 'This is a comparison of the embryo's DNA with the third profile. I'm assuming this is the profile of the potential father. There are far fewer of the red circles which leads me to conclude that the third profile has a negligible possibility of paternity.'

'This isn't exactly news,' Fiona said.

'I would have expected a zero possibility,' Van Espen said. 'But there are some similarities.'

'What are you saying?'

'There is a relation between the embryo and the potential father but it is not that of father and child.'

'What could that relation be?' Fiona asked.

'I have no idea. All I can say is that the two have a familial relation. It could be distant I'm not sure.'

There was good news and bad news in one package for Fiona. The good news was that her guess about someone close to the Canavans being responsible was correct but given the fact that a lot of people in the same area were related to each other, the potential pool of suspects might have become larger. It was one step forward and two steps back.

Van Espen printed the two sheets and handed them to Fiona.

Fiona took the papers and extended her hand to Van Espen. 'Thank you, doctor.'

Van Espen shook. 'Eva please.'

'We may be back.'

'Get me a swab from the father.' Van Espen shook hands with Tracy.

'Back to the station?' Tracy said as they left the GMIT building.

Fiona looked at her watch. It was a quarter past four. Going back to the station now would inevitably mean running into Horgan. 'Let's have a cup of coffee and discuss the way forward.

'Horgan won't be happy.

'There isn't much we can do about that.'

# CHAPTER FORTY-SEVEN

Ashling was pacing up and down in her small office. She had plenty of work to do but found it impossible to sit quietly at her desk. She had sent five texts to Fiona in the past two hours and hadn't received an answer. The first fault lines were appearing in a relationship that she'd felt was just about perfect. They'd met soon after Fiona had returned to Galway. It wasn't one of those love-at-first-sight things and neither had been hit with a coup de foudre. They dated for a couple of months and both felt confident enough of the relationship for Ashling to move into the cottage which was in the middle of being renovated. Tim's arrival and his impact on both of their lives was beginning to take its toll. Like Fiona, she had been upset at the level of tension in the cottage since she had invaded Tim's space. Every time she thought about Tim, she felt a ball of anxiety in her stomach. The existence of the second passport in the name of Michael Patrick Power was just one more piece of what was turning out to be a complex puzzle. She spent part of the morning working on a psychological profile of Tim but she found herself confounded by the anomalies. He appeared to be a calm eighteen-year-old who had a valid reason for wanting to find his biological parents.

But this placid teenager had been in a bar brawl within days of his arrival. There was the CCTV evidence from the pub and the confusion over his adoptive parents who were supposed to be uncontactable because they were on a world cruise. Then there was the issue of the absence of a social media footprint. Ashling was no fan of either Facebook or Twitter. She maintained a Facebook page but solely for professional reasons. But even she had a social media footprint. She picked up her phone and checked whether Fiona had responded. Nothing. Fiona must be pissed off with her. Despite her protestations to the contrary, she could understand that Fiona might be protective about her son. Ashling had taken on the task of looking into Tim's background because she had learned in her professional life never to take what people said at face value. She was sure that Tim, if that was his name, had created a narrative that fitted his agenda. That was the crux of her problem. What was his agenda? She had tried to tease it out of him but had failed miserably. Perhaps her failure had stung her professionalism and turned her quest to learn more about him into an obsession. She didn't think so. There was an established checklist of the attributes of a psychopath. She'd been through that checklist and Tim had ticked most of the boxes. The knowledge that Tim fit the psychological profile was a concern. He wanted something from Fiona but what was it? She'd passed the Michael Patrick Power name to Sok. Maybe he had some news. She dialled his office. There was a recorded message that he was working from home. Her phone pinged. She snatched it. It was a message from Fiona. She burst into tears. She tried to stop but the tears continued to flow. This wasn't her. Why was she so damn emotional?

# CHAPTER FORTY-EIGHT

Fiona strolled into the squad room happy in the knowledge that DCI Horgan would already be on the outskirts of Galway on his way to the picturesque village of Kinvara where he had a beautiful bungalow that looked out across Galway Bay. She was, therefore, more than a little surprised to see him stride through the door before she had even taken her seat. She glanced quickly at the wall clock and saw that she hadn't been mistaken. It was a credit to the gravity of the situation on the Sarah Joyce murder investigation that Horgan had put himself under the psychological pressure of staying late.

'DS Madden, from the look on your face you thought you'd succeeded in avoiding me. I need to know why you're treating me like a mushroom.'

Tracy made his *I-don't-understand* face.

Fiona looked at him. 'Kept in a dark place and buried in shit.'

Horgan pulled over a chair and sat. 'Illuminate me.'

'We've just returned from the Forensic Lab at GMIT. The bad news is that Mikey Canavan is not the father of Sarah's child.'

'And the good news is?'

'That he's related to that child.'

'And that's good news because?"

'It limits the number of possible suspected fathers.'

'Please tell me that most of the families in Glenmore are not related to the Canavans.'

Fiona wasn't even sure that her own mother didn't have some connection to the Canavans.

'Your lips aren't moving, Madden,' Horgan said. 'That might be a signal that we are back to square one.'

'We are following a definite line of inquiry,' Fiona said.

'Which is?'

'Sarah was selling drugs to some of the other kids. I think that she was getting the drugs from whoever impregnated her. We've been on to the drug squad and we'll soon have the name of a drug pusher in Clifden who the source may be. Hopefully, he'll give us the name of someone in Glenmore.'

'Have you bought a National Lottery ticket this week?'

Fiona could see where this was going. 'No, sir.'

'Well do so because this could be your lucky week.' He stood up and lifted his right hand. He left a small space between his thumb and forefinger. 'You are this far away from being taken off this case, Madden. If you strike lucky, I'll avoid the sack load of shite the super will throw over me.'

'Sarah's funeral is in Glenmore tomorrow morning. It's likely the murderer will turn up. Tracy will take a load of photos and we'll see if somebody behaves guilty.'

'I'm going home.' Horgan strode towards the door. 'If I'm leaving the force, I'd like to do it because I want to. Not because I was pushed.'

'He didn't seem pleased.' Tracy waited until the door closed behind Horgan.

'No, he didn't. Maybe he would have preferred it if you and I had walked in on the murder while it was in progress and arrested the miscreant. There was a murder in Dublin recently where a man chopped his wife into pieces with a samurai sword. The detectives arrived on the scene found the guy holding the weapon and standing over the victim. Case closed. That's the kind of investigation a lazy bastard like Horgan likes. We started with nothing. I don't think we've done too badly.'

Tracy pinned the two sheets with the results of the DNA comparison to the whiteboard. 'It would have been nice if Mikey had turned out to be the father.'

'Don't be like Horgan. It's pure luck if evidence drops into your lap. In most cases, you must dig deep and keep digging because if there's a flaw in your investigation, I guarantee that some smart-arsed barrister is going to find it.'

Tracy's phone pinged and he read the text. 'Message from our drug squad colleague. He suggests we connect with a guy called Steve Conway. He lives in Clifden and has been picked up several times for dealing.'

'Call Clifden and tell them to pick him up tomorrow morning. We should be there about eleven.'

'Anything else I can usefully do?'

Fiona thought. 'No school in Glenmore tomorrow, is Emma in town?'

'As it happens, yes.'

'Try pumping her, for information I mean.'

'You have a very dirty mind, for a lesbian.'

'I'm staying in town myself tonight. I've invited Ashling to stay over in a hotel, we'll have dinner and take in a show or a movie.'

'Sounds like a fun evening. I don't doubt that you'll be in perfect form tomorrow for the day ahead.'

'Try not to run across us on your date.'

'It's a small city.'

. . .

Fiona and Ashling ordered their drinks from the waiter in the bar of the g Hotel. They were seated in a quiet corner beside one of the windows that looked out on the inlet from Galway Bay.

'What brought this on?' Ashling asked.

'I didn't want to go home and I needed a secure garage for the Black Shadow.'

The waiter put their drinks on the table and Fiona signed the chit.

'What?'

'I've booked us in for the night. I couldn't take a repeat of the dinner last night. We're going to a movie and then dinner. It's my treat.'

'What about Tim?'

'I texted that we were spending the evening in town with friends.'

'I thought we were in trouble when you didn't reply to my texts.'

'We're not in trouble.' Fiona toasted. 'Slainte.'

'Good luck, we're not in trouble yet.'

'I'm having a little trouble fighting on two fronts. The clock is running and if I don't produce something tangible soon, Horgan will take me off the case.'

Ashling nodded. 'And you wouldn't like that.'

'I'd be gutted. The evidence is out there, I just can't get my hands on it. People have undoubtedly seen something that's pertinent to the investigation. Sarah was wrapped in black bags. Maybe someone saw a man carrying a couple of black bags into his house. She was dumped at sea. I come from here and I can tell you for a fact that no boat leaves a harbour in this area without someone spotting it. But there are more than twenty places that a boat could have left from and I bet if I knocked on every door someone saw something that was out of the ordinary. But that would take time and that's in short supply. My boss is on my back for a result and I can't see where it's coming from.'

'And I'm not helping with my paranoia about Tim, or Michael, or whatever his name is.'

Fiona slid her hand across the table and touched Ashling. 'I know that you're trying to help. Finding Sarah's murderer is my priority. Dealing with Tim must be put on hold. He isn't in play yet.' Who was she kidding? Certainly not Ashling. She wanted to concentrate on the murder investigation but she found thoughts of Tim constantly invading her consciousness. In his own way, he was as great a mystery as who murdered Sarah and therefore equally deserving of her time. Finding Sarah's murderer didn't have the ability to change her life, finding out what Tim's agenda was did. 'Let's forget the priorities for this evening and enjoy each other's company.' She smiled when she saw a tear creep out of Ashling's left eye. She squeezed Ashling's hand. 'Don't worry, it'll work out.' Fiona, you are so full of bullshit, she thought.

# CHAPTER FORTY-NINE

Irish funerals are legendary and the west of Ireland variety even more so. Glenmore was a sea of cars, most parked illegally. Every space around the church was occupied and a great mass of people surrounded the entrance to the pathway leading to the stone-faced building. The local Garda had co-opted several uniforms from Clifden to assist in managing the large crowd. The previous evening, Sarah's body had been moved from the Joyce house to the church where it had lain overnight.

Fiona and Tracy had parked their car some distance from the church and walked the last two hundred yards. Tracy had his mobile phone out and was videoing the scene. The church could accommodate a hundred and fifty people and Fiona estimated the crowd outside to be almost twice that size. She had given Tracy his instructions on the journey from Galway. He was to take as many photographs as possible and concentrate on the Canavans and their friends. She would stay as far in the background as she could. Taking a seat in the church would be out of the question judging by the looks she was receiving from the mourners on the periphery of the crowd. She recognised many of the faces and they recognised her. Several old schoolmates approached her for a handshake but there was no warmth in the greetings. She was the enemy. Eileen Canavan was near the steps at the entrance to the church when Fiona caught her eye. Thomas Canavan stood at her right hand and Fiona could just see the heads of the three Canavan children. She realised where she had seen Thomas Canavan before. He was the man who had been standing beside Eileen at the exit from the beach at Caladh Mweenish.

Eileen Canavan pushed her way through the crowd and made directly for Fiona. 'I hear you've been harassing my family.' Her voice was loud enough to attract attention from the people standing nearby.

'I don't think we should be having this conversation here.' Fiona spoke quietly to calm the situation. 'I'm a police detective and I don't have to answer to you or anyone else in this village concerning my investigation into Sarah Joyce's death.' Canavan's face was heavily made-up but Fiona saw the pallor underneath.

'You leave Mikey alone.'

'Please re-join your family and don't make a show of yourself.' Fiona looked towards the entrance. Mikey had joined his brother and they were staring in her direction.

'You bitch, it'll be the worse for you if you don't leave my family alone.'

There was a look on her face that Fiona hadn't seen before. The gentle look of the mild-mannered schoolteacher was replaced by the contorted face of hate.

The church bell sounded and the crowd began to shuffle. Fiona walked away from the entrance. Eileen tried to grab her arm but Fiona slipped the grasp with ease. Several people had their mobile phones out and were filming. They were about to be disappointed. There was going to be no repeat performance of the Molloy arrest. The crowd was steadily making its way into the church while Fiona was going against the flow. She turned. Canavan was no longer behind her. Thomas and

Mikey Canavan were at her side and the three of them were making for the church entrance.

Fiona reached the gate separating the church pathway from the road and found Jimmy standing there.

'I warned you about turning over too many rocks.'

'I've only just begun.'

'Are you going inside?'

'Not likely, judging from some of the looks I'm getting I might be in the next wooden box. What's your excuse?'

'I'm still in the phase of being prodigal. When I'm on my deathbed, I intend to throw myself on God's mercy, just in case.'

'Good plan, have all the bases covered.'

'I hear you're pissing the Canavans off. I'd watch my step there.'

'Why?'

'Forget I said anything.'

'Are you going to take what you know to the grave?'

'Who said I know anything?'

She laughed. 'This conversation is so Irish. Why do we always answer a question with another question?'

'Maybe it's because we're scared of the answer.'

'You're not scared of Mikey Canavan.'

'Possibly not. You ever hear of a guy called Billy Thornton?'

'The name doesn't ring a bell.'

'He used to box a bit when he lived in the States. He even entered the Golden Gloves competition. Some guy beat the living shite out of him. Gave him a bit of brain damage. Billy talks a load of rubbish now. He lives back the way on Mweenish Island.'

Fiona had forgotten what passed for conversation in Connemara. Jimmy was trying to give her a message but it had to cloaked in verbiage, everything was subtext. 'Is there a moral to this story?'

A hymn was being sung in the church. They both listened as Tracy joined them.

'I'd best be off,' Jimmy said. 'The Joyces have put three hundred euros behind the bar and there'll be a thirsty group of mourners to be served as soon as Sarah's in the ground. It'll be a busy afternoon.' He walked off in the direction of his pub.

Fiona had the feeling that their conversation hadn't really finished. She turned to Tracy. 'Did you get plenty of photos?'

'Lots.'

'Let's be on our way.'

# CHAPTER FIFTY

Ashling saw the notification of the arrival of the email as soon as she switched on her computer. Sok's name jumped out at her. Her finger hovered over the left click of the mouse. This was the moment of truth. This was the only morning of the week that she had no lectures. Their evening in Galway had been a wonderful interlude. They'd been to the cinema before having a late dinner in an expensive restaurant in a small lane off Shop Street. When they returned to the hotel, they had a nightcap before heading for bed and making love. It had been a relaxed evening, the perfect antidote to the tension-filled dinner with Tim. Fiona had been up with the larks while she had slept late, swum in the hotel pool, showered, and breakfasted before heading for the university. Now the spectre of Tim raised its head and she had that queasy feeling in her stomach. She looked down at her finger which still hovered over the mouse. This was what it was like when you opened Pandora's box. She had no idea what was in the email but she was reluctant to open it. She guessed that the information that it contained would prove at a minimum uncomfortable and at a maximum cataclysmic. She had started out on this road simply trying to find out information on Tim that he obviously wasn't happy to give voluntarily. Maybe her initial disquiet had been caused by jealousy. She wasn't keen on sharing Fiona's affection. She clicked the left button on the mouse and the email flooded the screen in front of her. Sok's message was short and sweet. There was a mass of records referring to Michael Power. He had saved the most relevant ones and they were appended to the mail. She looked at the attachments. There were more than a dozen. She clicked on the first. It was an article from the *Boston Globe* concerning a car accident in a place called Cohasset south of Boston. A middle-aged couple had drowned when their car had gone out of control and driven off a bridge into a river. An examination of the car had shown that the brake lining had been damaged and that brake fluid had leaked to the extent that the brakes were useless. The couple was named as Martin and Patricia Power. She moved on quickly to the second attachment. It was a follow-up article from the *Weymouth News*. The police chief was launching an investigation into the deaths of the Powers after an examination of their car revealed that the brake lining might have been tampered with. The police were searching for the Powers' son, Michael, who was not resident at the home address. The next few attachments related to reports of the funerals of the Powers. As she flicked through the rest of the attachments, the reports became sparser until finally there was a report of the coroner's inquest that listed the deaths of the Powers as misadventure. Sok had added a Facebook page for Michael Power. It showed a younger Tim and was typical of a teenage schoolboy. There were no posts that would lead her to think that Tim, as she continued to think of him, was harbouring psychotic intentions. She sat back in her chair. One of the great mistakes in life was to take leaps of imagination. A middle-aged couple had died in an accident. There was no proof that Tim played any part in their deaths. There might be suspicion but there was not a shred of evidence. But why had he disappeared? And why was he now living under the name of Tim Daly? And who did he know who was able to supply him with what looked to her untrained eye to be a bone fide US passport? She had learned a rush to judgement was not the most positive way to examine a situation so she printed off the attachments and put them into a plastic sleeve. She should talk this over with Fiona but her partner had enough on her plate with the murder investigation and she had a certain emotional investment in Tim as her son. It was possible that there was a simple answer to the questions she'd developed. If so, there was no need to involve Fiona at this stage. She'd come this far on her own, maybe she could go the rest of the distance. She would drop Fiona a line telling her that Sok had come through and leave it at that. No, it was easier to forward Sok's email without comment. She hit the buttons and leaned back in her chair. It was almost midday. She could return to the cottage and confront Tim with what they'd discovered. If he wasn't home, she could always do a bit of ferreting around.

# CHAPTER FIFTY-ONE

Fiona directed Tracy along the back road that led from Glenmore through the wild country that ran along the rocky coast of Connemara. Directly in front of their line of travel, the Twelve Bens were bathed in sunshine. It was a fine day for a funeral. She'd toyed with the idea of staying for the interment but such events elicit high emotions and she wanted the day to pass off without incident for Nora Joyce's sake. The trip to Clifden was another punt in the dark. She'd worked on several murder cases in Dublin that were still open after years of police investigations. She wanted desperately to obtain justice for Sarah but time and the absence of sound evidence were against her.

'We're not exactly popular out here,' Tracy said when they left the back road and turned onto the main road from Galway to Clifden.

'You're not the unpopular one.'

'Ever since our first visit to Glenmore to investigate Sarah's disappearance, I've noticed a vibe between you and the locals. Nora Joyce was the first and there have been others.' He flipped his phone to her. 'Take a look.'

Fiona played the video of their walk to the church and

then examined the photos that Tracy had taken. She closed the phone. 'You did a good job.'

'Who was the woman in black standing on the steps of the church? She never took her eyes off you.'

'That was my mother.'

'I thought she had a look of you.'

'We haven't spoken in seventeen years.'

'I don't want to pry and you don't have to tell me but what happened?'

Fiona wondered how to answer. 'Life happened. An event drove a wedge between us and that wedge grew bigger with the years. I suppose at one point there was a chance of a reconciliation but we both let it slip.'

'The look on her face wasn't hate. To me it looked like love.'

'Then you really are a naïve young man.' There had been a look of love between them at one point but that was well in the past. That was before her mother looked on her as the author of her own downfall. She was a victim. Like every other woman who was raped, she did nothing to encourage her rapist. But that wasn't how her mother saw it. Luckily, her grandfather stood by her. She'd seen her mother at the entrance to the church and there was a part of her that wanted to go to her and say enough. Life was too short. But the pain of abandonment was still there. It was one of the reasons that she understood the pain that drove Tim.

'Want to talk about it?'

She looked at him. 'Not right now. Someday maybe.'

'Whenever you're ready.'

'Any news from Emma?'

'Things are not back to normal at the school.'

'In what sense?'

'Your friend Eileen Canavan is inconsolable. Sarah must have been special for her.'

'That wasn't the impression I got at the church. She was

pissed that we were investigating her husband's family. If Sarah was so special, she'd be gagging to find the murderer.'

'Emma got the impression they were close. Maybe she was mistaken.'

'Maybe they were close until we took an interest in Mikey. Family first, student later.'

They passed a signpost indicating a speed limit of forty kilometres an hour.

'Clifden?' Tracy said.

'The police station is on the left two hundred metres ahead. There's a spot to pull in and park.'

The area in front of the station was empty. Tracy parked and switched off the engine.

Sergeant Glennan exited the station, opened the rear car door, and sat in. 'Welcome to Clifden,' he said. 'Mr Conway declined your offer to be interviewed in the station and I have no official reason to detain him. We'll meet him at his home.'

'Which is where?'

'Cleggan,' Glennan said. 'Into the town, turn right at the petrol station and straight ahead. You didn't say what you wanted with Conway.'

Fiona explained about the cider parties and Sarah providing weed and ecstasy. 'We need to know who her connection was.'

'Conway's a changed man,' Glennan said. 'Or so he says. He may not cooperate.'

'That's why you're along I suppose.'

'I know the local characters and they know me. My assistance is probably worth the price of a pint. I'd like a rundown on the investigation when we finish with Conway. That little girl's murder bothers me.'

They were travelling through an area devoid of houses and people. 'Does anyone live out here?' Tracy said.

'Precious few,' Glennan said. 'Take the second small road

on the right. A hundred metres on the left, you'll see a small cottage. Pull in there.'

The cottage was smaller than Fiona's and in a state of disrepair.

Tracy parked beside a beat-up Ford van. There were a wooden bench and two wooden chairs backed against the cottage wall. A young man lounged on one of the chairs supervising two small children who were playing outside.

Glennan exited first followed by Fiona while Tracy brought up the rear.

'Morning, Steve,' Glennan said.

'Morning, sergeant.'

Fiona stared at Conway. He was small and thin, he wore a rough-woven waistcoat over a grandfather shirt, jeans that had seen better days, and new trainers. If he was an example of the money to be made from dealing drugs, business was slack.

Glennan introduced Fiona and Tracy.

'Take a seat,' Conway said. He had a Dublin accent.

Glennan sat on the bench. 'Fine day.'

'It was until you lot arrived. You know I learned my lesson and I don't deal anymore. Why pick on me?'

'We're not here about you dealing,' Glennan said. 'DS Madden is investigating the murder of the young girl that was found on the beach over at Caladh Mweenish. She thinks you might be able to help her with her inquiries.'

Conway sat up straight. 'What would I know about the murder of a young girl?'

Fiona had taken the seat beside Glennan. 'We know that this girl was distributing drugs to kids her own age. We want to find out where she got them.'

Conway looked at his children playing ball on the grass lawn. 'I never sold drugs to children or young adults.'

'We don't think that you sold the drugs directly to her. Someone else was buying the drugs and using her to pass them along. We want you to look at some photos.'

'What if I don't want to?'

'You wouldn't really do that now,' Glennon said. 'Would you Steve?' He turned and looked at Conway's van. 'I hope that your tax and insurance on the van are up to date.'

'Are you threatening me?'

'Would I do something like that?'

'Show me the fucking photos.'

Tracy had been standing beside Fiona. He moved forward and held out his mobile phone to Conway.

'These photos were taken at the girl's funeral this morning.' Fiona stared at Conway as he scrolled through the photos. His eyes widened for a second and she realised that he'd seen someone that he knew.

'Sorry.' Conway passed the phone back.

Fiona looked at the children. 'Nice kids. Sarah Joyce was sixteen years old. The man who strangled her dumped her body in the sea like a piece of garbage. I get the feeling that you don't particularly like the Garda. Young Tracy here and me are only doing our job and we care about it. Now, think about your little girl. How would you like someone to choke the life out of her and dump her at sea?'

Conway looked at the children then held out his hand to Tracy. 'Show me the phone again.'

Tracy found the photos and handed the phone back.

Conway scrolled through the photos and then stopped. 'This guy was a client.' He handed the phone back to Tracy.

'Thomas Canavan,' Tracy said.

'That's a good man, Steve,' Glennan said.

'We're going to need a statement indicating that Thomas Canavan bought drugs from you,' Fiona said. 'Normally I'd ask you to come to the station in Mill Street but I trust Sergeant Glennan to do the necessary.'

Glennan nodded.

She turned to Tracy. 'Take a photo of Mr Conway.'

Tracy complied.

Fiona held out her hand. 'You've done the right thing and you've been a big help. Thank you.'

Conway shook.

Glennan stood and clapped Conway on the shoulder. 'Be at the station this afternoon. We'll get the statement over fast.'

They left Conway where they'd found him.

Fiona felt a surge of optimism. It was coming together. Thomas Canavan had bought drugs from Conway and used Sarah to sell them on. Mikey was related to the father of the embryo. The elder Canavan was the one who was having the affair with a child. The list of crimes the bastard had committed would be as long as her arm.

'Where to?' Tracy said.

'Let's drop Rory back at the station. We'll have a cup of tea and give Horgan a call. I bet the Canavan boys and their father will be at the drink in Tigh Jimmy. If it were up to me, I'd haul the fucker out of the pub by the scruff of his neck but Horgan might have other ideas. We might have to be a little more subtle.'

Glennan laughed. 'I didn't think that subtle was your style.'

'It isn't.'

# CHAPTER FIFTY-TWO

The parking area in front and to the side of Tigh Jimmy was packed with cars. The interment was over and the mourners could get down to the real business of the day. A group of smokers outside the door of the pub took no notice of the two men and one woman in the car facing them.

Horgan had reacted pretty much as Fiona had expected. He asked her to confirm that she, as SIO, believed that the person they were seeking for the murder of Sarah Joyce was Thomas Canavan. When Fiona confirmed, he approved the immediate arrest and detention of Canavan but insisted that the detectives be accompanied by the uniformed Guards from the area. She could hear the relief in his voice. With someone in the frame and about to be arrested, he would have been justified in informing his superiors that an arrest was imminent. Horgan wanted Canavan in the cells as quickly as possible. Fiona and Tracy had secured Horgan's career, for the present anyway.

'How do we do this?' Glennan said from the rear of the car.

'As gently as possible,' Fiona said.

'Thanks be to God for that,' Tracy added. 'They've been in

the pub drinking for the past couple of hours. Pulling Canavan out by the ears might be enough to start a riot.'

'Whatever way we do it,' Glennan said, 'it isn't going to go down well.'

'What do you suggest?' Fiona said.

'I'll go in alone,' Glennan said. 'That way I'm simply being a mourner. I'll ask Thomas to join me outside and if he agrees, you and Tracy can arrest him.'

'What if he doesn't agree?' Fiona asked.

'We'll cross that bridge when we come to it.'

A local squad car pulled in behind them.

'The cavalry has arrived,' Tracy said.

'We may be needing them.' Glennan exited the car, spoke to the two officers in the squad car, and entered the pub.

Fiona and Tracy watched his back as the pub door closed behind him.

'I don't envy Rory,' Fiona said. 'There's a healthy disrespect for the police in this parish.'

'Dates back to the bad old days when it was us against them.' Tracy started drumming his fingers on the steering wheel. 'How long will he stay inside?'

'My guess is that he'll have a pint and a jaw before he approaches Canavan. You can bet the old man and Mikey are there as well. So, there's an even money chance that something might kick off.'

Tracy's drumming intensified. 'If it does, you're probably going to kick the shit out of someone.'

'Only in self-defence.' The smile on Fiona's face belied her words. Thomas Canavan had probably raped Sarah Joyce, made her pregnant, introduced her to drugs, and used her as a conduit to other children, and more than likely murdered her. If anybody needed a good kicking, it was him. The problem was that it was all predicated on the presumption that his DNA was going to prove that he was the father of the embryo. Otherwise, all they had him for was contributing to the corruption of a minor by supplying drugs. 'For God's sake will you quit the drumming. If you're nervous, find another way of showing it.'

Tracy's fingers stopped. 'Who said I was nervous?'

Fiona wouldn't like to admit it but she was as nervous as Tracy. She understood Horgan's rush but Canavan was going nowhere.

The smokers dispersed and made their way back into the pub.

Fiona's eyes were strained from staring at the door of the pub. People came and went but there was no sign of Glennan. She was getting ready to exit the car and head into the pub when the door opened and Glennan appeared. She waited to see if Canavan was following. He wasn't.

Glennan retook his seat in the rear of the car. 'The bugger wouldn't come. We need plan B.'

'Shit,' Tracy said. 'Maybe Fiona should stay out of this. Phoenix Park won't accept another kung fu video.'

'You'll go a long way in the force,' Fiona said. 'The boys and girls at HQ are always looking for people on the ground who are minding their backs.'

'He might have a point,' Glennan said.

'We're the law,' Fiona said. 'We don't have to pussyfoot around when we have to arrest a potential murderer.' She put her hand on the door handle. 'I'm going in there and Thomas Canavan is coming out with me under arrest. If there's someone who gets in my way, they'll have to take the consequences.' She opened the door.

Tracy and Glennan exited the car at the same time and Glennan motioned to the men in the squad car to do the same.

Fiona strode towards the pub door closely followed by Tracy, Glennan, and the two uniformed officers.

# CHAPTER FIFTY-THREE

The cottage was eerily quiet as Ashling parked at the front gate. Her heart beat was so strong that her blouse was moving in concert with it. Along the road from Galway, her apprehension had been rising. Maybe Tim was responsible for the accident that had killed his adoptive parents. If that were the case, he wouldn't give a second thought to getting rid of anyone that could inform Weymouth police of his current whereabouts. Her plan of action was looking thin and stupid. But she owed it to Fiona to move forward. Reluctant to leave the safety of the car, she heard a knocking on the passenger window. She turned and stared into Tim's smiling face. She jumped involuntarily but forced what must have looked like a false smile. She wound down the window.

'Are you coming inside?'

'Yes, of course, I was daydreaming.' She wound up the window, switched off the ignition, picked up her plastic file from the passenger seat, and exited the car.

Tim was opening the door when she caught up with him.

'Fiona sent me a message that you guys were hitting the town last night.' He held the door open for Ashling to enter.

'We have a regular blow-out night: hotel, cinema and a nice dinner with copious drinks. It breaks the monotony of living in the wilds.'

'Sounds like fun. You want me to make you something for lunch?'

'Maybe a sandwich and a cup of tea.'

Tim went to the kitchen and Ashling heard water splashing into the kettle. She took a long breath and let it out slowly. Why was she so damn afraid? She wasn't going to accuse Tim of killing his parents. She was simply going to ask him to explain the false name and the reports in the paper.

'Is Fiona coming for lunch?' Tim placed a cup of tea in front of Ashling.

'No, she's still busy on that murder investigation.' She sipped the tea.

'Is it okay?'

'Tastes fine.'

'Ham and cheese sandwich good?'

'Perfect.'

Ashling wondered how she might bring up the car accident. She decided to get straight to the point as she sipped her tea. There were lots of noises from the kitchen but no sign of Tim. 'I don't need anything fancy. Just some ham and cheese between two pieces of buttered bread.'

'I'll be with you in a minute.'

Ashling looked at her watch. It was ten minutes since Tim had disappeared to make her sandwich. She was about to see what he was up to when he came into the living room carrying a plate with a sandwich and the teapot.

'Sorry for the delay.' He put the plate on the table and refilled her teacup which she hadn't noticed was empty.

'You're not joining me?'

'I already ate. Did you come back to have another poke in my stuff?'

She stared at him. 'That's a little passive-aggressive don't you think?'

'That's what you did the last time you came home. Learn anything useful.'

'Yes, Michael, I did.'

'That cat is out of the bag. Does Fiona know?'

'Yes.'

'So what's the purpose of today's visit?'

She handed him the plastic sleeve.

He took out the papers and read through them. 'You're a nosey little bitch, aren't you? I knew the day you started asking me questions that you were going to be a problem.'

Ashling was so staggered that she couldn't speak. She'd known there was a possibility that Tim had a nasty side but hadn't expected it to appear so soon.

'I know what you're thinking. What will Fiona say when you tell her that I called you a nosey little bitch? But I don't think you're going to be telling her.'

'Oh, I definitely will.' Ashling's tongue felt larger than usual and she had difficulty forming her words. She looked at her empty teacup. 'You put something in my tea.'

Tim smiled. 'Being a college professor you've probably heard of roofies. It's also known as the date rape drug. But don't worry, you're not about to be raped.'

'What are you really here for?'

Tim sighed. 'I suppose you'd say that I was after revenge but that's not what I'd call it. Maybe I want to put things right. There are two people here who owe me and I've come to collect.'

Ashling tried to speak but found that although the words formed in her brain, they didn't reach her vocal cords. She tried to stand up but fell back in her chair.

'I put one milligram into your tea. You're feeling the early effects. You'll be a zombie in two hours and you'll be out of action for eight to twelve.'

Despite the drug, a feeling of total despair overtook Ashling. He was going to kill Fiona and possibly her. She'd been stupid not to realise how dangerous he might be. She'd been right. He was a psychopath. Her eyes felt heavy. She had to warn Fiona. But how? She was a prisoner inside her own body and these were only the early effects.

# CHAPTER FIFTY-FOUR

Fiona pushed in the pub door. The room that constituted the bar was packed solid with mainly male patrons. Given the occasion, and the fact that a considerable amount of money had been deposited behind the bar to pay for drinks, the level of intoxication was pretty much what she expected. Funerals were not simply an occasion to say goodbye to a relation or trusted friend. They were social occasions where drinks to get the party rolling were on the deceased's family. The noise level was in the high decibels but it started to drop the second the first person in the room spotted Fiona until it was possible to hear a pin drop. The door didn't close and Fiona could feel the presence of Tracy and Glennan behind her. The two uniformed officers hadn't yet entered the room. Fiona glanced at Jimmy behind the bar. He shook his head slowly and leaned down to pick up a hurley. It was a sign that he anticipated a bar brawl.

'Good afternoon, lads,' Fiona said. 'Sorry to stall the festivities. My colleagues and I will be out of your way in a couple of minutes and the party can resume. If we must hang around, I'm afraid that nobody in this room will be driving home this evening. Most of you know who I am and I'm sure all of you know who Sergeant Glennan is. We have a bit of business to transact and then we'll be gone.' She looked to the back of the bar to where the three Canavan men stood together. Their jaws were set and they tried to stare her down. 'We need to have a word with Thomas Canavan. I'd be grateful if Thomas would accompany us outside.'

'Fuck off,' old man Canavan said. 'You'll not be taking my son out of here while I'm still standing. And I'm not the only one that you'll have to go through.'

'It's come to our attention,' Fiona said, 'that the children of this parish are being supplied with drugs. I know the tradition here of cider parties on the beach but lately the children...' She looked around everyone in the room. 'All your children are being offered something stronger than cider. I think Thomas Canavan can help us with our inquiries.'

A murmur started in the crowd.

Jimmy rapped the counter of the bar with his hurley.

Fiona could see the sweat on Thomas Canavan's brow.

Glennan walked forward and the crowd parted to allow him to reach the back of the room. 'Come along, Thomas, like a good lad.' He put his hand on Canavan's arm and looked around the crowd. 'You're doing a great disservice to the memory of a fine young girl. We don't want anybody hurt and there aren't enough cells in Clifden for everybody so let Detective Sergeant Madden do her job.'

The elder Canavan threw a punch that caught Glennan on the shoulder.

Before the crowd could react, Jimmy vaulted over the bar and whacked Canavan across the shins with the hurley. 'There'll be no trouble in my bar. This will either end or be taken outside.'

Fiona came forward and grabbed Thomas Canavan by his free arm. She applied maximum pressure with her fingers and

Canavan winced. 'Time to go.' She and Glennan marched Canavan through the crowd.

'Are you going to let her take one of your own?' Con Canavan shouted.

A man stepped out from the crowd and stood in front of Fiona. She kept a firm grip on Canavan but got ready to react. She stared into the man's eyes. It was a replay of the Molloy arrest. The squint in his eyes said that he was contemplating something stupid. He was drunk and his reactions would be slow. She was wondering how much pain she would inflict. Enough to disable him but not enough to incense the crowd. The margins were fine.

Tracy came behind the man and put his mouth to his ear. 'I'd get out of her way if I were you. She's a martial arts expert and the last guy who pissed her off is having a knee replacement.'

The man's eyes flickered and Fiona knew he had chosen well. He stepped aside and she brushed past him.

Outside, Fiona and Glennan rushed Canavan to the car and held him close to the rear door.

'Thomas Canavan, I am arresting you on suspicion of involvement in the murder of Sarah Joyce. You have the right to remain silent and refuse to answer questions. Anything you say may be used against you in a court of law. You have the right to consult an attorney before speaking to the police and to have an attorney present during questioning now or in the future. Get into the car.'

Glennan shoved Canavan into the rear seat.

Fiona waited for the car door to shut. She turned to Glennan. 'Find Canavan's car and impound it. I'll send a tow truck out from Galway to pick it up. They moved Sarah from the crime scene to get her into a boat. There'll be evidence in his car. Unless Mrs Canavan was busy with the bleach.'

A crowd was pouring out of the pub.

'We're out of here,' Fiona said

Tracy leapt into the driver's seat and Fiona the passenger side.

Fiona wound down her window. 'Thanks.'

Glennan stood with the uniforms. 'Any time, we'll hang on to pick up Canavan's car. Now get out of here.'

# CHAPTER FIFTY-FIVE

F iona stared at the sullen face of Thomas Canavan on the monitor in the observation room in Mill Street station. The return to Galway had been undertaken in silence. Canavan had uttered only one word since being arrested: solicitor. As soon as they arrived, Fiona had processed Canavan and taken his fingerprints and photo and swabbed for DNA. The swab was sent immediately to the lab. Canavan had refused to be interviewed without legal advice and now he and his solicitor were in a whispered conversation in the interview room while Fiona and Tracy sat watching the muted picture. The solicitor stood, walked to the door, and knocked.

'We're on.' Fiona picked up a file and headed for the door. Tracy followed.

A uniformed officer met them outside. 'They're ready.'

Fiona and Tracy entered the interview room and took their seats facing Canavan and his solicitor.

Fiona put her file on the table. She turned to Tracy. 'Do the necessary.'

Tracy switched on the recording equipment. 'Interview with Thomas Canavan at Mill Street Garda Station.' He gave the date and time. 'Present Detective Sergeant Fiona Madden, Detective Garda Sean Tracy.' He nodded at Canavan who gave his name and his solicitor followed suit.

'You understand that you have already been cautioned,' Fiona said. 'Is there any part of the caution that you do not understand?'

Canavan shook his head.

'Please speak for the recording,' Tracy said.

'No.'

Fiona opened her file and placed a photograph of Sarah Joyce on the table. 'Do you know this young girl?'

Canavan looked at his solicitor who nodded.

'It's Sarah Joyce.'

'And how do you know her?'

'She lives in my village and she's in my wife's class at the local school.'

'Do you know her socially?'

'She works sometimes at the local pub.'

'Is that all?'

'No comment.'

Fiona removed a photo from the post-mortem and put it on the table. 'Sarah was murdered. She was strangled and dumped at sea. Did you murder Sarah Joyce?'

'No.'

'Did you dump her body at sea?'

'No comment.'

Fiona put a photo of the embryo on the table.

Canavan looked away.

'This is an embryo that was taken from Sarah Joyce's womb. Did you know that she was pregnant?'

'No comment.'

Fiona put the results of the DNA comparisons on the table. 'Your brother Mikey gave us a DNA sample. On the left is a comparison of DNA taken from the embryo and Sarah's DNA. It confirms she was the embryo's mother. On the right is a comparison of the DNA from the embryo and from your brother. It shows that he was not the father but he is related to the father. We have taken a DNA sample from you and it has been sent to the lab. Will it show that you are the father of Sarah's child?'

Canavan looked at his solicitor who nodded.

'No comment.'

'I think the lab test will confirm that you are the father of Sarah's child. The post-mortem determined that Sarah was three months pregnant which indicates that the child was conceived when she was under sixteen years of age. Since she was below the age of consent, this constitutes rape. Would you please stand.'

Canavan and his solicitor stood.

Fiona remained seated. 'Detective Garda Tracy, please do the honours.'

Tracy stood. 'Thomas Canavan, I am arresting you under the Criminal Law Sexual Offences Act 2017, Section 34 part 2 for the rape of Sarah Joyce, a minor under the age of sixteen.' He repeated the words of the caution.

Fiona motioned them to sit. 'Have you anything to say to the charge made against you?' She stared at Canavan. His hands were shaking.

'No comment.'

'We will interview you again relating to this crime when the results of the DNA test are available. Do you know this man?'

Tracy held out his mobile phone showing an image of Steven Conway.

'No comment.'

'This is Steven Conway a convicted drug dealer. He has given evidence that he has supplied you with drugs on several occasions.' She reached into the file, took out a typed document and laid it on the table. 'This is a sworn statement that alleges you were the source of drugs supplied to minors by

Sarah Joyce. Did you supply drugs to minors via Sarah Joyce?'

'No comment.'

'Would you please stand.'

Canavan and his solicitor stood.

'Detective Garda Tracy, do the honours.'

'Thomas Canavan, I am arresting you under the Misuse of Drugs Act 1977. You are already under caution.'

'Do you have anything to say relating to the charge made against you?' Fiona said.

'No comment.'

Fiona stared at the solicitor then looked at Canavan. 'We're not making much progress here. Maybe it's time to put the situation clearly. The DNA analysis will establish your paternity of Sarah's child, so the rape charge will hold. We'll push on with the supplying drug change and I have no doubt we'll prove that also. We've impounded your car.' She noted the knowledge didn't impact on him. 'I think that we might find that you've washed the inside with bleach so I don't think the forensics team will find any DNA in the boot. But Sarah had a full head of hair and I bet in some crevasse or other they'll find a hair. Now that we know you're involved we're going to find people that have seen you together. The evidence will build and with the paternity established and some physical evidence from your car we'll have a strong case for the prosecution to present.'

Canavan turned and whispered in his solicitor's ear. The solicitor shook his head.

'Now is the time to come clean,' Fiona said. 'Tell us what happened. Did you want her to get rid of the baby and she wouldn't? Was there an argument that got out of hand?'

'No comment.'

Fiona put the papers on the table back into the file. 'We'll leave you and your solicitor alone to talk things over.' She nodded at Tracy who terminated the interview and switched the recorder off.

FIONA PUT two cups of tea on the table and sat across from Tracy.

'You nearly had him.' Tracy pulled a cup towards him.

'He'll confess sooner or later but we'll need more evidence.'

'Van Espen will establish the paternity.'

'Then we'll have him for statuary rape. I want him for the murder of that girl.'

'Maybe you're right about the car being used to transport the body.'

'I'm sure of it. But he's sure he did a good job of eradicating the DNA. Maybe we'll get lucky.'

'He couldn't have moved the body on his own.' Tracy sipped his tea.

'Did you check Mikey's alibi?'

'I tried to contact his flatmate but he didn't answer.'

'Get back onto him. Tell him it's a murder inquiry and if he lies to us, he's going to prison. Finish up your tea and contact the flatmate. We need to get back into the interview room.'

TRACY PRESSED the record button and did the preamble.

'Things have moved on a bit,' Fiona started. 'Mikey's alibi for the night that Sarah disappeared didn't hold up. I'm having him picked up and brought to Galway. You needed him to move the body. I'm going to charge him with accessory to murder. He can forget about his course in Sligo although I'm sure he'll have the possibility to study online. He just won't be able to work for five or ten years.'

Canavan shot a look at the solicitor who shook his head. 'No comment.'

'And there's the question of your mother destroying evidence.' She opened the file and placed on the table a photo of the contents of the burn barrel that Tracy had taken. 'She'll get two years for that. And all because you couldn't keep your dick in your pants. You've wrecked your family. Why don't you unburden yourself and tell us what happened?'

'You're right. I killed her. She wouldn't get rid of the child.'

The solicitor put his hand on Canavan's arm but he shook it off.

'We had an argument and I lost it. I have a temper. Ask anyone. They'll tell you.'

'Were you face to face when you had the argument?'

'Yes.'

'If that's the case, why didn't you just reach out and throttle her. You're twice her size. You've got hands like hams on you. Why didn't you strangle her?'

'I don't know.'

'Because you didn't do it. You're taking the blame because you want to protect someone. Who was it, your mother?'

Canavan leaned forward. 'No, please, it was me. Only me.'

'It's too late for that.' Fiona looked at Tracy. 'Wind the interview down.'

Tracy did as he was told.


FIONA AND TRACY went to the squad room.

'What the hell is going on?' Tracy said. 'We had a confession.'

'It's bullshit. If he'd had an argument with her, he would have hit her with his fists or strangled her with his hands. He could see that someone was going to have to go down and he decided to do what he thinks is the decent thing. There's no doubt that he's responsible for Sarah's death but he wasn't the one that put the ligature around her neck and strangled her. We'll get him for the rape and probably the dumping of the body. But he didn't kill her.'

'What do we do now?'

'We look at the evidence again.'

'Maybe it was Mikey.'

'He doesn't have a motive. I don't see him killing a sixteen-year-old girl because she's going to have his brother's child.'

The phone on Fiona's desk rang and she answered it. She listened for a while and then said, 'Okay.'

'The Canavan clan are assembled in the reception making a spectacle of themselves. They want to have Canavan released immediately. The duty sergeant wants me to go down and deal with them. Let's go.'

The scene in the reception area was one of pandemonium. The elder Canavan and Mikey were drunk and Mrs Canavan was screeching like a banshee. Behind his desk, the duty sergeant was doing his best to quieten the situation. Eileen Canavan was at the rear of the group with her three children in tow.

'Enough,' Fiona shouted. 'This is a police station and if this mini-demonstration doesn't stop, I'm going to ask the duty sergeant to arrest all of you for disturbing the peace.'

'Fucking bitch,' Con Canavan muttered.

'Thomas Canavan is helping us with our inquiries. He is going to be detained. I assume that he will be charged with various offences over the next few days.' She looked at the group and had a lightbulb moment. There comes a time in every investigation when the final piece of the jigsaw falls into place. That can happen when a vital piece of evidence is found but it's often when a confluence of thoughts form in the brain of the investigator. Fiona had just experienced such a moment. 'Mr and Mrs Canavan, you may leave.' She turned to Thomas' mother. 'We'll be interviewing you over the next few days concerning your role in destroying evidence in a police inquiry. Detective Garda Tracy would you please take Michael Canavan into custody and put him in an interview room.'

'You're going to ruin our family,' the elder Canavan tried to punch Fiona but she avoided him easily and he fell on the floor of the reception.

A uniformed officer came out from behind the reception and assisted Canavan to his feet.

'I'll overlook that,' Fiona said. 'Sit down and act your age.'

Tracy took Mikey Canavan by the arm and led him away from the reception area.

Fiona turned to Eileen. 'Since you're already here, I'd like to have an interview with you. The children can go home with their grandparents.'

Canavan gathered her children around her. 'I'm not letting my children go.'

Fiona smiled. 'They can keep the children here but only if they stay quiet. But I think it's important that you and I have a word.'

Canavan kissed the children. 'I'll be back soon. Momo and Dado will take care of you.'

Fiona held the door to the interview rooms open. Tracy and Mikey, accompanied by a uniformed officer, were standing at the door of one of the rooms. Fiona nodded at them and the uniformed officer and Mikey entered the room. The young man's head was down. Fiona realised that he was on the cusp of a confession. She opened an interview door. 'Eileen, can you wait for me inside. I'll be back in a few minutes?' Canavan entered and Fiona closed the door.

'How do you want to play it?' Tracy asked.

'You handle Mikey. Tell him his alibi is in shit and we know he helped to dispose of Sarah's body. He looks ready to crack. Just help him get it out. Don't forget to caution him and offer him legal advice.'

When Fiona entered the room, Canavan was already

seated at the table. She took the seat directly facing her. 'Eileen, I'm sorry about this but I'm obliged to caution you before we speak and I'm afraid I'll be recording what we say.' She gave the caution, switched on the recorder, and did the usual preamble. 'Would you like to have a solicitor present? Your husband's solicitor is in another room and I'd be happy to have him join us.'

'What do you think?'

Fiona thought that Canavan's voice sounded tired. 'I think we should ask him to join us. Is that what you want?'

'Okay.'

Fiona stopped the recoding, went next door, and returned with the solicitor. She restarted the recording and added the solicitor to the participants.

'Sarah was a student in your class?' Fiona said.

'Yes.'

'When did you realise that she was pregnant?'

'As soon as she began to show. She wasn't hiding it.'

'Did you have any idea at that time who the father was?'

'No, I thought it might be Mikey. They used to hang around a bit. But it could have been anyone. She'd become a bit flighty.'

'When did you find out that it wasn't Mikey but your husband?'

Canavan stiffened. 'That's not true. She was trying to bait me. Flouncing around in front of me. Showing me how young and beautiful she was. Wait until she has three children. That neat body will have turned more matronly.'

'Did you ask Thomas if the child was his?'

'Yes.'

'And what did he say?'

'He admitted he had sex with her but he didn't think that he was the father.'

'But you knew better.'

'Yes. The way she behaved in front of me at school was

indicative. The smirk on her face told me that she thought she could steal my husband away from me and my children. She was rubbing my nose in it.'

'What happened the night that Sarah disappeared?'

'I followed him when he left. I'd arranged for one of the neighbour's children to babysit.'

'What happened then?'

'He met her and took her to his parents' house. The parents were out. I watched through the window while she changed her clothes in front of him. He took her into Mikey's room and they had sex.'

'That made you angry.'

'Yes.'

'What happened next?'

'That's a bit hazy, like I dreamt it. I went into the house. She'd put that black dress on that showed every curve of her body. She was standing in the living room. A red mist whirled around my head and I felt a level of anger I had never experienced before. My children were going to be denied their father. I don't know where the scarf came from. It seemed to materialise in my hand. I instinctively knew what I had to do. I looped the scarf around her neck and pulled as hard as I could. I think she struggled for a while and then she went limp. I let her fall to the ground and she looked like she was asleep. The next thing I remember was Tommy coming out of the bedroom and going crazy. He bent and felt Sarah's pulse. He jumped up and hit me. He asked what I had done and said I must have been mad. I suppose I was. Then he told me to go home and he would deal with Sarah.'

'You realised that you'd murdered her?'

'I protected my family. I did what a good mother does. But I'm sorry I had to take a life.'

Fiona looked at her and saw the young girl that she remembered from school. Sarah had represented an existential threat to the Canavan family and Eileen Canavan had decided to remove it.

'Don't look at me like that,' Canavan said.

'How am I looking at you?'

'Like you're better than me and we both know that's not true.' She laughed. 'We're so alike that you could be sitting here in my place.'

Fiona looked at the solicitor.

'Are we done?' he asked.

'I think so.' She terminated the interview and turned off the recording.

'Can I go home now?' Canavan asked. 'The children will need to go to bed soon.'

'You'll have to stay with us a bit longer,' Fiona said. 'I'll tell their grandparents to look after them for a bit.'

'They can't. I'm their mother.'

'Stay here and talk to your solicitor for a while.' Fiona stood and left the room. She was suddenly exhausted.

'I was watching.' Horgan was standing in the corridor. 'Tracy got the young brother to confess to dumping the body at sea.'

'What a shitstorm. Canavan is done for murder and her husband and brother-in-law for disposing of a body. What will they get?'

'The brother-in-law will get two years and the husband three for the body and five for the statutory rape.'

'And the mother-in-law for destroying evidence?'

'Two years.'

'What about the kids?'

'You and Tracy did a good job.'

'It doesn't feel like it.'

'You got justice for Sarah.'

'But at what cost.'

'That's not your fault. A young girl is dead and you've given her justice. They've broken a lot of laws between them and they're going to have to pay. The justice system will take its course. The confessions will suffice. Go home. We'll keep them overnight and deal with them tomorrow.'

Fiona looked at her watch. It was seven thirty and Horgan was still at the office. She looked up at the sky. It hadn't fallen in.

# CHAPTER FIFTY-SIX

F iona sat on the Black Shadow but she hadn't inserted the key in the ignition. The super, Horgan and the hierarchy at the Phoenix Park would consider the investigation to be a major success. She was devastated. Three small children were about to lose their parents and possibly one of their grandparents. Over the next few weeks, she would be responsible for helping to destroy at least four people. Mikey Canavan might be able to finish his studies but he would do so from prison. If she'd been disliked in Connemara before, she was about to be despised. And yet life goes on. She would take the evidence and concentrate on the facts. Then the legal eagles would get at it and the court would be the usual circus. But the end would be the same. She and Tracy would play their part and perhaps there might be some blame that would attach itself to them. The bottom line was that those responsible for the death of a naïve young girl would be punished. She took out her mobile phone and called Ashling. The phone rang out but no one answered. She remembered receiving an email earlier in the day but events had taken over. She brought up her emails and opened Ashling's. It had been forwarded from a man called Makara Sok who she assumed was Ashling's computer contact at the university. She opened the first attachment and read. She moved on to the second. She snatched at her mobile and called Ashling again. No answer. This time she left a message: call me please. Michael Power aka Tim Daly was a possible murderer and Ashling was missing. Fiona turned the key on the Black Shadow and raced away from Mill Street. The journey to the cottage normally took seventeen minutes but Fiona did it in ten. Ashling's car wasn't at the cottage when she arrived. She parked her bike. The front door wasn't locked and she entered the living room. 'Ashling.' No response. The cottage was empty. Fiona relaxed. Ashling was a responsible adult and could be anywhere. But it was ominous that on the day she had received the information on Tim, she wasn't home and she wasn't answering her phone. That could be a coincidence but Fiona didn't like coincidences. She picked up a plastic sleeve that was lying on the table and examined its contents. Ashling had printed out the email attachments. She'd been to the cottage. But there was no sign of either her or her car.

'Looking for your little friend?'

Fiona turned. Tim was standing at the door. 'Where is she?'

'We'll get to that later.'

'If you've hurt her, I'll break every bone in your body.'

'That's not the way you should speak to your only child who you abandoned at birth. That could be construed as maternal abuse. You could go to prison for that.'

Fiona doubted very much that she could injure the son she'd abandoned. She was already subsumed with guilt for giving him away. And she didn't do red mist. Years of martial arts practice gave her a mechanism for calming wild emotional responses. 'Have you hurt her?'

'No, and I don't intend to. But as they say, beware the law of unintended consequences. Her future is very much in your hands.'

'What do you want?'

'Since I arrived, I've told you what I want. We need to be a family, you, me, and dad. Let's go find him and the three of us can have a talk about old times and the future.'

'Can we talk about this?'

Tim glanced at his watch. 'Ashling's situation is time-limited. I don't think she has time for us to have a lengthy discussion.'

Fiona felt a dart of fear. 'If I take you to him, will you tell me where Ashling is?'

'Yes.'

'Then let's go.'

Fiona climbed onto the Shadow and Tim sat on the pillion. She took a left at the main Galway road and drove deeper into Connemara, pushing the machine to its limits as they raced along the coast. When the road forked, she took the branch that led to Rossaveel. Ashling's situation was time-limited. Where the hell had he put her? It was somewhere her life was in danger. She didn't want to lose Ashling. At Rossaveel she passed the port and took the small road the led around the headland. She stopped at the field she'd inherited from her grandfather. 'We're here.'

Tim looked around. 'What sort of bullshit is this?'

Fiona unlatched the gate and walked into the field. 'You wanted to meet your dad.'

'Where is he?'

Fiona turned to face him. 'I didn't tell you that your father raped me when I was sixteen. You're the product of that rape.'

'You're lying.'

'That's why my mother insisted that we place you for adoption. You'd be a constant reminder of what happened to me.'

Shock registered on Tim's face. 'They abused me. The Powers abused me from the age of seven.' Tears ran along his cheeks.

Fiona extended her arms. 'Then we were both victims of the rape. The one that began the chain of events that coloured both of our lives was the man who raped me.'

'My father.' He allowed her to hug him.

She pulled him to her chest. 'We're both damaged goods. I've read the newspaper reports. You should go home and give yourself up. Tell them about the abuse.'

Tim stood back. 'Where's my father.'

'He disappeared several months after the rape.'

'You're lying. The whole rape thing is a lie.'

'There's a cardboard box under my bed. The reports on his disappearance are in it. But I brought you here because I have a notion about his whereabouts. My grandfather left me this field. He loved me dearly and he was a hard man who had served in the Special Air Service of the British Army. He knew how to kill people. I think we might be standing on your father's grave. That puts a pin in your plan for revenge, I bet.'

Tim turned and ran back to the bike. Fiona took off after him but he was fast. He jumped on the bike, started it in one movement, and was quickly fifty metres away and accelerating.

'Where's Ashling, you bastard?' Fiona screamed. She reached into her jeans' pocket for her mobile phone but she'd left it at the cottage. She raced down the road and back to the port.

# CHAPTER FIFTY-SEVEN

'Thanks for the lift.' Fiona jumped out of the car and ran down the short road that led to her cottage. Ashling's car was parked outside but there was no one in it. There was no sign of her beloved motorbike. She ran into the cottage. 'Ashling, where the hell are you?'

Silence.

She went into Tim's room. His small amount of luggage was gone. She felt tears rolling down her cheeks. Because of her, Ashling had to pay the price. She went into their bedroom. The cardboard box containing her prized possessions was open on the bed, the lid discarded on the floor. She took a quick inventory. Everything was there except for the newspaper story about the disappearance of Fahy. She cursed but right now nothing was more important than finding Ashling. She rushed through the kitchen and checked the bathroom. No sign of her partner. She couldn't be dead. She thought about Tim's adoptive parents. Perhaps he did murder them after all. Think, she told herself. The car wasn't there earlier. He must have taken it somewhere. Maybe Ashling was lying hurt in some remote place. What chance did she have of finding her? It was hopeless. She could be anywhere within a twenty-mile radius and that encompassed a lot of foreshore. On the way from Rossaveel, she'd noticed that the tide was fully in. If Ashling was dumped on the foreshore, she'd never be found. A wave of despair washed over Fiona as she looked through the open door at the car. She hadn't checked the boot. The car keys had been lying on the bed alongside the card-board box. She retrieved them and said a silent prayer as she approached the car.

Ashling was lying in a foetal position in the boot. Fiona put her fingers on her neck. The pulse was strong but Ashling was comatose. Fiona couldn't believe the level of relief she felt. She bent and pulled Ashling into a sitting position. Since Ashling was a dead weight, Fiona had to use all her strength to pull her out. She used a fireman's lift to carry her into the cottage.

'I SCREWED UP.' Ashling sipped her tea.

'No, you didn't. He knew the gig was up when you discovered the two passports. I'm not sure what he had in mind from the beginning but his plan was flexible enough to fit a change in circumstances. He didn't count on you playing Miss Marple.'

Ashling put her hands to her head. 'I have the mother of all headaches. He put something into my tea. And I have a memory of him giving me something before he stuffed me in the boot.'

Fiona went to the kitchen and returned with a glass of water and some tablets. 'Two paracetamol should relieve some of the pain.'

Ashling took the tablets, swallowed them, and washed them down with a slug of water. 'What about Tim, Michael whatever?'

'What about him? He's gone.'

'But he stole your bike.'

'So what, it's probably the least I owe him. You were right about the abandonment issues and to put the icing on the cake his adoptive parents abused him. The bike is a thing. It's replaceable.'

'I thought you told me it was unique.'

'Okay, it's not replaceable.'

'You think he'll be back?'

Fiona looked out the window. Her son was out there somewhere running from the US law perhaps and now he was running from her. She wasn't much of a mother. 'I don't think so.'

'Are you sad?'

'More than I thought I'd be.'

'I'd suggest a drink but I'm afraid to take alcohol on top of whatever Tim gave me. We must stop calling him Tim. His name was Michael.'

'I liked Tim better.' Fiona went to the kitchen and returned with two glasses of white wine. She handed one to Ashling. 'Take it. I don't think it'll kill you.'

Ashling raised her glass. 'Slainte.'

Fiona touched the raised glass with hers. 'Slainte.'

'In all the excitement, I forgot to ask how the investigation is going.'

'It's over. We have the culprit in jail. She's the mother of three children. Her husband and brother will go down for dumping the body and her mother-in-law for destroying evidence.'

'You don't sound happy.'

'It's the first murder I've worked on where I was as sorry for the miscreants as I am for the poor girl who got murdered.'

'Where do we go from here?'

'You're the university professor. You should know your Samuel Beckett. We'll go on.'

## CHAPTER FIFTY-EIGHT

Fiona had heard of a French saying: the more it changes the more it stays the same. Cleaning up the Sarah Joyce murder was messy but part of her job. She'd located Patrick Thornton and while he had taken a few punches too many, his recollection of seeing the Canavan brothers loading something wrapped in black bin bags onto a small boat in Mweenish harbour was as clear as a bell. It was another nail in the Canavans' coffin when none was needed. She and Tracy had collated the evidence and finalised the interviewing. The story was as old as the hills and the conclusion was inevitable. A rash act and an amateurish cover-up would lead to custodial sentences for all concerned. Life at the cottage had returned to normal. Fiona and Ashling seldom spoke of Tim/Michael although both felt the presence of an elephant padding around the living room. A month after Tim had left, Fiona received a postcard. On the front was a picture of Tim sitting astride her Vincent Black Shadow. The message on the back of the card was short.

Hi Mom,
Your secret is safe with me.

Fiona doubted it

# AFTERWORD

I hope you enjoyed this book. I depend on reviews to spread the word about my novels. I would be very grateful if you would write a review or at least give the book a rating.

Thank you in advance

# ABOUT THE AUTHOR

Derek Fee is the author of the Wilson series of police procedurals set in Belfast. This is the first book in a series featuring DS Fiona Madden.

ALSO BY DEREK FEE

**The Wilson Series**

Nothing but Memories

Shadow Sins

Death to Pay

Dark Circles

Boxful of Darkness

Yield up the Dead

Death on the Line

A Licence to Murder

Dead Rat

Cold in the Soul

Border Badlands

Mortal Blow

**Moira McElvaney**

The Marlboro Man

A Convenient Death

**Standalone**

Cartel

Saudi Takedown

The Monsignor's Son

Made in the USA
Monee, IL
17 July 2021

73795615R00184